Long for This World

A Novel

SONYA CHUNG

Scribner

New York London Toronto Sydney

SCRIBNER
A Division of Simon & Schuster, Inc.
1230 Avenue of the Americas
New York, NY 10020

This book is a work of fiction. Names, characters, places, and
incidents either are products of the author's imagination or are used
fictitiously. Any resemblance to actual events or locales or persons,
living or dead, is entirely coincidental.

Copyright © 2010 by Sonya Chung

All rights reserved, including the right to reproduce this book or
portions thereof in any form whatsoever. For information address
Scribner Subsidiary Rights Department, 1230 Avenue of the Americas,
New York, NY 10020.

First Scribner hardcover edition March 2010

SCRIBNER and design are registered trademarks of The Gale Group, Inc.,
used under license by Simon & Schuster, Inc., the publisher
of this work.

For information about special discounts for bulk purchases, please
contact Simon & Schuster Special Sales at 1-866-506-1949 or
business@simonandschuster.com.

The Simon & Schuster Speakers Bureau can bring authors to your live
event. For more information or to book an event contact the
Simon & Schuster Speakers Bureau at 1-866-248-3049 or
visit our website at www.simonspeakers.com.

Manufactured in the United States of America

1   3   5   7   9   10   8   6   4   2

Library of Congress Control Number: 2009027875

ISBN 978-1-4165-9962-3
ISBN 978-1-4391-0171-1 (ebook)

To the memory of my grandfather,
Song Yun-kyu,
who loved words

I want to unfold.
I don't want to stay folded anywhere,
because where I am folded, there I am a lie.

—Rainer Maria Rilke

Long for This World

List of Main Characters

Korean-American Hans

Han Hyun-kyu, second of three Han brothers
Lee Woo-in ("*Dr. Lee*"), his wife
Ah-jin/Jane, their daughter
Han-soo/Henry, their son
Paul, Jane's ex-boyfriend and Henry's best friend

Korean Hans

Eldest brother, married to Lee Woo-in's youngest aunt
Han Jae-kyu, Han Hyun-kyu's younger brother
Han Jung-joo, his wife
Hae-sik, their elder son
    Ji-eun, Hae-sik's wife
    Won-soo and Won-min, their sons
Hae-joo, their younger son
    Yoo-mee, Hae-joo's wife
Min-yung, their daughter
    Woo-sung, Min-yung's husband
Cho Jin-sook, their housekeeper
Cho Yoon-kwon, her husband
    Ji-hae, their youngest daughter
Chae Min-suk, Han Jung-joo's youngest brother
    Soo-young, his daughter

Book One

Explosions

Flight (1953)

The eldest brother was twenty years old when he left the island. His wife was eighteen. It was good fortune, the heavens smiling down upon him, that he was offered the position teaching sciences at a junior high school in Kyongju. He was young for the position, and less qualified than the other candidates, but the principal of the school was his wife's great-uncle and wanted to give the young couple an opportunity to move to the city.

The eldest brother hated the island. He felt trapped, did not like the feeling of being watched, and known. He wanted his independence, to start his own family afresh, and did not want his children to suffer the boredom and small-mindedness of island life. He knew everything there was to know about everyone in the village and did not like any of it. He did not like that nobody cared what was happening in the rest of the world. He did not like that every young man knew his future from the time he was a young boy—that he would take over his father's rocky plot of land, or rickety fishing boat. He did not like that learning to read and write Chinese characters, the standard pen for literature, was seen as a betrayal by the older generation. He did not like that the girls and boys were paired off when they were fifteen and sixteen years old—like animals, good only for procreation. He did not like that sometimes his uncle took one of his girl cousins into the back room and pulled the curtain closed, and that other men did the same with their daughters and nieces.

So when the opportunity came to leave the island, the eldest brother took it without hesitation. He and his wife packed a small trunk and were ready to leave within days of accepting the position. They did not yet know where they would live, but his wife's great-uncle would allow them to stay with him until other arrangements could be made.

His younger brother Hyun-kyu—next in line among the three sons—was about to start high school. Hyun-kyu begged his brother to take him along to Kyongju, to the city. He was a good student and had been studying hard. He wanted to leave the island as well. He wanted to go to college. From the beginning, the eldest brother had discouraged him from clinging to such far-fetched ideas, but Hyun-kyu was determined. Now that he was almost fourteen, he knew that the village high school—ten slothful boys and an *ajjummah* who knew little more than her students—would be of no use to him. And the village library was running out of books for him to read. Hyun-kyu begged and begged, but his brother refused him. There would be no room at the great-uncle's house, and certainly he and his wife would not be able to afford more than a one-room apartment. The eldest brother needed to make his own plans; he could not look out for anyone else. It pained him to think of it, leaving his sisters and brothers to fend for themselves, but he swallowed his guilt. He turned toward his own life.

The eldest brother and his wife arranged for the ferry to take them across the sea—a passage of some five hours, in good weather—early one Sunday morning. It was barely light out; the ferryman preferred to make the journey early, when the sea was at its calmest. The darkness of that morning was Hyun-kyu's saving grace: no one noticed as he slipped onto the boat and hid underneath a wool blanket that was thrown over a pile of rope and life preservers. By the time his brother discovered him, they were too far along to turn back.

The eldest brother was angry to discover Hyun-kyu's trick;

but underneath his anger, he was also a little bit pleased. *This boy knows what he wants,* he thought. His wife defended the boy and pleaded with her husband for compassion. The eldest brother feigned an even greater rage at her defense, and then relented. "Very well," he said, keeping back a smile. "We will help him along."

Flight (2005)

Han Hyun-kyu has not been on an airplane in nearly thirty years. The last trip was with his children, when Ah-jin, his daughter, was nine years old, and Han-soo, his son, was seven. He took them to California—to Disneyland and Hollywood—because they begged him. Their mother did not come with them, and in their absence she made a sudden and unilateral decision about the children's names—to start calling them Jane and Henry. "The schoolteachers and their friends call them by their American names," she had said, shrill as always. "So that is how we should call them as well. We don't want to confuse them."

What is confusing? he thought. In Korean, there are different names for everybody, depending on the relationship. A boy calls his older brother *hyung*, a girl calls her older brother *op-pah*; the children call their mother's sister *e-moh* and their father's sister *co-moh*. *What's confusing? Aren't they smart children?*

He recalls that trip now, the beginning of *Jane* and *Henry*—of traveling alone with the children—as the beginning of something else as well. Something long and unpleasant and persistent. Something he is trying to escape now.

He has not let himself fear or dread this flight. He does not like heights—hills, bridges, airplanes. But he had put the thought of it out of his mind for the last month, ever since he bought the plane ticket. He was determined, and he would not let his fear get the better of him.

He managed to secure an aisle seat, and as he boards the plane and finds his row, he is glad to find that his is the end of a five-seat middle section, across the aisle from any windows. He does not want to see anything, or feel the mechanical movements over the wing. He remembers this clearly from that California trip: holding Ah-jin's hand, trying to reassure her that all the sounds were normal—when in fact he was reassuring himself. He wonders now if she suspected his terror. He's almost certain she did, perceptive girl after all, and this thought unsettles him at a place deep and wide in his gut. It is a familiar discomfort, but somehow clearer, more solitary and uncluttered just now—here, as he begins his flight.

The attendants perform their routine safety presentation. He tries to focus on their instructions but phases in and out, finds the words and motions too much out of sync, like those old kung fu movies with dubbed dialogue that Han-soo used to love. As the plane speeds down the runway, then lifts off and begins its ascent, he is surprised by how little air travel has changed in the last thirty years: the script of the presentation—*please secure your own mask before helping others* seems to him as counterintuitive now as it did then—the bumpy feel of takeoff, the clunk of the wheels retracting into the belly of the plane, like a final word. He finds all this familiarity reassuring.

The seat-belt sign goes off. He reclines his seat, closes his eyes. Breathes deeply. The flight attendant rushes by, he stops her with a tug at her sleeve, calls her "Miss," asks her for ginger ale. She replies that beverage service will begin shortly, if he can wait just a few minutes. Her accent is thick. He realizes as she continues down the aisle that he should have addressed her in Korean. He doesn't even really know how to address a young woman of her station anymore. The word isn't the problem—

a-gashi is universal—but the tone. The waitresses at Korean res-
taurants in the States are more Westernized and familiar; this
woman is a Korean native, likely from a small town, judging by
her docile manner.

Eleven hours to Tokyo; another two to Seoul; then an hour's
flight to the south, to Pohang Airport. He is on his way. He has
done it. He has left it all, left *her*, behind. Without a word. For
what, or how long, he does not know. But he has done it. He is
on his way.

Half a century ago, he ran away from his home and family. He
had tunnel vision then, he was a survivor, and fearless. Today,
somehow, he feels uncertain and afraid, more like a child now
than back then. But he is still a survivor, and he is hopeful. It is
a desperate, frenzied hope—a second wind, begotten of nothing, born of utter depletion—which he has summoned up to get
himself this far.

He falls asleep, right away, before the beverage cart comes by.
But the flight attendant remembers his request and pulls down
his tray table, leaves an unopened can of chilled ginger ale. The
exhaustion of the last month—his plans, the secrecy, the pit of
anger that had risen, throbbing, in his chest; and now, facing
down his fears, all this *surmounting*—he didn't realize how much
it had taken out of him.

Minutes pass, maybe hours. Emerging from a fog (not sleep
exactly, too much awareness in the nerves), he feels dried out
and achy. Muscles like raw meat at the base of the neck, underneath the shoulder blades, between the ribs, red and tender and
vulnerable. He hauls himself upright. Rubs his neck and licks his
lips, runs a swollen hand through his silver, wavy head of hair,
now beginning to thin. He is sixty-five years old. He feels a hundred. Or like he's been hit by a speeding truck and left for dead,
life fluids draining.

The fears begin to inundate. What will *they* think? What do
they expect? What will he tell them of his life, his unhappi-

nesses, his disappointments? What will they see? He purposely did not call his brother's family to discuss his visit, but rather wrote a letter; for fear of questioning or awkwardness.

Drink, I need a drink. He notices the tray table, the ginger ale. He is thankful for this bit of mercy, opens the can and drinks. *She remembered. She remembered.* The young flight attendant rises to sainthood status in his mind. He can't recall a thirst like this, nor a quenching so sweet. He gulps until half the can is empty. The woman sitting across the aisle—a woman in her fifties, professional, blond bobbed hair—stares. Her gold earring catches the light. Han Hyun-kyu looks at her, squints to gain focus. Holding the can, leaning over now and peering through his fog, he appears drunk. "You can get so de-*hy*-drated in the air," the woman says, slight twang through a wide smile of large bright teeth.

"It was very nice of her," Han Hyun-kyu says. "She remembered."

Incoming (Wounded)

The news comes from Dr. Lee, a.k.a. Lee Woo-in, a.k.a. my mother. I am staying with Henry, I plan to start looking for my own place soon, but I need Henry's familiarity, another body around, just for a little while. The new muffledness of my world is slight, but enough to be disorienting; it slows me down in every way. The headaches are bad. I struggle to focus, on anything.

Henry knows generally what happened, that I was on assignment, somewhere, near an explosion—wrong place, wrong time—but nothing more. He teases me about my short, just-past-stubbly hair and tells me to eat, eat, put some fat on. We joke and poke at each other, sit in front of the TV with greasy pizza and watch *Lost*. It's been a while since we've seen each other, but we ask no probing questions, we let each other be.

Henry, for his part, is in his own fragile place, working through the Twelve Steps. Really working this time, putting days together. Almost two years sober, and half of that living on his own. My instinct, as always, is to protect him from everything hard and dark. He lives in a small, circumscribed world of rules and stability, which enables him to get through the day. I can see that he really is a different Henry. Humbled and worn. It seems he has decided, for now at least, that he would like to maintain stasis, eschew event or wild swings of any kind, and see where that leads. These days, it's enough for each of us to get out of bed in the morning (sometimes later), and we each seem to know instinctively to grant the other the gift of low expectations.

The accident, in a way, was fortunate. I mean that the timing was fortunate, the convergence of a forced hiatus with a needed one. Fourteen months straight I'd been in the field—after the split with Paul—taking every assignment that came my way, one right after the other. My photographs got picked up left and right; my agency was pleased. I was going going going, focused and efficient, straight to the story, often into danger, bam bam bam. I needed to work, to clear my head, clear my heart; and for a while, it was working.

I'd been away from fieldwork for almost a year, my longest civilian stint. When I was ready, my agency took me back right away, no questions asked; and the assignments came quickly. It was gratifying to find that the contacts I'd built up over the years held me in good stead, even after a break, and that there was work to be had for a girl with a good eye, quick hands, and the right measure of willing madness.

I stopped off in Paris to check in with my agency a few times, but mostly I went nonstop. Julien, my agency director, seemed to know every hotel and restaurant in the world with a fax machine, so he always got me what I needed for the next thing. Usually nothing more than a name, a location, a phone number, and a password of some kind, my "in": in the Congo, *Tell him it's for the* consul's daughter, *he'll know what you mean*; or in Colombia, *Remember: you're doing a story on* exploitation of farmers, *you have to talk* land reform.

It was nuts, the whirlwind pace of it—what veterans say you should avoid to keep from burning out. But for me, it was a welcome wave of hard work. I had nowhere else I wanted to be, nothing holding me anywhere. I didn't actually imagine I'd escape my demons, I knew better than that; but my instinct was to get far, far away and to pay them no mind for as long as possible. Neglect has its effects, one way or another.

Officially, the incident was unexpected and could not have been avoided. No one would fault us. There were four of us, experienced in the field and in war. But it was more than a coincidence, I think, more than just bad luck. For myself, I can't say that my reflexes were as sharp as they'd been at other times; somewhere—lurking, looming—I had things on my mind. There is really no forgiveness for distraction when you're in the field. Attention is everything. You feel, you sense from your center, and every nerve is live. Your skin is on alert. You are all there; or else you're in trouble.

I was in Baghdad, but I could have been anywhere. The bomb—planted in a parked car by the then just-budding insurgency—was meant for civilians. We were in the Green Zone, technically safe. But we were not even thinking about where we were; or at least I wasn't. And maybe that was it (if there is an *it*): our affront to the universe was in letting our guard down. Believing just for an instant, unconsciously, in some kind of essential peace.

We had just finished an interview with a Sunni family. The story was that they had voluntarily switched houses with Shiite friends, because they were each living on the wrong side of the tracks. It was human-interest, low-risk, supposed to be a soft gig for us in between frontline work. I was with Gerald, the London writer from *The Radical* with whom I'd been going inside for the last three weeks; Asha, the translator, a U.N. contractor; and Ali, a university student in journalism who had been tagging along as a kind of self-appointed intern. We were in good spirits. We knew we had something, something different. Their eyes—a couple and their two young children—were earnest and knowing and pleading; their stories real.

It was a lead that I'd gotten, quietly, from a university contact, someone for whom I'd guest-lectured years ago in Paris; the Shiite was a relative of his wife's. The timing was right, it came when we really needed it. We were tired, and relieved to find anything human—people helping people, friendship and decency. It came the way so many stories had come before—out of nothing, out of nowhere. (Of course, nothing comes for free ultimately. Agreeing to bring along Ali, my contact's nephew, was in fact "payment," and, fortunately, a good deal for both sides.) Those gifts had not come often, but at times when I'd been closest to some kind of final straw. Over the years I came to recognize that the universe and I, we had an agreement that way. And so time went on, and I kept going.

We'd been drinking a lot in the evenings, more than usual, and sleeping little. Gerald was looking terrible. I don't know exactly how old he was, I'd guess about forty. He looked closer to sixty, and not just because of his balding. But coming out of the interview, I noticed that he had perked up, his posture had opened, he was looking up, literally, and had a kind of gleam in his eye. He was telling me how the patriarch of the Sunni family reminded him of his favorite uncle back in Leeds—"a jolly fellow, a real lover of life," he was saying—when the car blew up.

It was a small explosion, relatively speaking. A handmade bomb, one of many planted simultaneously in civilian areas around the city to keep the insurgency at a steady clip. A reminder, a statement. Still, we were close enough. It was all noise and force, I couldn't tell you a thing about who was there, what the car looked like, or how far away we were. We were *inside it* as far as I could tell. All space collapsed; and then we were thrown, a million miles, or more. The word *blast* had never meant anything in particular to me before. In my line of work, it's a word as common as day, inert as milk. Now, for me, it has a singular meaning, specific to that moment.

Gerald must have died instantly, or at least quickly. A metal shard, likely a piece of the car's fender, impaled him from behind, straight through the neck. Asha was closest to the explosion, and she was also killed instantly, her body dismembered. I didn't see any of this, but was told by Ali, who saw everything and spared no detail, describing the deaths in absurdly flat tones, like a true reporter. He had fallen behind after stopping along the road for a Coke.

As for me, I was thrown hard into the side of a convenience store, a concrete building, but not hit by anything airborne. Somehow, the force of the explosion propelled Gerald and me in opposite directions—him into the path of the deadly detritus, me away from it. I came out with a concussion; second-degree burns; minor fractures in my left hand; a generous smattering of cuts and bruises. Because of the disorientation, it took three days to diagnose the real damage: loss of hearing. Partial—about 10 percent—in both ears.

Twenty-four people in all were injured, seven killed. Almost all civilians, many women and children because we were near a street market. There were two off-duty Iraqi soldiers in the vicinity—one spending time with his wife and children (all of them were severely injured but survived), the other on his way to visit a woman at a brothel.

Gerald had only his elderly mother, who lived in London, and an estranged teenage son who'd been adopted by a stepfather. While recovering in the hospital, I wrote his mother a short letter saying that I was sorry for her loss, and that I had come to think very highly of Gerald during our time working together. I asked if she would kindly send me his uncle's name and address in Leeds, but I never heard back.

Asha's ex-husband came from New York to identify and claim her remains—what were thought to be her remains. He stopped by my room to introduce himself and ask a few questions: How was she doing? Did she seem happy in her work? They'd divorced less than two years previously, after thirty-some years of marriage. She'd discovered his infidelity, an affair with her cousin's wife. This she'd mentioned to me one night after too much drink. Mister Asha (I never got Asha's last name; or maybe I did but can't recall) was a handsome, compact man in his fifties, wearing a tragic look of contrition. He clasped his hands together in front and looked down at his feet while we talked, which was for just a few minutes. "Thank you," he said as he left, avoiding eye contact and yet also trying to make it, "thank you."

Ali came to see me almost every day during my weeks in recovery. The burns were the worst and took the longest to heal, especially my scalp and arms. Ali did not flinch at the sight of me—my shaved head, pocked with scabs and abrasions; my swollen, scraped-up face, half-wrapped in gauze to absorb the fluids that drained and oozed before healing could begin. Nor did he seem to experience any particular posttraumatic stress; he was focused and coherent. This was his world, after all, it was all he knew. My own state of mind, on the other hand, was both foggy and flinchy—like a strobe light in a smoky club.

Ali came, initially, to tell me that he had taken copious notes at the interview and wanted to write the article, *in honor of Gerald*. I knew, of course, that it was really for himself, a big break for him since *The Radical* had agreed to accept his draft if he could submit it quickly. I was happy to help; it gave me something to focus on, other than the pain of the burns. So we worked on it together, there in the hospital room. Ali's ambition heartened me; without his daily dose of youth, I suspect that something inside me may have given in—curled up and withered away. I'd been there before, with Paul, I knew how easy it would have been. Ali's visits kept me awake and alert.

My recovery was slow, and boring. I did not have a TV in my room, but there was one down the hall in the patient lounge, where we all—strangers in war, compatriots in trauma—devoted ourselves daily to *The Family Ahmad*, a new soap opera, Iraq's first, to which nearly all Iraqi televisions (civilian and military alike) had been tuned since its premiere. The big wedding, the one viewers had anticipated for weeks, between a high government minister's daughter and a handsome soldier from a lower class, had just been ruined by an unannounced weapons search by American troops. The Americans were portrayed alternately as bullies and buffoons; the patients seemed to enjoy this especially.

After they discharged me from the hospital, I took a week to just sleep, take off-assignment black-and-whites with my Leica, and sit around in cafés, smoking and bullshitting with other journalists. Listening to their grisly bravado was strangely comforting. Some of them knew what had happened, but they didn't speak of it other than a few kind words about Gerald; and thankfully, they didn't tiptoe around me.

I checked in with Julien in Paris to let him know I was up and around but would be unavailable for an undetermined period of time. When I was ready, I sent an e-mail to Henry back in New York and bought a one-way ticket. I was on my way home.

I was returning with the idea of rest in mind—an idea that in truth sounded to me like a lot of work. But I was longing, I was ready, for a *clearing*. Everything I'd left behind had begun to back up on me, and I suppose I knew that this time, this readiness would come.

As I turned toward home, an image formed in my mind—of me hacking through a tall, thick brush, methodical and focused; the scythe a gracefully curved steel beauty, deadly sharp, solid and heavy in my hand.

But those notions and images scattered by the time I actually got home. I had a premonition of this—a vague tingling somewhere behind my heart, a nervous quickening as the plane touched down at JFK Airport—of something awaiting me, something unforeseen and yet inevitable. And what I've come home to is turning out to be a different kind of explosion.

Domestic Security

1

Han Jung-joo balances on one foot, lifts the other up to the hose, under the running water. It is ice cold—clear mountain water—but she does not flinch, does not cry out. She runs her other hand, the one that is not holding the hose, over her foot, smoothing away dirt and grass. She does this in slow, even motions, rubbing her pale, thinly veined feet with a small thumb, spreading toes apart with fingers, careful not to soil or wet her long wool skirt. She holds this position with ease and calm, like a yogi demonstrating stillness and balance.

Her blue rubber slippers—Adidas brand, which her son bought for her in Seoul—are also filthy. She sprays them clean, then switches feet, switches hands, repeats the motions. By the time she is done, both hands and feet are shiny and slick, bluish white, throbbing in slow, hard pulses. It is not an unpleasant feeling. She inhales once deeply, gathering the crisp mountain air—metallic in its sharpness—into her lungs, and holds it. Feels the cold moving through her blood, heading for her heart. Three solid beats in her chest, a slight pain at the top of her head; she exhales. The morning gray begins to burn off as the sun weighs in. Familiar big sky, their very own heavens. Blue mountains, heavyset and blunt like stern old Korean men, rise wide and formidable above Hyun Sook Lake, where she and her husband have built their two-story Western-style home.

Entering the house through the back door into the laundry room, she now finds a small pink towel, fringed on the edges (a hand towel should reflect a feminine delicacy as opposed to the thick mannish plush of a bath towel), and takes a moment to dry and warm her extremities. Cho Jin-sook, a dark-skinned woman from a village to the south, whom she has recently hired as housekeeper, is in the kitchen and hasn't heard her come in. Han Jung-joo brushes loose strands of bobbed hair—intolerably frizzy this morning and in need of a refresher perm (this after-noon's appointment)—away from her face and takes a moment to think. The woman must be reprimanded for forgetting to latch the dog pen again. Han Jung-joo spent a good part of the morning coaxing Bear, the German shepherd, back into the pen, and making a mess of her feet and slippers in the process. Last night's rains left the yard a muddy mess—good for the vegetable garden and grass seedlings that have sprouted, but even more important to keep the dog in the pen. With the cool weather settling in, it will be hard to get him to stand still under the hose for a wash. But this will be Cho Jin-sook's problem—the inevitable consequence of her lapse, circling back, as error is wont to do.

Han Jung-joo pauses one moment longer before returning to the main activity of the house. The cat—a timid, scrawny calico when they found her, now fat and presumptuous—has entered the laundry room, tail high, purring and rubbing against the bit of bare leg below the hem of her skirt, warming her cold ankles. The morning's trouble finished, she receives this bit of sweet-ness and returns it with a gentle scratch behind the cat's ear. All the animals content and in their places; time to tend to the humans.

Cho Jin-sook is a woman in her mid-forties, married to a poor rice farmer who only recently acquired a small paddy of his own. She married late, by country standards; they have three children under the age of twelve. She is not a pretty woman—

broad shoulders and flat bust, eyes narrow and spread far apart, dark leathery skin, a mouth full of crowded crooked teeth—and so her father had a difficult time finding a match for her. But she is strong, hardworking, loyal. Luckily, the man who agreed to have her recognized her qualities and has treated her kindly—no small bit of luck for a woman whose life could easily have gone the route of brutality at the hands of a more common man. Her previous situation, as housekeeper to a wealthy businessman's family in Taegu, had become unsustainable—two hours' commuting time by bus each way, a drain on both time and money. Now, from her village it was a forty-minute walk to the Han residence; and when her husband had time to drop her off, it was fifteen minutes by scooter.

Unfortunately, Cho Jin-sook does not like dogs. She tried not to let on during her interview a month before, but it has become obvious over time. It is the worst part of her day when she walks out to the yard, enters that pen, lays down food and water; then flees back to the house. This is the third time she has neglected to stop and secure the latch behind her.

Han Jung-joo smooths down her skirt and slips her feet into a pair of satin house slippers. She must make up for lost time now. Her husband will be down for breakfast soon. Cho Jin-sook must serve him first; she and her daughter will have their breakfast separately, after he has left for work.

The kitchen is warm and filled with the pleasant smell of stewed seaweed and garlic. Han Jung-joo enters calmly but swiftly, begins wiping down the breakfast table and setting her husband's place. "Auntie Cho, you must get the rice and soup ready for Dr. Han first. Miss Min-yung and I will eat later." Her voice is terse, and serious. "You must remember to lock the gate, Auntie Cho." She says this while keeping her eyes and motions focused on setting the table. Cho Jin-sook, who stands over the stove stirring the *guk*, pauses. *Ay!* she thinks to herself. *Idiot, not again!* She has gotten the message: Mrs. Han has spent the morning taking care of *her* work and is not pleased. She wants to apologize, explain herself—the dog was barking at her again, baring teeth, she was afraid—but this will only irritate Mrs. Han further. Mrs. Han hates whining and excuses, she knows this. And she likes Mrs. Han very much. She wants to keep this position.

Cho Jin-sook keeps the moment of silence, confirming that she has understood the reprimand. Then: "Miss Min-yung is not feeling well this morning. I will bring breakfast to her room later on. She is still sleeping now." Han Jung-joo nods her head. She suspected that her daughter might not make an appearance this morning. Four months pregnant, she has been staying in bed later and later, uninterested in eating and sickened by the smells.

"All right, then. We'll get ready for my husband, he will be down any minute."

The morning ritual is much simpler than it once was. When the three children were young, there was much more activity: lunches to pack, books and papers to gather, coats and shoes to button and tie. And they lived in a smaller house, the old Han family house, where they were crowded and had to coordinate so that each member of the family could use the one bathroom, eat breakfast, and go off to school and work. Han Jung-joo had become quite masterful at managing everyone's needs and schedules, her husband and each child invariably organized and ready for the day. She took a great deal of satisfaction from this, a well-run household. Even now, with just her daughter at home, she maintains many of the same rituals and makes sure everyone is on schedule. Possibly she does not need the help of Cho Jin-sook, but she does not like the idea of just one set of hands. She has always felt that a supervisor and a helper is the best way. And with extra help, she is always available to her husband, for social occasions and assistance at his office when needed—extensions of the household for which she feels equally responsible.

And they have just moved to their new home, not three

months ago. It is more than twice the size of their previous house, and requires more care and cleaning, as they built it using more sensitive materials. For example, the floors are made of soft fir, which dents easily, and so she is careful to make sure that the many area rugs are clean and in place and that the legs of all the furniture are securely adhered to thick felt pads. In the living room and dining room they installed track lighting, which makes the house bright and cheerful, but also reveals more dust, and so the dusting must be done daily now as opposed to twice a week. They also now have more modern appliances, so while Cho Jin-sook tends to the yard and garden, Han Jung-joo often deals with repair and maintenance people who drive in from town to assist her with problems that arise.

Han Jae-kyu now descends the stairs. Han Jung-joo is still getting used to the sound of footsteps on a stairway—they have never lived in a two-story home before—and likes the warning aspect of it, which helps her prepare. She can now tell the difference between her husband's steps (*clop clop clop clop*—even and unrushed) and her daughter's (*CLOP-clop . . . CLOP-clop*—one foot heavy, the other following, increasingly reluctant and obligatory these days). It has not occurred to her until just now to think whether either of them can tell her own footsteps; or what they might sound like.

"Good morning," Han Jae-kyu says as he sits at table.

"Good morning." Han Jung-joo brings his soup and rice and coffee. Coffee is a new element in the ritual, since they've moved into the new house. She was surprised when he brought it home one day—a bag of Starbucks whole beans and an elaborate machine that grinds the beans and brews the coffee all at the touch of one button. It was a gift from a patient who had just returned from a trip to Seoul. People often brought things to her husband from their travels—specialty foods and smart clothing and accessories from big cities—and most of the time, he accepted them graciously but either stored them away or gave them to his sons. This time, he showed an enthusiasm for the gift and asked her to put it to use right away. Han Jung-joo herself liked the smell and taste of coffee but did not like the jarring noise the machine made when grinding the beans. But he was so pleased when she served him his first cup, held it to his nose and inhaled deeply before drinking. He even brought home a box of new beans when the first one ran out, which he ordered from the city for delivery. "Put these in the freezer," he had said. "They will keep longer."

She does not sit down at the table, but returns to the pot and ladles a small bowl of soup for herself, which she sips slowly, lifting the bowl to her mouth and standing over the counter. Cho Jin-sook has gone to start on the laundry.

"Min-yung is sick again?"

"Yes, she is still sleeping."

"Too bad. It will get a little worse before it gets better. Make sure she has some *guk* later. She has to gain weight."

"She has lost three kilograms." He considers this, but moves over it quickly.

"It's all right for now, but she has to gain soon. You should take her to the *oncheon*, it may do her some good."

"But they say . . ."

"Yes, they say that, but it is not true. Pregnant women have been going to the hot springs for centuries. There is no reason to think anything has changed. She can stay in the cooler pools."

"Yes, well . . . maybe it will make her feel better. She is very unhappy. She is upset with Woo-sung."

"Why should she be upset?"

"He has been in Taegu over a month now." Han Jung-joo says all this matter-of-factly. She is careful not to express opinion, but to simply let her husband know the facts.

"A man has to work, make a living. He is doing as he should be doing."

"Well . . . you were never away when I was pregnant." She is speaking affectionately now, not making argument. Always careful-careful with her tone.

"Those days were simpler, we lived and worked in the same place. I worked long hours but I could come home during the day because it was so close." His tone is playful. He seems in a good mood.

"Min-yung does not want to move to the city."

"It is not a matter of 'want.' She has to go where her husband finds work. These days, there is no work here in the country."

"Too bad he is not a doctor."

"Why should he be a doctor? A business adviser is a good occupation. A stable company, very respectable."

"If he was a doctor, then he could work for you, here in town." She is flattering her husband now. He is the most successful and well-known physician for several towns and villages around. People come from long distances to see him. Han Jung-joo takes pride in this. And she makes sure to find ways of expressing it regularly.

"That is true. I have too much work. I am getting old."

"You are still young," she says teasingly. She finds her husband not exactly handsome—he has large ears and round eyes spaced close together, is short-legged and bony in build—but has always admired his competent, decisive temperament. "Only fifty-eight. Look, your older brother in America is sixty-five and still working."

"In America it is different. People live to work instead of working to live. I do not think my brother is happy working so hard all these years. I think sometimes we should feel sorry for him."

Han Jung-joo is silent. She is surprised by her husband's words, which is unusual. There are very few surprises in their life now, after thirty-five years of marriage and three children raised

and grown. He is also silent for a moment. Then: "The air is turning cold. Night is coming earlier. Make sure Min-yung wears a
sweater, even in the house. And thick socks. She should sleep on
a bed, not on the floor. What will you do today?" Dr. Han asks
this question each and every morning. Han Jung-joo's answer is
more or less the same each day, with a few varying details.

"We will go to the market in town this morning, then tend
to the garden and yard this afternoon. Hae-sik and Hae-joo will
be here Friday afternoon for the birthday celebration, so I must
prepare their rooms and do extra shopping, special treats for the
children. I will have to keep an eye on Min-yung. If, as you say,
she gets worse, she will need me throughout the day." Her voice
trails off, imperceptibly, even to herself. Her thoughts in relation
to her daughter have lately begun drifting away from her, like a
strange music drawing her into dark shadows; but she does not
follow their lead, her will to focus is strong and instinctual.

Han Jae-kyu nods his head, brings his soup bowl to his mouth
to slurp noisily the last of the *guk*. Han Jung-joo has intention-
ally neglected to mention her hair appointment. He will notice
her fresh perm later, but better not to discuss it. It pleases him
that she minds her appearance, but in a way that does not draw
attention or make a fuss.

"All right, then. I'll be off."

Han Jung-joo ascends the stairs, pausing in front of Min-yung's
door. She sees that it is open just a crack and peers in to see if
her daughter is awake. She sees that Min-yung is sitting up in
bed, reading.

"Is there something you wanted?" Min-yung's voice is a
monotone; she does not look up from her book.

"We're going into town now."

"All right."

"Is there anything you need?"

"No, nothing." Han Jung-joo taps the door open, steps into the darkened room.

"You need more light. If you open the curtain behind you . . ."

"All right."

"Min-yung *ah* . . ." She looks up, eyes only. *Such a look*, Han Jung-joo thinks. *Why does she look at me so, what have I done?* . . . She catches herself, smiles at her daughter. Min-yung's expression softens as well, and a kind of truce—a faint sadness—opens up between them.

"What are you reading?"

"Nothing. I mean . . . it's an old one. Baby Uncle gave it to me, long time ago."

"A novel?"

"Stories. Strange ones, but also funny. From Russia. *Na-bo-kuv.*"

"Well, I am sure they have some good meaning. Baby Uncle always sends you nice things, from his heart."

"Yes." A half-smile, then Min-yung's eyes are back to her book. She pulls her knees to her chest, still under the *tamyuh*.

Han Jung-joo looks around the room, takes stock of her daughter's things—so many girlhood treasures, now crammed onto shelves—neat and orderly enough, but three layers deep and not an inch of empty space. She cannot imagine what the closets look like, or under the bed. When Min-yung was younger, they enjoyed showering her with dolls and figurines and other pretty things—she was the only girl after all. But the girl's attachment to them, the way she packed them away and refused to part with them over the years—even this time, this move to their new house, now as a married woman, soon to be matron of her own home—troubled her. "What's to worry about?" Han Jae-kyu said. "She is a girl, and she loves her toys, they keep her company. At least nothing goes to waste; most girls tire of things so quickly." It seemed to Han Jung-joo that he was always defending their daughter, and she was always worrying.

Mostly, this gave her comfort. Her husband's unconditional love and approval of the girl, their closeness. He, too, always fed her reading habit, with everything from old folk tales to the new fantasy adventures. Together they had read the first two Narnia stories, but then he became busy with his work and was too tired when he came home, so Min-yung would read on her own, on the couch next to her father while he watched the news on TV or napped in his chair. Han Jung-joo would sometimes find them there in the late evening, her husband snoring lightly, mouth open, and Min-yung asleep also, book on her chest, legs up over the back of the couch (she liked to read lying upside down). She was always happy to find them there like that; her daughter in those moments seemed so much at peace, so perfectly herself— not the nervous, inward girl she was in every other setting.

"You haven't eaten."

"I will go down later. I will fix something."

"*Ku reh*. All right, then. I will have my cell phone." Han Jung-joo steps back and closes the door. She thinks to open it again, to ask if Min-yung would like to go to the *oncheon* tomorrow, maybe she would enjoy it. Instead, she continues on to her bedroom— changes her clothes, fixes her face. Sets herself to the day's tasks. She moves quickly down the stairs and calls to Cho Jin-sook: "*Ajjummah*, let's hurry. It is time to go."

2

In town, the shop owners have begun bringing their wares in off the street. Some years, they are able to stay out through November, but the cool air has descended swiftly this October, and the winds coming in from shore already have bite. It is abalone season, the *ajjummah dul* are squatting over hotpots, stewing up *jeonbok juk*, abalone stew, to sell in large tubs. They talk to one another in loud, husky voices, smile silver-capped or toothless smiles, balance their weight over bow legs and slippered feet. (Only a few of them still wear *hanbok*; many now wear wide-legged wool pants and puffy ski vests instead.) The smell is everywhere—warm and fishy, but sweet—along with roasted chestnuts, radish kimchi, barley tea. The smells of autumn in this small seaside town.

Han Jung-joo remembers the days when she and her mother stewed *jeonbok juk* themselves—an all-day and overnight affair. She began working with her mother in the kitchen at an early age, seven or eight, while her brothers focused on their school-work. She was the only girl, and so her mother relied on her for help. Jung-joo's father lived three hundred miles away in Seoul, where he was a mathematics professor at Ewha University. Her mother, her three brothers, and she stayed behind in North Kyongsang province, because, as the wife of the eldest son, Jung-joo's mother was obligated to care for her father-in-law; his wife, Jung-joo's paternal grandmother, had already passed away. He was ailing and getting on in years and required much care. A hardworking rice farmer and successful agricultural businessman for many years, Jung-joo's grandfather nonetheless deteriorated quickly after his wife's death, and, along with his body, his mind began to weaken. He became like a child—demanding, fussy, irrational; and jealous for Jung-joo's mother's constant attention. When Jung-joo's father came twice a month for a weekend stay, her grandfather would scowl at the two of them sitting on the same side of the dinner table and ask why they had to sit together like that. "You go away!" he would shout at his son. And so, even when Jung-joo's father was present, he was often banished—the upside of which was more time with the children. But it was mostly the boys who enjoyed their father's attention in those days, as Jung-joo took on many of the other household duties that her mother could not tend to because of the senior male's demands.

It was four years of this all-consuming devotion that Jung-joo's mother paid to her father-in-law. During those preadolescent years, Jung-joo became like a mother to her brothers, two of whom were her elders, and one, Min-suk the baby, five years her junior. He was too young to keep up with the other boys, and so he became her little helper. It was Min-suk, through all the years, who stayed close, never forgetting her care of him during that time.

Even with all the work that fell to Jung-joo, she managed to go to school and make high marks. Her father knew she was a bright girl; Jung-joo's was a practical, sharp mind, good at problem-solving and getting to the heart of things. He had seen her manage the household, settle conflicts among her brothers, even advise her mother on how to appease and handle her grandfather when he got especially difficult. She was precocious, wise, effective. By the time Grandfather Chae passed away and the family moved to Seoul, Jung-joo was twelve years old, about to enter seventh grade. Her father wanted her to try for entrance to Kyong-gi, the top girls' school in Seoul. The most distinguished and affluent families sent their daughters to Kyong-gi Girls, and their sons to Kyong-gi Boys. Her mother thought it a waste of time to educate girls, to enlighten them and teach them literature and history and the arts, when their futures would lie in serving their husbands and children anyway. Why get their hopes up for some kind of independent achievement? Jung-joo's mother was not bitter about this, but rather more or less complicit: a woman's place was in the home, caring for her husband and raising children, not reading philosophy or developing opinions. Besides, the more opinions a young girl developed, the less marriageable she would be. An unmarried, educated woman was not only useless, but doomed. Jung-joo was a pretty girl, with a long, narrow face, lively eyes, and smooth fair skin. She was well mannered and already knew how to run a household. Why ruin her chances?

Jung-joo herself was torn. Not that her own preference would have borne any weight on the matter, but, precocious as she was, she did consider the implications of her situation. On the one hand, she adored her father and loved him for believing in her abilities. On the other, she wanted what all young Korean girls of her age wanted—to find a good husband and to raise a healthy, prosperous family. Her father's interest in her education seemed well-meaning but ultimately frivolous. In that, she agreed with her mother. What was the point? She also felt a certain measure of defensiveness on her mother's part, having seen her suffer those years under the tyranny of her grandfather while her father lived away, not having to deal with the day-to-day torments of a demanding old man on the edge of senility. They managed so much on their own without him, who was he to now introduce these impractical ideas?

In the end, Jung-joo sat for the entrance exam, just to please her father. She never learned the results of the exam, but in the fall, she enrolled at the local middle school near their faculty apartment in Sinchon. She went on to pharmacy school at Ewha, but did not finish her degree. In her last semester, she was introduced to Han Jae-kyu, a residency classmate of her older brother's. He was a hotshot handsome young doctor from North Kyongsang province—one town over from Jung-joo's family's hometown—who had made it to prestigious Seoul University. Within a month, they were engaged. In the meantime, young Min-suk was preparing to graduate—one year early, having shown great promise in both religious studies and the visual arts—from Kyong-gi Boys.

Those days of spending hours upon hours stewing the abalone to the right flavor and consistency are long gone. She and her husband, although back in North Kyongsang province—having returned to her husband's hometown to set up practice after he finished his training in Seoul—have become modern people. They have in fact become *the* modern family in town, the model of success and progress. They keep up with technology and the latest in appliances and personal gadgets, and now they live in a Western-style home—a kind of Tudor variation, made of all imported materials. Her husband's practice is famous for its advanced Western-style know-how, having abandoned all traces of traditional *hanyak* in favor of the hard sciences, current research, and pharmacology. They have family roots in the region, but have also both been to Seoul and have brought their big-city experiences back with them. They are self-made in the way that one can only be in the country—where professional success can compete with social birth. It is fair to say that the Hans have established themselves as the most prominent family in town, perhaps for several towns around. They are the big fish in this small pond.

This is not to say, however, that they have lost all taste for the traditional. Ironically, Han Jae-kyu often uses *hanyak*—crushed deer antler, mushrooms, ginseng—for his own personal ailments. And of course he still loves his *jeonbok juk* for breakfast and lunch. In fact, Han Jung-joo will be sure to stock up today at the market and freeze the stew in meal-sized portions, to be microwaved later.

After the shopping is done, Han Jung-joo sends Cho Jin-sook home with the car to unload, check on Min-yung, feed the dog and cat, and start on dinner. Cho Jin-sook usually manages all the preparations, then Han Jung-joo takes over from there, relieving her and sending her home to have dinner with her own family. Often she will send along leftovers from previous meals. The Hans will eat a simple meal of broiled mackerel, rice with beans and grains, and *daen-jang chigae*, along with assorted vegetable *banchan*. The mackerel is expensive, but easy to prepare. Since there are no messages on the cell phone from her daughter, Han Jung-joo assumes everything is fine and is free to keep her hair appointment. Afterward, she will walk to the post office to pick up the mail, then over to her husband's office, just a few blocks farther, to ride home with him.

At the beauty salon, Shin Won-hae greets Han Jung-joo effusively. "You look well! Getting younger every day! Gaining some weight finally, always too skinny! How is Min-yung? How are the boys? I missed seeing them when they were home last time. You should tell your daughters-in-law to come in, I will do something special for them. But maybe they only like those big-city stylists in Seoul, not the outdated styles we do here!" Shin Won-hae is a distant relative of Han Jung-joo's, her brother's wife's second cousin by marriage. Han Jung-joo does not particularly care for her aggressive chatty manner, her brightly patterned, tight-fitting clothing, or her nosy questions. She is what they call a *muht jengee*, flashy and overly made-up and always concerned with the consumer trends and gossip of the day; but even worse, because she is in her late forties and much too old to be concerned with such things, which are likely for her a distraction from the fact that she was unable to have children (for everyone else a reminder of it). But she is good-natured overall and does most of the talking so that Han Jung-joo can relax and reply vaguely without having to think too hard or worry about proprieties. Sometimes, she even a little bit enjoys hearing the latest gossip about certain people in town with whom she interacts on a strictly formal basis—some of her husband's patients, the town mayor, the Christian minister and his family. And Shin Won-hae does a good job at a reasonable price. She does what Han Jung-joo asks—despite her repeated refusal to let Shin Won-hae give her *hah-ee-lah-ee-tze*, bright auburn or purplish streaks, the way all the Korean women are doing these days.

Today, Han Jung-joo takes a moment to examine the tufts
of gray at her temples and the strawlike silver strands emerging
from her crown. She has not given this advance thought, but
somehow—perhaps it's the abrupt change in the weather, the
exhilarating throb of this morning's muddy battle with the dog,
or something else she can't quite name—somehow, she is clear,
she has decided: "Color it black. Let's get rid of it." And in her
mind, as Shin Won-hae prepares and slathers on the black dye,
she explains to herself, and to her husband: "I don't want the
children to start thinking their mother is getting old. They will
feel sorry for me, and for themselves. I won't have it."

Two hours later, and it's done. Shin Won-hae has washed out
the chemicals and blown dry the black curls with low heat and a
big round brush. "It's good, Mrs. Han. It's very good. Very natural. Not like me, so obvious trying to look too young. Looks like
a professional woman, a city woman, very sophisticated. Beau-
uuutiful." Han Jung-joo studies herself in the large hand mirror
Shin Won-hae has given her—the reflected reflection of the back
of her head in the large vanity mirror behind her like a bizarre
funhouse trick, especially now that she has done this thing, this
alteration, this . . . artifice. She shifts the angle of the hand mirror, swivels her chair slightly left and right, raises and lowers her
head to try to get it right, to find herself straight-on. But the mirrors and the chair and her own face seem to be too many moving
parts. Vaguely she feels a confusion, an unsettling, originating
deep within and making its way through her blood, outward to
the surface of her skin, just beneath her facial expression. She
smiles, pats down lightly the puff on top of her head, tucks a
few stray strands behind her ears. "Yes, that's it, thank you. It is
very good. Just what I wanted. Let me pay quickly now, I must
be going. The post office will be closing, and my husband will be
leaving for home soon."

Outside, thin yellowish clouds sail overhead, high over the
squat mountains. They seem to be passing through, rushed, on

their way to some other town, some other time. The motion is enough to draw Han Jung-joo's eyes upward, a momentary connection with the heavens before getting back on the clock—imminent closing times, crosswalk light turned green, the setting sun signaling that it's time to *finish up*. The day is settling into evening, a heavy green-gray encroaching. Bit by bit, evening swallows more of each day into winter.

At the post office, the lines are long, there is an energy of impatience. Families to get home to, dinners to prepare. The clerk locks the door behind Han Jung-joo as she enters, she is the last one allowed. Thankfully, she has no packages to send or retrieve, just the post office box to check. The clerk smiles at her, his eyes meet hers and rest a little too long, a few seconds after she looks away. She can sense his lingering gaze behind her and is irritated by this. He is a man many years her junior, he should know better. Then she remembers: the artifice.

Careful-careful. She scans to find her box and inserts the key slowly, deliberately, turns it to the right and, in a single firm, smooth motion, pulls the little door open. She removes the stack of envelopes and closes the box, swift and hard. Removes the key. These actions calm her, focus her energies. One *must* focus on the tiny actions that make up the events of one's life. She has always believed, perhaps more deeply than anything, that the details matter. If one tends to the small things, the larger things fall beautifully into place; order is created and maintained. She turns to leave, walks past the clerk, leaves him with an icy smile—remote, possessed. Outside it is nearly dark.

Under the street lamp outside the post office, Han Jung-joo takes a moment to sort through the envelopes. The mail stack has decreased gradually over the last year or so, as she and her husband have become more adept on the computer, communicating more, both personally and for business, by e-mail. She stands to the side of the entrance, just out of the way, as several people, one after the other, approach, pull on the locked door, look at their watches, rush off. A few curse within earshot. She glares after them, into the backs of their heads, both condemning and pitying; how easily rattled they are, how lacking in self-control.

In her stack: three of the familiar government-stamped envelopes containing insurance payments for services rendered by her husband; alumni news from Seoul University, plus an invitation to the annual Alumni Achievement Awards (of which her husband was a recipient several years ago); an invoice from the heating contractor who installed *ondol*, the underfloor heating, in their house; a letter from Woo-sung for Min-yung (it has been too long since the last letter; she is relieved and annoyed to see it); lab results from Min-yung's most recent doctor's visit.

A postcard from Min-suk. Famous artist now, but still and always baby brother. The card is large and square, a reproduction of one of his paintings—a new one she's never seen before, from his latest exhibit in Tokyo.

> Greetings, *nu-nah*. Good turnout here, Yoshio finding enthusiastic collectors, especially for the peonies. But this city drains me, a violent assault on the senses. Everything in flux, too much ugly noise and motion, and everything about money. Worse than Seoul. Next time I won't come, Yoshio is my good and trusted proxy. Regards to *hyung-nim*, wishes of good health to my dear niece.

She likes his note, even in its brevity; it's just like him to be so forthright, no holding back. When he likes something, he likes it very much, and he is expressive, even joyful about it; as if finding something to your liking were a small miracle each and every time. And when something offends him, when the unbeautiful crosses his path, he is equally vociferous—near heartbroken, and sometimes ruthless. *Why* should such awfulness exist? What she likes best is that he always manages to find something to like, even in what he disdains. *Yoshio is good, even in this bad place.*

Given the tortoise slowness of rural mail in their area, it is likely that he has long returned to Seoul by now. Still, it gives her a tiny thrill to receive international mail; her brother's elegant handwriting—both careful and offhand, the artist in him too well trained for scribbles, too busy for neatness—like a tickle of glamour, a glimpse of the cosmopolitan life to which she can outwardly genuflect and inwardly condescend, happily, from her humbly prized perch. *Remarkable Min-suk. Poor Min-suk.* She studies the postcard painting for a moment; it strikes her: an unusual shape for him (square), and a bit monochromatic for a landscape. She knows little of art, of form or composition or the artist's process, but this makes her wonder—a small thought, a slight amplification of an ever-present thought—how her brother, with his sundry personal troubles (his daughter, Soo-young: *remember to send birthday gift*, she writes a note to herself on the postcard), is faring.

Finally, there is one more letter: an airmail envelope from the United States. How odd, she thinks, before even checking the return address. They have only one relation in the States, her husband's older brother Hyun-kyu, whom they have just mentioned this morning. And yes, in fact, it is a letter from him. She opens her purse and drops the full stack into the side pocket. Without checking the time, she knows she must hurry to catch her husband before he leaves the office. She prefers not to call; it is smoother, less troubling, to arrive on time and blend seamlessly into his schedule. Together they have built their lives around such well-conceived convergences.

The letter from Han Hyun-kyu will of course wait. It is addressed to her husband, he must open it. Likely, he will take his time, relax and unwind over dinner, read a bit while drinking a small glass of *soju*; then summarize the contents of the letter later in the evening. Han Jung-joo will tuck away her curiosity, tend to the evening's rituals, wait patiently for her husband's interpreted account of the news—as she has done so well these many years.

3

Friday morning. Cho Jin-sook is up earlier than usual, 4:00 a.m. instead of 5:30. Her husband has not yet left for the fields, he is finishing up his breakfast—silently, as always—which he prepares for himself: rice, squash fried in flour, half a pear (the other half goes into the oldest child's lunch box). When there is meat left over from dinner the night before, he will have a piece, but always leaves the rest for the children.

The children are still sleeping. Cho Jin-sook splashes warm water on her face, fumbles in the dark looking for her best dress, the one her mother-in-law made for her to wear to her niece's wedding last year. It is nothing fancy, a plain long-sleeve wool dress. But the material is thick and good-quality, with a large rose-petal pattern. It is simple, but has a Western style to it, what her cousin from Seoul calls "A-line." She cannot turn the lights on, because the children's room is not separate, but an annex to the room where she and her husband sleep, and the lights are all on one switch. She does not want to wake them too early, especially the youngest, Ji-hae, who is six and running a fever.

Cho Jin-sook reaches with her right arm across her chest to rub her left shoulder. Her body aches and throbs with exhaustion—an allover tingling just under the surface of her skin, and deep nuggets of tight pain, hard and solid like chestnuts, beneath her shoulder blades and in the small of her back. She has been going nonstop for the last five days, staying late at the Han residence, and up and out early. She was prepared to put in extra time Friday evening when the two sons and their families, along with Min-yung's husband, Woo-sung, would arrive for the older grandchild's birthday party. But then the Hans received the letter from Dr. Han's brother in America, dated a month before but only now arriving, with the sudden news that he would also be arriving on Friday.

Much of the work of the last week has been not only preparing for the guest, but also making the preparations appear as if they have been long in the making. Dr. Han's older brother must not in any way feel that he has put them out or troubled them with this visit. And so, even the work itself must not feel rushed, must be efficient and unhysterical. There was, for example, no discussion about sleeping arrangements; preparations for Han Hyun-kyu to stay in the master bedroom were simply carried out: a *boryo* was set in the corner of the dining room for Hae-joo, the younger son, and his wife, Yoo-mee; Hae-sik, his wife, and their two sons—the older of whom is the birthday boy—will take the large guestroom. Min-yung and Woo-sung will stay put in Min-yung's room, where she can be comfortable and sleep on a bed. Dr. Han will sleep in his den on a *boryo*, and Mrs. Han will take the couch in the living room. Of course, she will be the last to sleep and the first to rise, so no one will ever see her there. She sleeps little anyhow, usually no more than five or six hours. When the children and grandchildren leave, Dr. and Mrs. Han will move into the large guestroom upstairs for the remainder of Han Hyun-kyu's visit.

In fact, the household is generally kept up so well that most of the preparations are for Friday evening's meal. It is to be a great celebration and homecoming welcome, a feast fit for royalty. Cho Jin-sook spent all day yesterday going from market to market with Mrs. Han, gathering ingredients for a total of nine courses, even driving down the coast thirty minutes for baby crab from a specialty fisherman's market. They will serve traditional royal dishes such as *sinseollo*, gourmet hot pot with sea cucumber, abalone, and gingko nuts, and *gujeol-pan*, a nine-part dish with wheat pancakes, which Han Jung-joo would normally reserve for Chusok, the harvest festival, or family weddings or funerals. In the evening, they soaked and boiled beans, tenderized and marinated meat, set the broth to simmer overnight. They did have to concede a few shortcuts: store-bought *gochu jang* and *daen jang*, for example, since there wasn't time for homemade and the *ajjummah* who sold fresh jars door-to-door had sold her last batch of the week.

Cho Jin-sook finds the dress and slips it over her head. It fits a little tighter around the hips and buttocks than it did the last time she wore it, but the fabric has enough give so that it's still comfortable enough for the long day ahead. She pulls on a pair of thin socks—no tights or *naning goo*, she will be in the kitchen over the stove all day—and a pair of sweater pants, just for the walk. She is about to leave the bedroom, but then pauses, opens the top dresser drawer, and pulls out a small purple-satin zipper bag, which contains a lipstick and compact—gifts from the same Seoul cousin a few Christmases ago, which she has never used— and tosses it into her tote bag. Cho Jin-sook has never met an American before. Perhaps, she thinks, American housekeepers wear makeup.

In the kitchen, her husband is just finishing his half pear. The smell of fried grease is strong and pleasant, a daily reminder to both of them that these are good times, there is food and fat enough for the whole family. The cock has not yet crowed, but the chickens are beginning to flap and cluck.

"The children are still sleeping?" he asks. He is standing close to her, hovering in his way. He is a good foot taller than her, but somehow unaware of his own stature.

"Yes, but Ji-hae is stirring, the fever makes her restless."

"It is still high?"

"Yes. Mother-in-law will arrive soon, she will be all right until then."

"You won't wait for her?"

"I cannot. I must be leaving."

"They know that you have a sick child?" Cho Jin-sook does not answer. She moves away from him, looking for her shoes. In truth, her husband does not expect her to answer, or rather, he knows the answer by her response: it is no use, a waste of words and thought. As she puts on her coat and shoes, her husband feels sorry for this, he knows what he has done. He says, to make up for it, "My mother raised nine children and sometimes three of us had fevers at the same time. The child will be fine."

"Yes," she says hurriedly. "She has a strong constitution. The others should keep quiet in the evening so she can sleep. They will both have hangul exercises and mathematics to do." He grunts in assent, looks out the window toward the fields, imagining the swaths of bright yellow that will emerge, as if painted onto the world, as the moon fades into the broad sky of day.

"At eleven, then? At the crossroads?"

"Yes. Eleven. No, better say eleven-thirty."

"If you are not there, I will come out a little farther."

"All right, then. I'm off." She hurries down the path to the road that leads to the main road. He watches her go. He feels what it is to be the one left, to watch as someone goes away from you. There is an unnaturalness to it, which he finds unpleasant. But he will endure it for just these few days, the special circumstances. The Han family has been good to her. The pay has been fair. And things are generally settling well for them. He knows better than to complain.

When Cho Jin-sook is out of sight, he turns back up the path toward the house, his long, lanky strides a funny contrast to his wife's short-legged hurriedness. In the entryway by the main door, he gathers up his thermos and satchel. Time to head out to the fields. He laces up his boots slowly, thinking maybe his mother will arrive soon. He hates to leave the children alone, especially the little one with her fever. But there is no sign of her yet, and he must be going. The laborers will be waiting.

They are good men, reliable and hardy. They all worked together on a farm ten miles to the west for many years, starting as boys. Cho Yoon-kwon was older than the others by a few years, more serious and focused. He knew somehow that he would be the first to get his own land, destined to make his own way. It was both a determination and a foregone conclusion in his mind, and so when the time came, when he counted up his savings and made the deal with the old farmer who had no heirs (a tragedy— his son lost to tuberculosis, his wife now barren), he did not celebrate. He barely took the time to acknowledge the accomplishment. In his mind it was always there, it was what he had worked for every day.

The men were glad to leave the large farm to come work for Cho Yoon-kwon. They knew him to be an honest and hardworking man and did not begrudge him his success. There were some who resented that he had been made foreman ahead of them, and that he received rice bonuses more often from the boss. These men did not come to join the new venture but stayed on and vied for Cho Yoon-kwon's position. The men who came knew that it would be difficult in the beginning for their friend to pay as much as the former boss; but they came anyway. If they could not have their own plots, they wanted to work Cho Yoon-kwon's. Their wives balked: How could they leave the better wage? Cho Yoon-kwon knew the sacrifice they were making and felt the weight of it.

He walks a mile and a half to the paddy every morning. There is no time to linger, he walks briskly toward his purpose. But it is a good time of the day, the best time, when he is aware, physically aware, of something like pleasure. The world is mostly still asleep, and this fullness, this sense of well-being and anticipation, is a kind of secret. He walks, this furtive gratitude coursing through his blood, even as—perhaps because—he walks toward the myriad unforgiving tasks that comprise his ultimate responsibility as landowner and employer of men. When he arrives, the first face he sees is always his friend Lee Joon-ho—an old and cheerful bachelor, ever the early bird. "Skies are clear," his friend says, referring to yesterday's prediction of rain.

"Unh," says Cho Yoon-kwon. "Maybe it will hold."

When the time came for her husband to leave his position for the new venture, Cho Jin-sook, too, knew better than to make a fuss. Her own father had also worked his way to independence, acquiring a piece of land with his brother. But life continued to be hard, and money was even tighter in those first years. She, her sister and brother, and her cousins all stopped going to school to work full-time for the family. She knew farm life, its relentlessness, better than anything. She and her husband determined that their own children would stay in school, no matter what, and knew it would be even harder for them, having to pay laborers.

Cho Jin-sook knew the wives of the workers and felt with her husband their new responsibility. She immediately began looking for a new position. She heard about the Hans' new home and their need for a housekeeper through a neighbor who sold kimchi to Mrs. Han at the market. Cho Jin-sook went to market every day at midday for a week, waiting for her opportunity. Finally, one day, her neighbor pointed out Mrs. Han to her. Cho Jin-sook had said extra prayers that morning (to her Christian God, the one her husband believed in and whom she adopted when they married) and was thus emboldened to approach her.

A bit surprised, but not put off by her forthrightness, Mrs. Han wrote down her address and asked Cho Jin-sook to come the next day at noon. Cho Jin-sook knew right away that she would like working for this woman—she had a special quality, and such elegant handwriting!—and set her heart on winning her confidence.

At the interview, Cho Jin-sook marked the wonder of the new home. Two stories, shiny wood floors, so much space, the appliances all electronic and compact. She had never seen anything like it, except in the glossy magazines they were now carrying in town. It was strange for a family this well-off to live in the flats. The rich usually moved to the city, or at least up the mountain. The house stood out, with its odd pointed gables and crisscross woodwork, like something out of a Western fairy tale, but it had a modest quality and was not off-putting; Cho Jin-sook felt in awe of the place, but not unwelcome. Han Jung-joo's manner was calm and straightforward, neither condescending nor overly familiar. Cho Jin-sook liked Mrs. Han's formality, as it made her want to mind her manners as best she could in turn. The man of the house was of course not at home, but she could sense, just from the way that Mrs. Han referred to Dr. Han, that they were a good match—that they lived in harmony. The two sons had married and moved to the city, so it was just the daughter at home now, newly pregnant. Cho Jin-sook did not ask why the young miss was at home and not with her husband, but thought she sensed a slight unease—a sadness—in Han Jung-joo when she mentioned Min-yung, who was, as she put it, "resting."

Everything about the position was appealing. The house was large but new and orderly, with automated conveniences, and there were no small children to pick up after. Mrs. Han's husband was apparently particular about his food, but she could learn that. The distance was manageable, and the pay was better, not even counting what she would save on bus fare.

Yes, she liked everything she saw and learned. Everything except the dog. How she hated dogs! Her husband wanted to keep dogs at the house for security when the children were home alone, but she refused again and again. In general, Cho Jin-sook proved fearless in the face of physical challenges, but a long-ago episode with a mangy stray, the scars from which remained prominent on her hand, reminded her of something deeper than plain fear. She'd loved the farm dogs previous to the incident and had approached this stray affectionately, attempting to feed it. She could never forget the animal's sudden turn, from meek to aggressive, or the painful consequences of being caught so completely off guard.

"The dog will need to be fed morning and night. He can be a bit temperamental. Only Dr. Han can calm him fully." Cho Jin-sook swallowed hard and nodded her head. She made tight fists in her lap and willed her blood to quiet and slow. It was all she could do to keep from getting up and leaving. "It is a good job. A reasonable amount of work, but I expect everything to be done just so. I am looking for someone who can be trusted. I do not like to remind or to make requests more than once."

"Yes, of course," Cho Jin-sook said with a slight quiver, finding her voice again.

"You have a family of your own, I assume."

"Three children. My husband has his own rice paddy."

"Where is that?"

"Down the road past Kangpoong Village."

"Did you come by foot?"

"Yes. About three miles. My husband can sometimes pick me up on his scooter."

"Your husband must be a hard worker."

"Yes. Both of us."

"Your children are in school?"

Cho Jin-sook nodded. "The youngest has just started."

"Your mother is alive?"

"No. My father neither. My sisters and brother have all moved to the city. I am the oldest. My mother-in-law watches the children while we work." Cho Jin-sook spoke too quickly; she stopped herself, took a breath. Han Jung-joo also paused here, collecting the data in her mind. This seemed a good sign to Cho Jin-sook, who thought perhaps she was imagining having her in her home, how it would feel, did it fit.

"All right, then. When can you begin?"

They agreed that Cho Jin-sook would finish out the week with her current employer and begin the following week. Cho Jin-sook thanked Mrs. Han, held her hand firmly with both of her own, and was careful not to make eye contact upon taking leave; although something about her new employer attracted her, tempted her curiosity. She must mind this, watch herself. She hurried down the driveway, short-steps-short-steps, then at the bottom dared to turn and look back. Han Jung-joo was not in sight. Cho Jin-sook paused a moment to listen. In the distance, from the back of the house, she heard a noise: the squawking of a chicken, she was almost certain, that familiar shriek, in the grip of imminent doom—then a hard thud. Silence. *Sae sangae!* she thought. *Incredible . . . the woman must still be wearing her blouse and skirt!*

Han Jung-joo set the headless, lifeless chicken aside in the shed. It was cool enough to keep until tomorrow, when she would take it to market for plucking and cleaning—a task she had done herself as a girl but thoroughly disliked. She wiped her hands on her apron and went inside to wash. Perspiration beaded lightly on her forehead and nose. The shepherd whined and fidgeted as she passed, but she paid no mind. Thinking of the woman she had just interviewed and hired, she felt satisfied with her decision. The woman was rough but had a solidity to her, and an honesty. It would be difficult for her to keep the children in school, but it was a noble goal. And ultimately none of her affair. But if they knew they would not put the children to work, they should not have had so many, she felt. Foresight was everything to Han Jung-joo, and the world sorely lacked it at every turn.

"The dog," she thought to herself, more amused than concerned. "The dog will be a problem for her."

Returning to the day's tasks, thinking of the training and preparation required in the coming weeks, she sighed—a mixture of fatigue and relief. Memories of raising her own three children, back when her husband was still in training came into her mind; such a difficult time that was. Things got better when they could afford help, but even then, the constancy of caretaking never subsided. Those were years of persistent worry. It seemed to her that she slept very little, if at all, during those years. But she never let on how filled with anxiety she was every minute of the day. Sometimes she worried over specific things—Hae-sik's asthma, Hae-joo's trouble with reading, Min-yung's sullenness—but mostly her worry took on an amorphous cast: something gray, a pulsing cloud cover, a threat. She did what was required—meticulously, diligently— it was what she knew, what she believed, must be done to fend off danger, of every kind. And she trusted this diligence utterly.

But that day, the day she hired Cho Jin-sook, Han Jung-joo battled an unease. It was not Cho Jin-sook herself, or her decision to hire her. Rather, it occurred to Han Jung-joo, thinking of the woman and her three young children at home, that her worry had in fact never left her. That even now, here in her new, bright home, thick clouds hovered and filled her mind.

Her husband would wonder why she had slaughtered the chicken so soon; it was still a bit young. She would, as always, find just the right answer.

4

The little boy, Won-soo, sulks as his mother pulls him by the arm up the hill toward the house. He has a fresh crew cut, which he hates, and is wearing the green Ralph Lauren sweater his grandparents gave him for Christmas last year, which he also hates. The rounded collar feels too close to his neck. He forgets, however, that every birthday up until this year he has had to wear *hanbok*, and that last year his mother promised him he would not have to wear it anymore on his birthday after he begged and begged and begged. Won-min, the younger boy, with matching crew cut and the same sweater in yellow, is still groggy from the journey from Seoul. He sleeps heavily in his mother's other arm, drooling over her shoulder. Hae-sik lifts what seems like an endless number of duffel bags and diaper bags and toy bags out of the trunk of the car. His early-graying hair is disheveled, his forehead and underarms moist with sweat. He seems to be sulking as well.

"You've arrived!" Han Jung-joo comes hurrying toward them in her blue slippers. Hae-sik's wife, Ji-eun, lowers her head and half smiles in respectful greeting. When Han Jung-joo arrives beside them, smiling and lightly huffing, Ji-eun nudges the sulking boy toward his grandmother. "*Halmuhni hantae insa hae*," she says. "Greet your grandmother."

"*Anyong ha sae yo, Halmuhni*," he mumbles, looking at his feet.

"*Aigoo, whae gu rae, Won-soo ya?* It's Won-soo's special day today, why so grouchy?" The boy shakes his head, back and forth, resolute. Han Jung-joo looks to his mother. She shrugs and shifts the weight of the little one on her hip. She takes her mother-in-law's glance as a sideways scolding and now resists her own grouchiness. Four hours in the car with the children did not pass quickly.

"Ap-pah says Uncle from America is coming, so I have to share my party and Uncle is the more important guest." Han Jung-joo laughs, but then gets serious, now bending down and looking directly into Won-soo's eyes.

"Won-soo *ya*, you should not be unhappy about paying respects to your family, to your elders. Respect should be cheerful, and unthinking. Your mother and father should never have to scold or lecture you about it. Do you understand? It's very important. You are getting older, six years old today, you must learn this well. Grandpa will never put up with this kind of moping. Are you ready to see Grandpa?" She puts out her hand. He takes it, nods his head. Hae-sik joins them with bags hanging off every limb and shoulder, greets his mother. They all walk toward the house.

"*Ajjummah*, please show my daughter-in-law to their room, and help with these bags." Cho Jin-sook greets Hae-sik's family and leads them up the stairs to the guestroom. Hae-sik greets his father, who puts his arm around him affectionately.

"*Chal eet suh*, Hae-sik *ah*? You are fine?"

"*Neh, chal eet suh.*"

"Work is good?"

"Yes, work is busy. I work night shifts these days. The other emergency doctors have done it, so it's my turn now. Ji-eun doesn't like it, she worries that I will fall asleep driving home."

"Every doctor-in-training must work the late hours at some point. Part of the—how do they say it in English—*paying dues*, right? Your wife will always complain about something. At least you are finally making some good money."

"Yes, finally. The boy just started private school."

"Why private school? In my day, the best schools were the public schools, especially in Seoul."

"Not these days. The government is practically socialist. The public schools are terrible. They try to make them 'equal,' but instead they are all poor quality."

"Ah, it's too bad. The government should leave things alone. Whatever they try to improve, always they make worse."

Hae-sik bows his head, a moment of silent assent. "I like your house, Father."

Dr. Han smiles, but with heavy eyes. "Yes, it is a good house. We used an English architect. All the materials from Europe. I will give you and Hae-joo a tour. Hae-joo is here already; they are resting. But I will rouse him and show you the rest of the house."

"And my sister?"

"Min-yung is not feeling well, you know." Han Jae-kyu smiles, laughs uneasily. "Woo-sung was supposed to come for the weekend but had to stay in Taegu for work. Women have a way of upsetting themselves to sickness. I have been practicing medicine thirty years, but this kind of sickness, I tell you, it cannot be helped."

"*Uhn-ni*, what do you think of this house? Didn't you study architecture in school?" Han Jung-joo, Cho Jin-sook, and the two daughters-in-law have gathered in the kitchen, tending to final preparations. Cho Jin-sook stands over the simmering oxtail soup while the two young women sit at the table arranging *mandu* on a large platter. Han Jung-joo skillfully snip-snips baby radish—candy-red and white—into floral shapes for garnish. Ji-eun hesitates to answer the question that Yoo-mee, Hae-joo's wife, has asked her. Yoo-mee is several years younger than Ji-eun and was born and raised in Seoul. She is petite but solid in build, wears her thick and very black hair short ("like Winona Ryder"), and speaks directly—sometimes too directly, in Ji-eun's opinion—with both her raspy voice and her round, eager eyes, to no matter whom. She recently confided in Ji-eun that she does not intend to have children and that she wants to be a movie producer (another in a long line of revolving prospective professions), "jet-setting" frequently overseas.

"Yes, I did," Ji-eun says. "But that was so many years ago."

Han Jung-joo's upper half is now buried in the refrigerator, looking for something, but Ji-eun is, as always, keenly aware of her
mother-in-law.

"Do you think it is a good design, *uhn-ni?*" Yoo-mee persists.
"It seems to me it is trying to bring together Eastern and Western
styles. But there is something . . . I don't know . . . *strange.*"

Han Jung-joo reemerges from the refrigerator with a ginger-
root in hand, which she passes to Cho Jin-sook, and returns to
her post with the radishes. She is attentive to the conversation
that is occurring while tending to her tasks. She and Yoo-mee
have a kind of implicit agreement to be pleasant and to let each
other be. The differences, it seems, are too great. For Han Jung-
joo, it would be almost undignified to spend too much effort on
Yoo-mee, to attempt a motherly shaping of manners. And Yoo-
mee's sense of entitlement, inherited from her high birth, is too
great for her to feel any sort of obligation toward her mother-
in-law, as far as reserving her opinions. In this way, surprisingly,
their relationship has been mostly smooth.

"Ji-eun *ah*, do tell us what you think," Han Jung-joo says. "I
am curious as well." Over the years, Ji-eun has become adept at
reading her mother-in-law's tones—as perfectly even as they are
on the surface—like learning perfect pitch in music. Today, she
seems to Ji-eun in a light mood, and slightly distracted, which
is unusual. Ji-eun has also noticed Han Jung-joo's new hairstyle
and the dark coloring. She wonders if her mood is somehow
related to this change.

"Well," she proceeds cautiously, as if at a blinking yellow traffic light, "it is interesting, this 'strangeness,' as you say." She looks
to Yoo-mee, the safer audience. "It is as if . . . ," she pauses, considering both her thoughts and her manner of expression ". . . it
is as if it began with a Western conception, but then held back,
like a restraint. It stops short of the heaviness, the weight, of an
English home. These open beams, for example. It's the restraint
that is most interesting. As if the house is aware of itself, of its

roots. There are these horizontal panels. They keep things low, and level, almost like railings. . . ."

"I keep thinking they'll come back to finish it." Min-yung has appeared in housecoat and slippers. The women look up, surprised and pleased to see her.

"Min-yung, we were wondering when we'd see you." Yoo-mee goes to hug her, and in that moment—the stark contrast between Yoo-mee's buoyancy and Min-yung's infirmity like a bolt of reality—a hush blankets the room, dulls the activity. It is more than just her paleness, or the cloudiness of her eyes; Min-yung's presence, and the unspoken knowledge that Woo-sung will not be coming, opens up a kind of gray vacancy among them.

"It feels like they didn't quite know how to finish this place," Min-yung continues, "so they just left it . . . I don't know . . . half-done. But it's intentional, I know—like what Ji-eun *uhn-ni* was saying. I'm not complaining or anything," she says, directing her comments now toward her mother, sensing, like a single-degree drop in room temperature, her displeasure. "It's such a nice house. We're glad Ap-pah likes it so much."

Han Jung-joo smiles, arranging her radishes on a plate. "You girls know so much these days about so many things. In our day, we left things like buildings and houses to the men. It's wonderful that you all feel free now, to voice your thoughts and opinions, even questions, about anything." They are all quiet for a moment, uncertain. Han Jung-joo's smile has not altered, it is a commanding smile, opaque and final. But she seems to be thinking of something else, trying to recall something just out of reach that has slipped her mind.

"Look at how many hands it will take to make this meal!" It is Cho Jin-sook who breaks the silence, a relief to all. "Miss Min-yung, come help me with this, we'll need a *looooot* of ginger."

⁏   ⁏   ⁏

Dr. Han and his two sons stand in a distant huddle in the front yard, beholding the house, rubbing their hands together and breathing white smoke into the air. Hae-joo is the most dramatic about the cold, hopping from one foot to the other, breaking into jumping jacks at one point. Dr. Han finds his youngest child, the *mangnae*, mostly charming and amusing. He is a good-looking boy, with almond eyes and dark freckled skin, gregarious and cheerful, always very popular; but sometimes his father wishes he would shape up a bit, take things more seriously. He and his wife were pleased when he finally decided to settle down with Yoo-mee—an intelligent, youthful, albeit somewhat aggressive young woman from an aristocratic family in Seoul. Yoo-mee's father was a German literature professor at Seoul University, now retired, and her grandfather a well-known research scientist. Her older brother is finishing his doctorate in business administration, also at Seoul University, and her older sister married one of her brother's classmates. Dr. and Mrs. Han worried a bit about the match—two *mangnae dul*—but they put their hope in Hae-joo, that marriage and family would turn him into a more responsible young man. And besides, Yoo-mee's family was quite taken with Hae-joo and seemed to expect very little of him, for better or for worse, in exchange for what seemed a bottomless financial generosity. So they knew, at the least, that the two of them would never want for money.

"It is the best house in town, that's for certain," says Hae-sik.

"But not *too* good," says his father. "We wanted comfortable, and modern, but not . . . flashy. People look to us, you know. We don't want to separate ourselves, or act better than others. We have a responsibility."

"You can leave that to Reverend Lee's people," Hae-joo says with a sarcastic snort. His father smiles and says nothing, his way of assent. "Just promise you and Mother don't start sounding like Imelda Marcos or anything. Saving the common people, that sort of thing."

"They call this style *Tudor?*" Hae-sik asks, instinctively running interference on his brother's impertinence.

"Yes, that's right. Our style is very simple. The wealthy English had three or four stories, and carvings in the timber, and covered the interior beams with plaster. We just kept everything plain and simple and open. The materials themselves, the wood especially, were expensive enough."

"Saved your money for all the technology," says Hae-joo. "Those toilets are amazing; hardly any sound at all."

"Right, and save gallons of water. That's important in a small town these days. Population is growing, resources stay the same." The three men shift their weight and look up at the good-but-not-too-good structure before them, rising up over the scattering of smaller homes here at the foot of the mountains along the perimeter of Hyun Sook Lake. Hae-joo's restlessness gets the better of him. He leaves the circle to get reacquainted with Bear, who has been barking and whining ever since the guests began arriving. Han Jae-kyu and his elder son stand together in silence as Hae-sik waits for his father to speak. "You look a bit worn, Hae-sik *ah.*"

"Ji-eun says I am looking more like you. Like an old man, I guess." They both laugh. "The children keep us busy."

"You will wake up from these years. I hardly remember them myself. Those years I worked and worked, and always had you children on my mind. I wonder if you three knew that—how much I was there with you even when I was not home." Hae-sik is surprised by his father's words, his candidness. A measure of tenderness and self-revelation that is new between them. Hae-sik is at once comforted and disturbed by his father's mood. Han Jae-kyu's eyes are fixed on the house, but it seems to Hae-sik that he is seeing something else, something from long ago. Or perhaps something to come.

"Father?"

"Yes."

"Shall we go in?"

He nods, but doesn't move. Hae-sik waits.

"Your wife is happy, Hae-sik?"

"Father?"

"Your wife . . . she is happy? She is satisfied with you?" Hae-sik purses his lips, considers the nature of his father's question, the answer he must give. It is a strange word he uses—*satisfied*—a strong word that refers to an active and whole-being kind of fulfillment, a word often used in a religious context.

"*Kul seh* . . . Hard to say. She is so much focused on the boys. . . ."

His father nods. "Yes. The children are the most important; it should always be this way. But it can become almost an obsession." They stand without speaking a few moments longer. Hae-joo is running around the yard playing fetch-and-chase with Bear. He is huffing and puffing; the dog growls playfully. "*Ko mahn, ko mahn*, Hae-joo *ya. Jaaaahhh-shik.* Time to go inside. Don't make a mess. Your uncle will arrive soon." He throws the stick one last time, runs after Bear, pulls at the stick, which the dog holds tightly in his jaws.

"*Ko MAHN*, Hae-joo." It is his older brother who now urges him to cease and desist.

"I have to win," he says, now pulling with both hands and the full weight of his compact body. "In a tug of war with your pet, you must always win. You must establish dominance." Finally, he wrests the stick from the shepherd's mouth, jerks backward, and trips on a large rawhide bone. He lands hard on his bottom on the damp grass, laughing and pleased with his triumph.

5

Ji-eun and Min-yung have begun to cover the dishes with plastic wrap to keep them fresh. Min-yung asks her mother if she should put the fish and the shrimp in the refrigerator. *"Ah-nee,"* Han Jung-joo says, waving her off. Yoo-mee is playing *yuht* with the boys in the living room—not exactly playing by the rules, but they love to throw the wooden sticks in the air and watch them fall, over and over again. The red markings look to Won-soo like ribbons fluttering. "Not too high, Won-soo. You're going to hit someone in the eye or break *Halmuhni's* pottery." Ji-eun is thankful; the boys love their young auntie, and she is good with them. As it nears 8:15, Ji-eun knows that without Yoo-mee's distractions, Won-soo will kick into high-gear whining, especially since it is his birthday; and that once he starts, he will not stop.

As it is, Han Jung-joo is the most irritable. Not visibly, of course, and yet all the family knows how much she does not like to wait, to have things veer from the plan. Han Hyun-kyu was expected on an early-afternoon plane arriving in Pohang. After customs and baggage claim, then the ninety-minute trip from the airport by taxi (they would of course pay the driver the fifty thousand won when he arrived), he should have arrived close to 6:00 p.m., 7:00 at the latest. When they spoke on the phone during his layover, Han Jae-kyu had specified (at Han Jung-joo's request) that his brother should call if there were any delays and, at any rate, to call from Pohang Airport when he arrived. They have as yet heard nothing.

Dr. Han and his two sons sit on the leather sectional in the family room. He and Hae-sik recline with their feet up on the low table. Dr. Han smokes a pipe. Hae-joo sits forward, leaning on his knees, remote control in hand, flipping back and forth between a popular soap opera drama and soccer. He crunches loudly on walnuts. "I'm surprised how good the reception is here," he says. "You must have a very big satellite dish."

"These days they are not too big. You probably did not even notice. It's at the side of the house, next to the cherry tree."

"We have no TV these days," Hae-sik says. "We think the boys will become too absorbed in it. We want them to develop in other ways."

"You are becoming like one of those funny Pusan families," says Hae-joo. "Hippie types. Yoo-mee likes that kind of thing, wants us to leave Seoul for Pusan, maybe join up with some of those communal-living groups."

"No way, we are nothing like those hippies. We are too old for that. Those are the college kids. The ones who work the film festival. We're just concerned about all the consumerism. The teenagers these days are unbearable."

"Here, too," their father says. "When we were children growing up we didn't have enough to eat or shoes to wear. We went door-to-door with your grandmother selling potatoes and hand-made socks and hats. Now the young people spend money on everything—clothes, cars, cell phones. They don't think about their lives, just how to get money and buy things. They don't even study.

"My brothers and I all studied hard; but your uncle who is coming tonight, he studied the hardest. When we were young, our family lived on a small island in the East Sea, five hours by boat." Hae-sik smiles faintly; he has heard this story before. Hae-joo is distracted by the TV, but listens with one ear. "No one from that island ever went to college. Your uncle would stay up late with a single candle and read science books late into the night. He asked one of his teachers what he had to do to go to college, and the teacher told him he had to pass a test, so he asked the teacher what was on the test, and the teacher gave him a list. This was when your uncle was only in sixth grade. He started studying for the test as soon as he got that list, always getting books from the village library. Then, when he was old enough to go to high school . . ." White lights flash through the window. The taxi has arrived. "*Aigoo, owhat goonyo!* He has arrived!"

The three men stand. Dr. and Mrs. Han rush to open the front door. Everyone else gathers at the window looking out to the driveway. The younger boy, bouncing in his auntie's arms, squeals. *"Ay ay!"* Han Jung-joo hands her husband a wad of bills, and he slips his feet into outdoor slippers and steps into the night, into the brightness of the taxi lights, coatless. Han Jung-joo squints and raises her hand to her forehead as a visor, her other arm wrapped across her middle, to steady herself as she shivers from the sudden cold. She sees her husband leaning into the taxi window, then stepping back to behold a larger figure who has just exited the car. She is not sure if her eyes are playing tricks on her, or if the angle of her view coupled with the intensity of the headlights has created an optical illusion; but the second figure strikes her as utterly gigantic—like a creature from another world.

Captor and Captive (1968)

Lee Woo-in did not like the tie Han Hyun-kyu was wearing when he left the house. It was not a silk tie, but some imitation fabric, much too shiny, clearly something purchased at one of those bargain-basement warehouses. Something-Mart, or Something-Rite. And that color—was it aqua? Disgusting. He infuriated her with such daily blunders. He had no sense for things, for elegance or sophistication. He was a country bumpkin, a *chun nom*. The other doctors laughed at him, at his thick accent, which hadn't improved even after four years in the States. She didn't know this for a fact, as she didn't much socialize with his colleagues; but she was sure of it. How could they not? He was ridiculous. Working like a dog, never gaining recognition or promotion at the hospital. The worst was that he didn't seem to mind it. He appeared content with his lot, almost proud of what he'd accomplished—bootstraps, undignified beginnings, et cetera. She was supposed to be impressed by this, apparently, but found it boring. Such a hackneyed story—the island, the older brother, hiding on the boat. He lived for these simpleton stories, telling the same ones over and over, as if life was one big country folk tale. She cursed her luck, and herself, when she thought of how she had stumbled, blind and impulsive, into such a life. Greater things awaited her. Yes, no doubt. Much greater things.

Her work. Her work would be her salvation. She was on the cusp, she could feel it. Her research was going well, a breakthrough was imminent. Dreams. Post-Freud. Beyond sexual inter-pretations. But she was racing the clock, she needed to finish her study and publish quickly. The stress was tremendous; some days she thought she might collapse from the intensity.

This morning, her husband has left earlier than usual, a morning surgery scheduled at the last minute. She is left to mind the children until the nanny arrives, which won't be for two hours. Han-soo, sweet Han-soo, is sleeping. He has always been a good sleeper; she kept him in the bed with her up until a few weeks ago, and he seems to be transitioning well. Ah-jin has been up since her father left, always cranky when she senses his absence. Lee Woo-in sets the girl down in the playroom with some toys and leaves the door open. She is hoping she can fin-ish reading Jergensen's paper on the recurring dream before her first clinical session later this morning. She is close, very close, to confirming the hunches upon which her study is based. But now the child starts to fuss, banging on—what is that cursed thing, noisy metallic instrument Han Hyun-kyu brought home for the child?—the *glockenspiel*. Lee Woo-in hears anger in this, not exploration. She rubs her temples and marks the pain in her stomach.

The child unnerves her—a temperament incompatibility, nothing more, she tells herself. Terrible twos, as they say. A pass-ing phase.

She reaches for the cocktail glass that has become her close companion these last months: first in the evenings before bed, then as a ritual preamble to her studies after dinner—a fast and businesslike affair centered mostly around the children—and now also mornings, when she must calm her nerves to focus. She finds her stomach relaxes immediately after the first sip, her shoulders and back after the second. One more sip, and her mind begins to settle, and open. She holds up the glass just as a vague glow from the morning sun illuminates the room through sage-colored linen curtains—curtains she picked herself, along with all the furniture for this office, in anticipation of the day she would use it for private practice.

The shift in lighting, although slight, startles her, draws her full attention to the glass in hand, whose clear golden liquid has caught some of the glow. For an instant, she becomes aware of the glass's power, its beguiling hold. Provoked, she tips her head back and drinks the full volume at once, finishes the act by placing the glass down with intention, and authority, but withholding just before contact with the hard wood of the desk is made. Her determination, her focus, must be quiet, and steady. Yes, now she is ready, this is her time, the mustering of her life, this, this is what matters. Presently, a disturbance fills the hallway beyond the threshold: the child crying, shrill clang of wood on metal. But Lee Woo-in does not hear.

Entry Wounds

1

I have not spoken with either Dr. Lee or my father since my return, now nearly two months ago. It is not unusual for me to be back in town without contacting Dr. Lee, who is less likely to notice the length of my absences; but I usually try to check in on my father. It comforts him, I think, and maybe me, too, just to know that the other is *still there*, details notwithstanding. But this time, somehow, I just haven't had the strength. Or maybe I'm just not as certain about how *still there* I really am.

Henry has been good—remarkably good—at keeping the news of my return under wraps. He's less in touch with them himself these days. And anyway, I shouldn't be surprised. Henry has an impeccable poker face, it's how he's always operated; and how, ultimately, he got himself in so deep before we knew it.

He holds the phone out to me as I'm coming out of the shower. He says something, but I'm rubbing my head with a towel, and he's playing something loud on the stereo. "Who?"

"Mom-o." He shrugs his shoulders, anticipating my next question. "She just knew. I don't know. She asked for you. Something's wrong." I take the phone, he goes back into his room.

"Hi there."

"Jane? It's Mom." I am holding the phone two inches from my ear out of habit. Dr. Lee's voice is almost always loud, too loud—in person and on the phone. My theory is that it helps her think more clearly, because she's always got so much going on in her head. Like she's chasing out distractions with volume. I've wondered if she speaks so loudly to her patients (pity the poor souls). Right now, realizing I can barely hear her—the phone is somehow the hardest since the blast—I press the receiver close and plug my other ear with a finger.

"Sorry, what? Are you all right? Is something wrong?"

"Yes, well . . . yes, I'm fine. How are you? Are you all right? You've been back a little while?"

"Just got in," I say vaguely. "Had a few things to take care of. Work things."

"Your father doesn't know you're back? Have you been in touch?"

"No, not yet. I just got in . . . there's been a lot . . ."

"Yes, right, you said that. Well . . ." It's strange, this hesitation. Dr. Lee rarely hesitates, and even more rarely does one wait for her to complete a thought. The thoughts are complete far in advance of their expression, with far more complete thoughts than time and space in which to express them. Henry knows it too and must have sensed the same strangeness. I bear the pause for as long as I can, which isn't long.

"Mother?"

"Well . . . it's your father." Her voice is taut and low now, also unusual.

"What is it?" I walk toward Henry's door, put my hand on the knob.

"He's gone. He's disappeared." She says this somehow with emphasis and dissipation at once, her voice trailing off as I take the punch in the gut.

My mother is tall for a Korean woman, a towering five foot nine, and lanky—long-armed, long-fingered, even long-toed. With her physique you'd think that she would saunter and pirouette

through life like a ballerina; instead, she is flitting, like a drag-
onfly with a clipped wing, buzzing and pouncing, here and away,
always. A freakish energy, a frenetic presence that is no presence.
By now, I should be used to it, I should expect her disruptions,
her antics. She is like a child ringing doorbells and running away,
trampling on all the carefully tended flowers and kicking the cat
in the walkway. She is quick, and invisible; and thus inculpable.

But she is saying something now, she is telling me something
real, and surprising.

"Disappeared? What do you mean?"

"Your father . . ." She pauses. Dramatic effect or genuine anxiety, I can't be sure. "He left. Over a week ago. I thought he'd
be back soon enough, so I didn't say anything. I hate to bother
or worry Henry, you know. But he's gone. Not a word. He's put
things away around the house. I found airline charges on the
credit card. Korean Air. He's gone . . . home. I think. No, I'm sure
of it. To his family. To Korea."

Home? Family? Korea? The words land flat, inert, like crypto-
grams on a cave wall. And like a cave, it is dark and airless in my
head as she proceeds to tell me that my father has left—left *her?*
left *us?*—without a word, without warning.

I have a flash of déjà vu. Or maybe, is it something I've
dreamed, or wished? My mother is hanging on the line and I
can't quite get a handle on a response to what she's told me.
Words spill out, clumsy ones, I'm like a gum-smacking teenager
responding to the latest gossip: "For real?"

When I first arrived on Henry's doorstep, within a few seconds
of seeing him I knew that something had really happened to
me, in a way I hadn't quite grasped while still in Baghdad, in the
zone with other photographers and journalists. Here, back in

New York—from the airport to the taxi ride through Queens, to the quaint streets of Gramercy, to Henry's front steps, an impossible parallel cosmos of beings strutting and rushing about all confidence and blind assurance *as if nothing at all could befall them*—the blast suddenly seemed enormous, and still happening. The white-noise nonsound of it filled my head, and I thought for a moment I might be deaf—fully deaf—in its wake. In the doorway, Henry, with his slumping shoulders and chalky face, moved his mouth at me and smiled sadly with his eyes. Henry. Henry was not impossible, thank God. Henry was in *this* cosmos, and he was very probable, bodily and real—confidence and assurance shot to hell, and dealing with the plodding gloom of it. Together, we've pulled a big puffy blanket around us, literally and otherwise, and hunkered down in our respective grief.

But now Dr. Lee has single-handedly burst the bubble. I suspect on some level she has no idea—her ever-reliable emotional war-waging. Dr. Live Grenade.

After all these years, all this time, he's done it. Finally. My father of sorrows, he's done it. I snap back into the probable, the possible, and suddenly the brush grows up again, taller and thicker around me.

2

They called her in whenever possible for these cases. Sometimes, when she wasn't on duty, it fell to whichever nurse happened to be there. But it was better when she was there: she could step in, sit with the couple, especially the woman, for a few minutes, an hour, sometimes longer. She would come back to see them, right after breakfast the following morning, and always walked them out. It was her job, she felt, to escort them over the threshold, to wish them well, in words and inward thoughts. She always said a short prayer as they parted.

That night, it was all quiet in the maternity ward. The couple that came in looked perfectly normal, except that the young woman was brought in by wheelchair; they had come from the emergency room. The nurse on desk duty had buzzed her in Room 32, where she'd just finished chatting with Maddy Ritter, a sixteen-year-old who would be giving her child up for adoption. She came down the hall and saw them there by the desk, waiting. They were a young Asian couple, handsome pair. The man wore sweatpants and a college T-shirt, most likely the clothes he slept in, his hair was mussed and spiked in every which direction, and he wore very thick glasses—probably not his daily habit, but there wouldn't have been time to put in contact lenses. The woman had long black hair pulled back in a low ponytail, a few moist strands hanging forward in her face. She wore a hospital gown, which they gave her in ER, and she held loosely in her lap, as if she'd just as soon let them fall to the ground, a bundle of clothes. Good, she thought; the medical part was done.

The lights around reception are too harsh—especially during the night shift, when the hall lights are dimmed. As she approaches, she can see all too clearly, as she knew would be the case, that there is nothing perfectly normal about them—about what they are feeling, what they've just been through. These two are blank, completely blank in the face. They look like terribly bored children, with poor posture and lack of grooming habits. Like brother and sister, orphaned. She sees it ten, sometimes fifteen times a day, and yet each time, something plummets deep in her chest, takes her breath away. She recognizes the awful singularity of it, the way it changes each person irrevocably, but differently. She knows the experience firsthand—three times she's gone through it—but never assumes, never pretends to know just what they feel, what is going on inside them, between them, around them. She just knows that they need a quiet place, a place

to rest, to talk or not talk, where they don't have to *explain* anything. The next day they will reenter a world much crueler, more
precarious and absurd than the one they'd known before. She
generally resists predictions of what will come after, whether
they will "make it"—as some couples didn't, as she and her ex-
husband didn't. Sometimes it depended on how far along they
were when the child was lost; sometimes not.

They seem not to notice her, even as she comes close, right
up in front of them. She puts one hand gently on the woman's
shoulder, holds the other out to the man. He takes it, out of some
past learned reflex, but without understanding, without hearing
her introduce herself as . . . *Kathy? . . . Carrie? . . . a social worker . . .
maternity ward . . . must be very difficult* . . . She holds them like this
for a moment, breathing deeply, calming herself first, taking in
their bewilderment. She notices that there is no contact between
them, none at all, physically or otherwise, and mourns the vast
distance that separates these two; either long in the making or
breaking in all at once, this part she can't detect. She finds herself
trembling, imperceptibly except to herself, feeling how, at this
moment, her hands are all that hold them together.

3

My freshman year out in the field, I'd learned quickly, on the
spot really, most of what I needed to know, what most took
years to get: that you have exactly one second to think, not a
moment more (or less); that you always and immediately run
toward the danger, but never at full speed; that ignorance and
naiveté can work in your favor if your instincts are good and
motives clear; that you trust no one but are always trustworthy; that no assignment is a dud, but rather a chance to show
some ingenuity. That your camera is your precious instrument,

and also, yes, your weapon—wielded properly, it's your ticket in; squandered, your one-way pass to nowhere nice.

These lessons were somehow not difficult for me to learn, and natural. Something about quick reflexes came easily. Reacting is as strong a skill as I've got, a basic mode of existence. As is inconspicuousness, flying under the radar. People opened up to me, allowed me wandering rights in their territory. I suppose they sensed no threat, no covetousness (I am a tallish person, but plain-styled and slight). From the get-go, I pushed as far as I could in every situation, and minded my limits.

For me, it's never been about *breaking the story* or *exposing the subject* anyway. It's always been about the moment. Freezing time, holding space. The enormity of an instant. Later, when you see what you've got, what you've managed to seize from time, you feel somehow like the world has stopped turning, everything and everyone suspended, waiting; and the moment you have, there in your hands, before your eyes, it's spinning out into its own deep and wide eternity.

Everything happens in a moment.

And yet, string them all together and you can still somehow find yourself nowhere. Time and space flattened out into here, there, yesterday, tomorrow. Years gone by in a blink.

The parade of cameras over time was fairly conventional. First, it was my hands—baby fingers curled over into O's, binocular lenses to frame objects of interest. The ornate patterns of kitchen-floor vinyl, the cat's front paws stretched out in front like baby boxing gloves. Clouds. These, my first cropping exercises, everything cast within circles. Then it was the Fisher-Price Zoo Camera. Prefab images of zebras, lions, tigers that went click-click, an artificial flash to simulate the magic.

But I was impatient for *actual* magic; I could smell a rat. So I lobbied hard for a Polaroid.

I was eleven, I think. The world had begun to seem an unpleasant and unstable place. *Magic.* Magic was everything. *See, click, poof!* That first real camera seemed the answer to everything, a revelation—like a crime with no punishment. The world was mine for the taking. From the beginning, I somehow knew: behind the lens, I had my footing. It was a place of instant solitude, and safe.

Looking back, it was probably best that my parents refused my pleas for a complex manual-focus Pentax until I was older. Those first few years I had one variable to work with: the frame. Within such parameters, your eyes begin to work hard. You learn to tilt your head, bend your knees, step back, step forward, look away then look again. You learn to scan. Pause. Wait—for the light to shift, the subject to turn, the wind to blow, your eyes to adjust until texture and dimension come into relief. You learn to always keep your eyes working when they are open, sometimes even when they are closed.

I am on the younger side among my colleagues, in good part because of some luck early on. The thing about luck is that you don't need a whole lot of it; but it must be well timed, and you've got to be paying close attention to receive its full benefits. Lesson #1—that you have exactly one second to think—applies especially when luck breezes by.

When I was in college, cobbling together art and photography classes alongside a poli-sci major, figuring out how my future life as a photojournalist was really going to work, there were still only a few women out there tromping through minefields wearing burkas and camping out in desert caves dressed as men. One of them was a French *femme* named Eloise Martine, who came to give a special weeklong lecture series during my senior year called "Love and Lust: The Concerned Photojournalist"—which, despite its racy title, proved to be a seminal philosophical treatise on the complex morality of war photography. The lectures were subsequently published in photo-essay format by a major art publisher, with blurbs on the back cover from the likes of Nachtwey, Amanpour, Salgado.

By that time, Paul and I had been together a couple of years. He was out of graduate school and had just begun working as a civil engineer for a large company, a major government contractor. He was a rising star, the only junior engineer managing his own projects, meeting sometimes with senior government officials whose identities he claimed he could not reveal (I suspected sometimes that he said so for the fun of it, knowing I'd eat up the intrigue). He was very busy, and the difference between my listless, self-determining senior schedule and his heavily deadlined professional one had begun to set us on different paths. We were drifting, the way couples do, I guess; especially the young and the ambitious.

So I had some time on my hands: I was ripe for something, and searching.

I attended Eloise's first three lectures. At the third one, I braved up to ask a question—something about how much thinking and planning went into the work, intention versus instinct—which apparently made an impression, sending her off into a gripping story about photographing women in coca-growing cooperatives in Bolivia, which, many months and even more rolls of film later, eventually got her access to traffickers, their brothers and husbands and fathers—the real story. Afterward, I lingered at the front of the auditorium as she held court, catching bits and pieces of Q&A. When she began to pack up her things, signaling the end of the session, I headed toward the exit; but then I felt her turn toward me and point in my direction. In response to a question I didn't catch, she said, "Ask that one over there; she knows what I mean." I looked over, and I am almost sure she winked at me.

It was spring term of my senior year. I had a "Totalitarianism and the Modern State" mid-term exam awaiting me, but I thought *what the hell*—and I had exactly one second to think. In that second, she'd left, and I rushed out the door. I pushed my way through bodies and backpacks, out into the campus square. It took a near sprint for me to catch up to her, and when I did, she was, miraculously, alone. "Excuse me," I called. She was a few steps ahead, and walking very fast. "Madame Martine!" I was yelling now, people were turning to stare. She stopped short, did not turn around, but allowed me to catch up. Just as I reached her, she immediately started moving again, as fast as before.

"Oh, it's you," she said. She hadn't turned to look at me, but identified me peripherally. "There is always one. I am very fast, you know, I know how to get away. But there is always one. I am glad it's you. *Viens.* I have some time, you are in luck."

She led me to the faculty lounge, where mostly younger faculty congregated. There, she had stowed her things in a corner, behind a chair. "It's my camera, really, that I am worried about. It will be okay, you think?" I looked over to see a pile of lumpy canvas bags, edges worn and torn, colors faded. It could have been a homeless person's life possessions. "You learn to disguise your treasure, your instrument," she said, reading my thoughts. "Subtlety, always. You never announce yourself as *The Photographer.*"

Some time turned into an afternoon and then an early dinner at a nearby café. It was like a dream, this bit of luck—my first lesson in what can happen when you *act*, when you plant your feet in *that second* and do what needs to be done. She started our chat with this: "Yes, I am glad it is you. Did you notice how many women were in that lecture hall?" I hadn't, really, though I knew the answer. "You are very lucky that your *université* has brought me here. In France, in Paris even, they don't ask me to speak. They would rather silence me. These wars, all of them, they are still about *le machismo.* Penis wars, you know. We are not welcome in their matters. These nations which are at war, they are nations in the grips of patriarchy. We women work not twice as hard, but ten times as hard to get inside, to earn *entrée*. We are trouble, we invade their male space, you understand?"

She spoke quickly, as if time was short. And it did feel like time was spinning, releasing for just this moment something wild and mysterious, and I would be waking up from the hallucination very soon. It was a moment, I suppose, of pure youth. The young Rilke had his statue of Apollo—*You must change your life.* I had Eloise.

"You ask a good question, the kind with no exact answer, and yet one must ask it, over and again. Don't lose that, it's very easy to lose your self in all this mess, your sense of *what* and *why*. I see you are serious, you want *some*thing. I was like that. I will speak about this—*le sexisme* in journalism—at the end of the week, to that roomful of boys, after they have heard my stories, after they have seen my pictures and I have proven myself a worthy source. But you, you are getting this little talk from me now, *entre nous*, because I do not like wasting time. Those boys, most of them will not care or understand what I am saying. I am talking about love and lust.

"I think that, yes, perhaps women, they have a harder time with the physical challenges of fieldwork. We need toilets and hair-washing and the skin of our feet is soft. But *enfin*, I tell you, what we know better is the difference between love and lust.

"Many photographers, they lust for that moment, the height of violence or terror or destruction, when they can swoop in with a camera and shoot—like a gun, you know? But listen, we are not combatants in the war, we are not there to crave and consume violence. War and violence, these are male adolescence, unenlightened instincts—don't forget. You love your work, you love the art, the craft, of capturing those instants"— she said these words with drawn-out vowels, savoring them— "because the world and all *humanité* exists in an image. But at the same time, you hate it, you must always also hate what you do, you make your living off of suffering and ugliness and despair.

You mustn't love that. If you do, then you are mercenary, you have built your work on lust. You may get away with it, perhaps even make money. I don't know you, I don't have time to know you—but I have my instinct. . . . You asked me about instinct, and so, here you have it. . . . I gamble here and there. Try to do something *real*. I tell you, it will not be easy."

We drank, she smoked, and the whole evening I had the strange sensation of seeing everything, for just these few hours, through a telescope. And simultaneously feeling as if the two of us were the image *inside* the telescope—participating in the immensity of the stars and the sky and the planet. Time spun, a glorious whir, and when I stepped back, beholding the image, a shape of a life presented itself to me; and it looked something like my own shape, but also the shape of everything.

It was both terrifying and exhilarating—that someone *expected* something of me, like being anointed and picked out of a police lineup all at once, God and the law pointing her finger: *You.* Eloise was in fact not much older than I—about ten years—but seemed a lifetime away and ahead. She was petite, muscular, with frizzy auburn hair, pale freckled skin, watery blue eyes. Isabelle Huppert with a shot of testosterone.

When we parted that evening, she told me to send her my photos when I was ready, but not before. I told her I would. I was twenty years old, she had me by the collar, and I wanted to say something like "Thank you" or "I won't let you down, Madame Martine," but instead, possessed by a sincerity that seems all but impossible to me now, I said this: "I hope to learn what you mean by 'love.'" We were standing on a street corner, it was late on a warm spring evening, the nearest streetlight was just far enough that we were mostly in the dark, the distant brightness illuminating the space between us. Eloise held my face in one hand, very close to hers, and kissed both cheeks. My headless Apollo, *from every edge exploding like starlight.* "You will, Jeanne. I believe you will."

I did not attend any more of Eloise's lectures but instead spent that time and the bulk of that semester finishing my senior portfolio series—Asian-American kids with money, bankers and lawyers, dressed to the nines, shooting up and snorting coke in brightly lit, marble-countered club bathrooms (Henry got me in, a friend of a friend). It was shock-value stuff, but the photos themselves were understated and had a warmth to them that I knew somehow worked. I sent prints of the best ones to Eloise. The series won an award in the senior exhibit, which meant my own one-week show at a scrappy gallery in an up-and-coming neighborhood. I sold one photograph, and had money to tide me over that summer, so I went to work on another series: Chinese prostitutes in Queens. This one I got on my own, through one of the subjects of the first series who came to the show and liked it. The girls let me shoot them while they passed time, smoking dope and giving each other makeovers, during off-hours. No clients, they said, the johns would never allow it. I explained that I would be discreet and didn't want any faces; they said I'd get myself killed if I tried. I believed them.

I sent these to Eloise as well. I was so hopeful, I sent originals. When I didn't hear back for a long time, I grew listless and despondent.

"She's probably traveling," Paul assured me, always the level-headed optimist. "Give it some time." When finally I did hear from her, it was an e-mail, and not much to go on: "Jeanne, come to Paris, your work is good. Come right away." I had exactly one second to think.

She included an address, which meant nothing to me, since I'd never been to Paris. But I went right out and quit my respectable entry-level job in the photographic preservation department of the public library; Paul and I discussed it for all of two minutes for formality's sake ("I'll be back soon enough, who even knows what this is about"); and off I went.

That was it. That was the beginning.

4

To: Paul@company_x.com
Fr: JaneintheJungle@hotmail.com

P,

I'm here. We've been moving nonstop since the day, the minute, I got here. Sorry it's taken so long to write, it's not so easy to find a computer, let alone a connection. Anyway, back in Paris now. Haven't had even a second to look for a place, been crashing on couches, wherever there's room and a reasonable (not disgusting) bathroom. We're off again tomorrow, then hopefully back for at least a couple weeks so I can find a place, get in with an agency (Eloise may help), sleep a full night. Will write again when I have an address. Tired. Miss you. Smacks to Henry, don't let him too far out of sight. —J

P,

At Pristina Airport in Kosovo. Laurent, my partner on this one, is guarding me, we think this Internet terminal is for military personnel only. The place is all guns and uniforms, and it's impossible to tell who's who. How will I ever get it straight? Who's on whose side? I'm trigger-happy, and I know it. Laurent looks at me knowingly, the freshman who isn't sure what she's shooting or why. It's all instinct out here—there's no time to think, there's no *knowing* anything. If you see it, you shoot it. I don't know what I'm doing. When we get back to Paris—if we get back to Paris (two flight cancellations already)—I'll develop my first set of rolls and see what I've got. Everything's coming out of pocket until I sell something. The pressure's on. Julien at the agency is a macho s.o.b. so I have to double-prove myself. Gotta go . . . —J

P,

I just have a sec. You should take the promotion. It'll be a stepping-stone, don't think of it as permanent and don't overthink it. Send pics of Henry's bash to the Paris address . . . it's nice to come home to mail, and I want to see his face, his eyes . . . I believe you when you say he's ok, but I want to see for myself.

I sold another one, the stupid polar bear. Check the *Times* next week, Travel section on Saskatchewan. Julien is backing off, he's stopped calling me "petite fille." I'm getting a feature! Paid travel, materials, and per diem. We're going back to Bogotá. The other kids with cameras are dropping like flies, every day I hear of someone else going home, throwing in the towel. Why am I still here? Who survives and why? Last week my period came early, we were on the road to a coca farm, hitching with a "delivery" guy, and I had to . . . never mind. Anyway, I'm alive, I'm here, everything hurts, everything's dirty, I think something very bad is happening to my digestive system . . . but I'm here, and I think I'm starting to know what I'm doing . . . —J

Dear Paul,

Don't worry. I'm safe. Or, at least I think I'm learning to know the minute I'm not. Julien doesn't send me out alone. Not yet. Soon maybe, but not yet. Two is better than one, especially when one of you is a petite fille. And I have learned how to identify the right local to help with translation and getting around. You can always spot him, he's hanging around the train station or the bar where the journalists congregate. There's always one you want to stay away from, because he's 100% hustler. But there's always someone, and God, they'll do it for next to nothing. Next to nothing is a million times more than nothing.

When does the new gig start? So you're officially switching
teams, you'll be one of them now, a Fed? GS-xx? You'd better
burn all traces of connection with me (!) when they want to
appoint you to the Cabinet . . . the things we have to do to
get inside . . . Why am I still here? Why can't I bring myself to
gripe and moan like the others? Why does this feel like . . .
a privilege?

It's 2 am here. I can get warmish water for a few minutes
at this time, so I'm going to try to get a wash. Tell Henry to
e-mail me. I know he won't, but tell him anyway. —J

Paul,
I don't know what to say. You're mad, obviously. You have a
right. There is no way to explain the schedule, the pace . . . I
couldn't get out of it. It had to be me, it had to be now. You
know how it works. I can't say no to a feature. Not yet, not
now.

I'm sorry. Time speeds by like nothing now. The days are the
weeks are the months. Have I really been out two years?
Honestly, I wouldn't even know it if you didn't remind me.
I'll be home soon. I'm clearing three weeks, two at the least.
Henry's pissed too, I know. You guys take care of each other.
I mean it.
    —Jane

5

It's ironic, I suppose, that I would speak with Eloise about love.
She seemed to know *something*, although I would come to learn
later, not surprisingly, that Eloise had an illustrious and tumul-

tuous love life—that she was more faithful to her Nikon and her Leica, to her stories and captions, than to any one human being—and that many would claim survivor status on her trail of wreckage. *Love and lust*. Did she truly know the difference?

At the time, Paul and I were attempting something like love. Before we met, he was Henry's teaching assistant, assigned to lead a study group that Henry had joined to get close to a fair-haired, hazel-eyed girl named Liv. It became clear soon enough that both Henry and Paul wanted to date her, but she spurned them for a swarthy Italian guy named Marco. They found themselves commiserating one night over beers, bemoaning their emasculated Korean male plight. Neither of them took it seriously, but it was a kind of common language for them. They probably shouldn't have ever hit it off, if biology really does rule and males are driven innately by competition. They were too alike. But perhaps intuition also clued them in to their differences: Henry the more typically masculine—taller, stockier, more brash and gregarious—and Paul a bit softer, his temperament more spacious, and patient. As their friendship grew, it was not long before both recognized Paul as in fact the stronger, the more staid; the older brother to the prodigal son.

The beginning, of Paul and me, was as natural as anything. We met for the first time at one of Henry's birthday bashes. He threw them every year, starting on his sixteenth. Neither Dr. Lee nor my father was crazy about it, but they preferred he held it at our house as opposed to somewhere else, where God knows what would happen, and agreed to go away overnight as long as I was there to monitor and keep it under control. I'm not sure why he was so set on it, why he looked forward to it; since every year, without fail, about midway into the festivities he'd get very depressed, because of who didn't show, or who left early—either the girl he was chasing or the one he'd just broken up with—and then he got very, very drunk.

This time, he'd started to get out of hand early on. He was falling into that *honest* mode—the depressed drunk, telling his friends what he really thought of them, yelling over the music and making a scene. "Is there anyone here that even knows my real name?" he bellowed over Nina Simone singing "Feeling Good," standing precariously on a folding chair, and waving a red plastic cup. "It's Han-soo," I said, and grabbed him by the arm, pulling him down off the chair. Paul had grabbed his other arm, and we escorted him upstairs to his bedroom. "It's the second one on the right," I said. Paul was leading Henry, he'd taken control. I opened the door for them so they'd have a clear path. "Take a load off, Henry," he said. "It's *Han-soo*," Henry said. "My father calls me *Han-soo*." "Okay, Han-soo," Paul said. "Take a load off." Paul pulled off Henry's socks and shoes and laid him down on the bed. He even pulled the blanket over him.

I was impressed. He seemed so capable, like he'd know just what to do in any sticky situation. And it was nice to have some help with Henry, for once. I had grown so used to bearing the responsibility, I hadn't even recognized the weight until some of it was lifted. Within moments, after mumbling a few unintelligible things, Henry was asleep.

"Nice work there, Barney," Paul said, holding out his hand. I smiled, gave him mine, and he flipped it over, delivering a playful five.

"Barney?"

"You know—as in Fife?"

"Riigghht." I smiled at my feet and let out a breath, halfway between a laugh and a heavy sigh.

"They won't miss him. A party's a party."

"I know. It's like this every year. Have you been to one before?"

"A party? Once or twice."

"Ha-ha. That's cute. I mean a Henry birthday bash."

"No, this would be my first. I only just met Henry last semester."

"You're in school with him?"

"I was his teacher." I puzzled at him. "His T.A. Mechanical Systems 300. I'm old, but not that old."

"Not as old as Andy Griffith?"

"Mayberry or Matlock?"

"Whatever. Never mind. In real life, I'm Jane. Who are you?"

"Big sister, I know. I've heard about you. I'm Paul."

"How come I haven't heard about you?"

"Because you don't go drinking with Henry. You'd know all sorts of things about him if you did." He seemed to be telling me something, even back then. He didn't know either me or Henry well enough to get too personal, or to interfere, but he wanted me to know something. A slight expression of concern, friend to relative. I already had my suspicions, and appreciated his subtlety.

"I'm supposed to be minding this party, it's the only reason my parents let him have it here. Shall we?" He motioned a charming "after you," and we went back downstairs, going our separate ways—me stacking cups and straightening furniture, he socializing with some of the other engineers. I saw him lean over Liv, who was alone by then (Marco had gone back to Italy). I watched him the rest of the night; he seemed both easy with himself and a little out of place. There were moments when he had no one to talk to, and he'd just sit on the couch, drink his beer, flip through magazines. I liked him right away. He had a kind of dignity about him, something solid. And somehow, he felt . . . familiar.

We started spending time together as a threesome, then gradually Paul and I would go out alone. We never made any grand pronouncements. It just happened, and Henry seemed to understand from the beginning. It worked for all of us, that was the beauty of it. Henry had always taken up significant real estate in my worries; now I had someone with whom to share the burden—we were his caretakers, his ass kickers, his absolvers—and also the love. And Henry, I think, felt good about it, more safe and sound with the two of us working together.

Henry. Baby brother. My father liked to tell the story—he is prone to repeating stories over and over—about the time when Henry was turning one, at his *dohl*, his first birthday party, and someone put a candlelit cupcake in front of him to blow out. Of course he didn't know that he was supposed to blow it out, nor was he capable of it; but he *was* at the stage of grabbing and swiping at things, and so when he saw the bright hot light in front of him, he went for it. My father saw the whole thing, captured it with his Super-8. Dr. Lee, busy talking to a guest sitting next to her, had Henry in her lap; I was sitting in a booster seat on her other side. Henry batted with his right hand, and the cupcake-with-candle fell over, lighting the paper napkins on fire. I have no primary recollection of any of this, but I've seen it on film: Henry giggles with delight, leans in toward the fire, then feels the heat and begins to cry. At this point, Dr. Lee sees what's happened, but I'm already pushing hard on Henry's face with both hands, knocking him off her lap into the guest's lap, and knocking myself over into Dr. Lee's lap. Everybody is up out of their chairs by now, the guest has Henry, Dr. Lee has me, someone is throwing fruit punch onto the fire, disaster efficiently averted. Dr. Lee is furious, holding me under her arm like a rolled-up rug, and scolding the cameraman for continuing to film.

She hated it when my father told this story, mostly because the repetition grew tiresome to her. But my father would tell it, again and again—about how Janey saved Henry, how Henry is always the baby, with poor judgment. How his big sister always knows what to do and takes care of him. Which, I suppose, is true enough.

But I remember a different story.

We were older, old enough to be left alone. Both Dr. Lee and my father were working all the time that summer. My mother had an office in the house, where she met with patients, but we were not to disturb her. This was the last summer before my parents discovered "summer activities"—tennis lessons, art classes, Korean school—and so we were pretty much on our own, Henry and me. Left to our own devices, we alternated between dreaming up fantastic fun together and hating each other. And there was one particular day when the former took a nearly irreversible turn toward the latter.

We'd been running off into the woods in the afternoon, through a path at the end of our street. There was a creek, and we made a hot-summer idyll of it. Henry threw stones, I squatted down to watch for fish and other swimmy things, we splashed around mildly when we got hot. That spot calmed us, and we liked that, but it was far in, through dark and dense areas off the path, easier somehow to get there than to get back. The first time we went, we got lost coming back and barely got home before dark. Henry was scared, and so was I, but I pretended to know the way all along. "It's just a little farther this way," I kept saying, even when I had no idea where we were. The next time, we had the idea to tie pieces of string to tree trunks along the way so we could find our way back more easily. It would have worked, except that we didn't bring enough string, and so we still got lost, looking for the next tree trunk. Luckily, it had rained a few days before and the ground was damp, so we tracked our footprints back to the path. By the third time we went, the way had become familiar to me. I could see in my head the shapes of the trees and the contour of the hill, and I knew I could trace the way. But Henry was at my mercy. He'd followed my lead and didn't memorize the way for himself.

I can't say for sure what made me do it. What is it in a child's soul that tempts her to torment the weaker? Or is it just a pre-developed morality—no context for compassion, no sense of responsibility? I did not hate Henry, not really, but I was curious about things. And there he was, an unsuspecting object in my path. I wanted to see what would happen. I wanted, perhaps, to *make* something happen.

"We're lost again," I said to Henry, lying. It was late afternoon, the sun was dark orange, almost brown, and sagging low, barely visible through the trees. It was hot and muggy, even in the shade, the sour smell of our dirty little bodies settling in and thickening. Swarms of gnats and mosquitoes feasted on our sweet blood. "Wait here. I think it's this way, but I'm not sure. Let me check first." Henry was tired out from the heat, happy to let me do the exploring. He sat down cross-legged, leaned up against a tree. He had some action figures and a windup flipper bath toy in his pockets, with which he proceeded to occupy himself. His hands and his clothes were filthy. I can see him now, absorbed in his play, sweaty and flushed, foggy-headed from the heat. I can feel the distance between us, then and now, how he ceased to be Henry to me, my brother. How I saw him as a thing—an experiment, an idea. I snapped his image with my eyes, I saw the *him* beneath his basic identity. And I left him. I climbed the hill through the forest I'd come to know, and guided myself home.

Some time later that evening my mother came to my bedroom. I was doing a word puzzle in a *Highlights* magazine. "Where is Henry?" I did not look up at her. A few moments passed; I felt her towering, lingering. "Ah-jin *ah*? Where is your brother?" Slowly, I raised my eyes to meet hers. "I lost him," I said calmly, holding her gaze. "I lost him in the woods."

I believe that my mother—the scholar of human psychology—understood something about me then. Something that no one else knew, something I did not understand myself. Her eyes widened, but she said nothing. She turned from me and rushed away. I heard rummaging in the closet—presumably a search for a flashlight—then the slamming of the front door. Some time later, she returned with Henry and my father, who'd driven up just as they were walking up the driveway. Henry was bawling, but he was safe.

I learned later that he'd stayed put the whole time. As it got dark, he started to yell and cry. When no one came, he curled up and cried himself to sleep. On top of fear, it was hunger that really did him in. My mother went looking for him in the woods, yelled his name into the blackness. He awoke, heard her, and answered. They kept yelling until they found each other. In total, he probably sat there for about two hours. My parents did not say anything to me about the incident. To this day, I don't know what they discussed. I went into Henry's room later that evening, after he'd had dinner and a bath and was in bed. I crawled into the bed and wrapped my arms around him. "I got lost," I said. "I got to the street somehow and then didn't know how to find you again." He made a noise, like a small animal in distress; and then he started to snore. I slept with him that night. My mother found us there together in the morning and woke us for breakfast. We read each other jokes from our cereal boxes and kicked each other under the table. "Ah-jin," my father said. "Take care of your brother." And that was it. I've tried my best—and failed, no doubt—to heed him since.

I told that story to Paul, late one night, lying in bed. It was the first time I'd told it to anyone, the first time it occurred to me to tell it. It began with a confessional impulse (*There's something you should know . . .*), but as I spoke, both of us lying on our backs, naked and hot in the dark (it was July, the thick of summer), my body still buzzing from the pleasure of our lovemaking but my mind already elsewhere, I found myself shifting tone, changing perspective. As if the part of the narrator were now being played by another actor, with a new interpretation. The whole thing seemed distinctly funny to me. And the revelation of cruelty and wickedness I'd been gearing up for, the whack of ugliness displayed by the villainous older sister, somehow dissipated in the telling. It was a good story, not a bad one. It was, in fact, one of my happiest family memories.

"After they brought Henry back, the house was so peaceful," I said to Paul, to the darkness. "Everything was fine. Everything could have been awful, but everything was fine."

"You got away with something."

"We were all okay."

"Were you worried?"

"About Henry?"

"About anything."

"I was not worried about Henry. Come to think of it, it may have been one of the few times I was not worried about Henry."

"About what, then?"

"About nothing. I wasn't worried. That peacefulness was a respite from the worry. It was unusual. It was nice."

"You won. You conquered your mother."

"She saw me. That's all. Not through me, not past me. And . . ."

"And?"

"And . . . *she* found him."

"Come here." In the hot, in the dark, we made love again. It was strange, though. Paul held me, he moved over me, gently and soberly, as if to console. But at that moment I wanted something different. Something had opened up, something was lifted. It was a good story, not a bad story. I wanted to jump for joy.

When I look back on that time, on Paul and me, it feels like another life and continent and planet. It feels small, like high school when you return for a visit, or like your childhood bed-

room. I find it puzzling that things always feel like the whole
world at the moment in which you live them; and then the
world, what you thought was the whole world, telescopes as
you move away from experience. One minute you are the image
in the telescope, you are so close that you are *inside*—like when
I first met Eloise. The next minute you are the viewer, you
are standing at a remove, zooming in, drawing the image as
close as possible, and yet knowing that what you see, what you
long to see in detail and immediacy, is ever and always far, far
away.

How can you live or experience a moment in its full present,
knowing that it will only diminish as soon as it has passed? It's
like the new car that loses value the minute you drive it off the
lot. What's strange is that I can't even say for sure whether I was
all there even at the time, or if I was already telescoping into
the future, or maybe the past, or perhaps even an alternative
present.

When I think about Paul now, he eludes me. He has faded
into a ghostlike sensation. Much like the child we made and lost.

6

A month passes without event. A stagnant pond, murkier by the
day. He is looking for a reflection, a tiny ripple, signs of life.
But there is nothing. She lies in bed most days, sits up when
he brings her the paper, or food, which she picks at and pushes
around the plate. Her back hurts, sharp pain in her abdomen,
head pounding. He grants her whatever she asks, whatever she
doesn't ask, this first month.

They have been apart more than they've been together.
There were times, more frequently as time went on, when he
thought they were fooling themselves. He had not cheated, but

had wanted to. He couldn't say for sure whether or not she had. He suspected not. The impression they'd each given was that of extreme and persistent work and exhaustion, which presumably meant no time for distractions, or indiscretions. It seems now beside the point.

They are a Modern Couple, not married, putting no stake in institutional commitments; allowing each other freedom, choice, advancement at whatever cost at any moment. Far be it for either one to stand in the way of the other. "I won't be the reason you hate your life," they each promised. Something told them that this was love, love in a new age. It was the nonbinding clause, the only way intelligent, ambitious men and women could work out the complexities of love and work. And it functioned in its own delicate balance.

But not without cost, or dangers. They would meet in different cities, most often in Paris, where she kept a flat in the Marais. She'd asked him to consider moving there, look for work in France. More and more her work brought her to Europe, and to Africa. Paris was a more sensible home base for her. She came back to New York less and less frequently, always arguing that he needed a "vacation," he should meet her in Paris, or London, or Berlin. Nothing about this appealed to him.

She was changed: she belonged to a particular kind of life now; everything outside of that was either boring or overwhelming. In one of their long-distance arguments, he told her that if it wasn't exploding or bleeding, it didn't interest her. Which he sometimes really believed.

There was, in fact, someone else. At work. He'd known her—Caroline—for over a year, but only recently had the tension between them grown. She and her boyfriend had split up; he knew it right away, even before she said anything. You can tell—he could tell—a new sense of availability.

He did not consider it seriously—taking action, making something of it. Worse, it made him *think*. It made him review, rehash the last six years. With Jane. Without her. The affair with Caroline happened in his mind, in the alternate-path imaginings. Someone near, someone close. They had lunch together sometimes, she often talked about her big family, Cuban Americans from Jersey, she was close with her aunts and uncles and cousins, nieces and nephews. She smiled a lot. She had a pretty round face, dark button eyes. She wore earrings and sheer tops and colored bras. Her work in another department was different enough that inquiries were required to understand the other's job, but they both knew well the agency culture. He assured her that her ex-boyfriend was a jerk and hinted at fixing her up with friends and colleagues, but never did.

She asked him about Jane. Six years was a long time, were they going to get married? He said they had time for that, they were in no rush, they were both putting time in, working at working. *She must be strong, she must be talented, she must be really something.* Yes, she is. We've sort of grown up together.

And you must have a lot in common? Did your families know one another?

Our brother . . . Jane's brother. I knew him in school.

It's hard, the long distance?

We're used to it. It's how we are now.

In his mind, Caroline became a measuring stick. Jane fell on one side or the other of Caroline in all things. More this, less that, so glad she's not this, would be nice if she was more of that. It was wrong, all this going on in his mind. It was small, it was wrong, it was unenlightened. Or was it . . .

You forget. Why you love someone. Why you loved her. Someone said—someone on the radio, a scientist or anthropologist, someone cynical, someone arguing for physical determinism or polygamy or something—that love is nothing but a convergence of need, convenience, and pleasure.

So what is left, Dr. Cynical, when those three things run out?

He hated the sound of the nagging, neglected spouse in his own voice and resented her for provoking it. And Henry was slipping away. Jane was less and less aware; she'd abdicated their shared responsibility.

There was a time—wasn't there?—when he understood her. There was certainly a time when he wanted to. But something happens. You've put your feet in her shoes so many times. You lose interest. You hate those shoes, they are ugly and they don't fit. The walking has gotten you nowhere, your feet are blistered and tired.

Her work began to take on the cast of obsession and self-absorption. Nothing more, nothing less. She was no longer building something—a career, a reputation—she had succeeded at that, she was the kid wonder. They lived in a time when you could see no end, no shortage, of war, poverty, destruction. The work would come, she had established her place. She did not exactly revel in it—no, not so cruel as that—but it seemed she could not live without it. The next assignment always called. And the next. And the next. He was not there with her, he did not know what it was like. But something did not seem right. Something was missing. Like she was becoming a blank—nothing but casing, lens, and shutter. She used to share with him her photographs, talk to him about what she saw, why it struck her, *Look how she's tensed up in her jaw, but her blouse is so free, it flutters*, or *From that angle, it's like you're being drawn up, and you can almost feel it, like reverse vertigo*. But now her work was *relentless*, it was *professional*, without the pause or the wonder. Now. Now they are no longer novices, kids-in-training, everything fair game, for the *experience*. Now what was it for? What was next? Just more, and more, of the same? Deeper and deeper into a life based on—thriving on— *what?*

It was their last rendezvous in Paris. The first night, she obliged his suggestion to walk along the Seine at dusk but made clear the effort required on her part—the scene and the mood apparently too charming, too placid. It was cold, she said, she wanted to find a bar, a place where they could sit and people-watch and get warm. They found a place, a noisy and smoky café, gritty and local, where she was able to eavesdrop on French-speakers, but he sat bored. He was not able to find the moment, a clearing, to tell her what he came to tell her: that they should end it, the time had come, had passed long ago. It was over.

The week wore on, she was able to wind down from the intense rhythms of her most recent assignment, and she fell into a torpor. He, too, was worn out from the trip, from the pressures of his own work (of which she knew little), from the loneliness of fidelity to an elusive love. In the end, they spent much of their time in her flat, she sleeping and he watching TV.

The morning of his return flight, he awakes to the sun streaming in, muntins casting elongated shadow patterns, a distorted order of gangly grids, over the bed, across his face. It is early, the sun barely up, finding its way to a full bright white via faint, wispy strokes of purple, peach, rose. All quiet, and Jane is awake. She has slept nearly fifteen hours. She sits by the window in a wobbly wooden chair, looking out onto rue de Picardie. Her hair is very long, tangled and stringy. She has pulled her T-shirt over her knees, hugging them tightly with long, slender arms. She has lost so much weight, all he can see of her bottom half are bony ankles, long feet and toes. The flat is a mess of magazines, proofs, ashtrays, and camera equipment. But she is beautiful. He misses her. God, he misses her.

The night before, over a mostly wordless dinner at a quaint café in the Latin Quarter that Paul had picked from a travel book, they'd begun toward the end of the meal to speak of things familiar and shared when Jane asked about Henry. It wasn't what Paul wanted to talk about, but it was something. She was showing interest in the real world, their life together.

"What have you heard from him?" he asked.

"Nothing directly. Not for a long time. Months?" It was becoming more like her to lose track of time, to mistake weeks for months for years. He was silent for a moment. At this point, he wanted to leave her out of this. It was no use anyway. But she asked, so he had to tell her.

"Your father and I got him into rehab. He had to go. In the end, he went willingly, but we had to press, it wasn't pretty. It's a good place, though. Your parents agree." She looked away.

"How long?"

"Two months ago."

"Let's go," she said, downing what was left in her wineglass, swallowing hard. "I'm so tired."

They returned to her flat, she went straight to bed. It was still light out. He joined her but lay awake through most of the night. Something was coming to an end. He and Jane. Henry. Where is the leak that drains away the sweetness? Where does it all go?

But now, this morning, something is different. There is light, ample and brightening. Purple, peach, rose. Jane is awake, she is *here*, he can sense it. For the first time in a very long time, they are together, present to a moment, simultaneous. He stirs, sits up, waits for her.

She stands and comes to him. She is long and slight and perfectly plain. In an instant, the sweetness returns, all of it, in a rush. They make love. Searching, searching, touching, smelling, moving. Finding. Distances crossed, mysteriously and at last. Familiar. Consoling. Found.

At the airport, their embrace is a confirmation of rediscovery. She will return from Africa in three weeks. She will go straight to New York, she will make it for Christmas. She says she will stay for "a while." He says, "Okay." He kisses her on the forehead.

It turns out to be four weeks instead of three. She misses Christmas, which he'd planned for them. They argue about this as soon as she arrives.

Then she tells him that she is pregnant.

They are both stunned; and then they are happy. The timing is right, they both agree. This was the direction they were heading in, after all. She was going to stay, and now this confirms it. *Yes,* she says. *Yes, I suppose this was what I wanted all along. I'm glad, I'm glad it happened. I needed a wake-up. It's right. It's a good time. We'll settle down.*

They are young, they are starting anew, it's all rolling out before them. They change their diets. Clean out closets. Start a savings account. He is still nervous, scanning for signs of restlessness. But she seems happy, seems to be settling in. When she talks on the phone to colleagues, she says, "I'm loving it, don't miss it at all. I feel like a person." She gets good local assignments from the *Times*. The farthest she's traveled is Pittsburgh.

She doesn't want to share the news yet. They've passed the mark, but she doesn't want to tell. She just doesn't. She is nearly four months along when, one night, an unspeakable pain overtakes her. When he comes to her in the bathroom there is *so, much, blood.*

Another month goes by like the first one. Stagnant, murky. A variation here and there, small patches of relief. Mostly, they are ghosts, haunting themselves. The moment has passed. She can't stay. They both know it. Neither wants to say so. Instead, they pick fights. They say terrible, petty things. "Fine," he says. "Fine," she says. Everything is "fine."

They wait for the call, both of them. Waiting. He doesn't care how she does it, letting the agency know she is available again, that she's ready to go. By dropping a hint through a colleague, a direct line via e-mail. It doesn't matter at this point. He will do it himself if he has to. Finally, it comes: the assignment in Darfur.

She leaves most of her things, which isn't much. Nothing in particular is said. After she leaves, he piles everything into a closet. Out of sight. For a long time, in the room with the closet, he keeps the curtains drawn. He continues to visit Henry in rehab, but keeps a new distance, and never asks about Jane.

He will always remember the early-morning light in Paris, Jane's bony ankles, the clarity of discovery and being found, at the very moment when loss seemed so vast and final. He will never understand why something so delicate and hopeful, the creation of life in such a moment, should end as it did.

7

I started out those fourteen months in a town called Gereida, in South Darfur. It was an unusual assignment that came to the agency not through a news organization, but directly from an American reporter. His name was Clayton Warrick—a crusader type, sort of—who'd been covering the atrocities there and had started working on a series of articles called "Genocide: The New Tolerance." He was on his own mission-driven time clock and felt the major newspaper for which he worked, not to mention the United Nations, was pussyfooting around. He was not clear as to what specific purpose these photographs would be used, nor to what end ultimately; but he fronted the money, out of his own pocket most likely. He was a mid-career type, ambitious, Ivy League, all the right creds; what he was doing would probably make him or break him, but I wasn't going to tell him that.

Clayton, it turned out, was a very smart reporter. He made friends with the right people, kept his friendships with the wrong people quiet. He was also utterly sincere. He'd gone out there for love, initially—an aid worker named Sarah, a fiery blonde from Raleigh, trained as a nurse, who'd seen terrible things, especially among women and children. Through Sarah, Clayton stayed close to the daily effects of the violence on civilians. At the same time, he kept up on the numbers, and the politics— death tolls, troop withdrawals, budget cuts, semantic wrangling by Western officials doing everything they could to keep their hands (on paper) clean.

"This isn't about hanging anyone," he said to me. "My first month here, I was livid. I was so enraged by what I saw, by everything Sarah told me, I was determined to expose any and every culprit I could find. Especially Western diplomats sitting on their asses, calling this thing 'tribal war' and saying we shouldn't get involved. *Chickenshit bastards*, I thought. Looking the other way, as always. It was very personal, it became obsessive. But after a while, after seeing the senselessness of it, and the relentlessness, I started to understand what they meant, why they didn't want to step in. It's beastly what they're doing here. We're beyond a moral universe. Christ, it's barely human. And you start to think, Jesus, if they want to butcher each other like this, if this is in their blood and their souls, then what the hell, let them do it. Get out, get away from this evil, leave them to their own ghastly undoing." We were walking and talking, which was Clayton's way, he always needed to be moving. He preferred to be on foot whenever possible. "Eventually, it really just becomes a matter of numbers. You see, you realize, that the ghastliness is the work of a few; and the suffering borne by many. There's that African proverb: 'When two elephants fight, it is the grass that suffers.'" He spoke with a slight drawl, the suggestion of a New England pedigree. "I started out as an international economist. Statistics, numbers—it stuck."

I'd been in Gereida all of three hours, and already we were getting to work, he was touring me through the villages and camps. The perimeters of the town creeped outward, with rows and rows of tents and other ramshackle shelters filling the plain, growing, it seemed, by the minute. We stayed on foot, swimming our way through seas of migrants, many of whom appeared to be just arriving, on foot and by donkey, some with horses and carts. "The wadis are filled with water, which makes it harder for the trucks with supplies to get here," Clayton said. "Soap. There's never enough soap. When the latrines flood, disease will be everywhere. Have you ever seen someone with cholera?" I nodded. I had. Clayton's eyes bore into me, affirmative. "The population here has tripled in the last year. When the wadis dry up, we will have a different problem—not enough water."

My camera stayed in its case but I was framing and snapping with my eyes, clocking the light, zooming long and stretching wide. The textures were simple and clear: dark, smooth skin, black as bitter chocolate. Sun so hot and strong you couldn't see it, you were *in* it, and colors so rich and bright as to confound— such vibrancy in this place of bare survival. Everything powdered in fine, mustard-colored dust, drier than bone, with one exception: the eyes. Eyes so big and wet, you thought you might slip into them and drown.

I liked Clayton's way, it was just what I needed to get going again: no time wasted, moving moving moving. This was the work, the living stage; you kick into a kind of trance, almost like a high. I was surprised—a little—at how quickly I adjusted to the kind of visual shock I'd been away from for over a year: the cholera, children on the edge of starvation, mothers carrying around their dead infants, drifting about like ghosts, half alive in this place of no-place. The truth is, I was in my element.

I stayed and worked with them, day and night, for three weeks. Mornings I'd hover around Sarah, keeping some distance at first, allowing the villagers to get used to me on the periphery. With Sarah, things slowed down. First thing each day, the aid workers met with the sheiks, who reported on urgent problems, while the workers mostly listened. "These meetings are productive because we keep good relations with the leaders," Sarah told me. "If the sheiks don't trust us, nothing gets done. But the real work happens with the women. We show them how to sanitize the water, use the mosquito nets, spray the latrines." Sarah spoke softly and slowly, more like a teacher in a placid country school than a worker in a desert refugee camp. She smiled at everyone she spoke to, no matter how frantic or angry, and many people came to her in these states. "Your child is looking much better today," is something Sarah said at least twenty times a day; and somehow she meant it—even when she didn't.

Afternoons I joined Clayton, who, after filing his stories by noon, would assist the men with building projects, delivery of supplies, gathering firewood, collecting and burning solid waste. A young boy, maybe nine or ten, an orphan who'd been taken in by relatives, tagged along with the men, eager to be useful. He'd taken to Clayton and was often by his side. When I started taking photos, the boy became both self-conscious and animated, whispering with Clayton and covering his mouth when he smiled. Only later did I learn from Clayton that he was actually a girl. "She's strong, and she wants to work with the men. Her uncle and her boy cousins are all she has, she feels safer when she's with them. In these circumstances, they allow it, they loosen their conventions—there is no one else to look after her."

"What is her name?" I asked.

"I don't know," he said.

When I wasn't working, I slept, or found a bar in town with a TV and watched CNN. Sometimes, Clayton and Sarah and I would eat together in the evenings, and we'd help Sarah with chores around the camp. I watched them, their wordless togetherness, the way they seemed to debrief their day through shared work—sweeping out the tents, washing clothes and towels, inventorying medicines—like any couple, tending to their household in tandem. A few times, I managed to photograph them without them knowing; I knew they'd object, they didn't want the story to be about them.

You wouldn't think it, there's an illogic, I know; but after what I'd just left—those long days and weeks, the end of Paul and me—it was a very restful time. Nights, lying in bed in my tent, solitary and exhausted, I felt relief wash over me, a balm of healing.

Months later, I received a letter from Sarah at my Paris address with the news that they'd been married, in a tribal ceremony by a local chief. A snapshot was enclosed, Clayton and Sarah squinting under the midday African sun, wearing traditional wedding garb—all color and brightness, no confusion about it. A few months after that, just before heading for Baghdad, I received a brief, matter-of-fact e-mail from Clayton: Sarah was dead. A Janjaweed attack on a nearby village, where she was delivering medical supplies.

8

"You're leaving?" It's the day after Dr. Lee's phone call. All at once I'm moving quickly again. Henry doesn't quite know what hit me.

"Yeah."

"You just got back. Don't you think you need, maybe, some more time?"

"Probably. It's been two months, though. It's not like I'm going back to work." I hear my own voice, a familiar tone, a not-quite-honest one, from the days with Paul.

"Should I go with you?" Henry says this while helping to fold the pile of laundry that I am packing. He doesn't look at me. He doesn't mean it. We both know this.

"You should look after Dr. Lee."

"Yeah, whatever. Dr. Lee looks after herself."

"She sounded strange."

"Are you kidding?"

"Strange in a different way. He's never done anything like this. To her."

"I know." Henry and I share a silence, an anxiety, for this moment. But then it breaks. "Why are you doing this?" He stops folding. We are no longer together. Henry seems to up the anxiety level to panic, to an urgency that will halt all motion. But I'm *moving*, I'm running with it; the brush is rising, rising all around me, and I've got the scythe, newly sharpened, in hand. *Pick a direction*. What else is there to do? I take the abandoned T-shirt from his lap and fold. "Maybe he just wants to be left alone."

"Maybe. I guess we don't know."

"What does she want you to do?"

"She didn't say. She didn't exactly ask me to go. I offered."

"You offered?"

"She didn't know what to do, she was at a loss. It was bizarre. It just came to me as what had to be done. I want to see . . . where he is."

"You're glad, aren't you? You're glad he left." He's back to folding, not looking at me.

"*Glad*? C'mon, Henry. No, not *glad*. I just . . . I think he's done something. He's *done something*." I stop here. I do not tell Henry that I am a little bit proud of my father. That I want to see for myself *what he's done*. Henry does not defend my mother, not out loud. We have learned to keep our alliances, tenuous as they are, unspoken.

"When will you be back?"

"Soon."

"I'll be all right." I think maybe he is saying this to himself.

"Yes, you'll be all right. Call Paul if you need to."

"I've been fine without you, on my own. It was a year in August."

Yes, I think. We've all been counting too. "Call Paul."

"He called the other day."

"Did you . . . ?"

"No. You didn't come up. You told me to keep it on the QT, I'm keeping it on the QT. He just calls, once in a while, to check in."

"Don't take on too much of Dr. Lee. You don't have to. . . ."

"Someone has to." I sigh. I suppose I deserve that. I suppose he's right. "I'll be fine. I've been fine. I'll call Paul."

At the airport, Henry is even more unsettled. He keeps at it.

"You don't have to do this, you know."

"I don't know."

"I don't get it."

"Me neither. I'll try to come back with something that makes sense." It is difficult for me to explain—about the scythe and the clearing; about the blast; about Gerald, and Asha, and Sarah; about Paul, and Eloise, and the telescope.

Dr. Lee called; I had exactly one second to think. I am running toward the danger.

"They should fucking figure out how to take care of themselves." Henry's voice falters, and he looks away. He is fighting back something, and suddenly neither of us can bear it.

"I gotta go." I hug him hard and walk fast toward the gate.

Book Two

Foreigners

Domestic Disturbance

1

She hears him stir, listens carefully, has learned his routine. First, he stands to do his stretches—an odd but fully established regimen of arm-swinging and back-bending, accompanied by mild, intermittent groans. Then to the bathroom: a long, cascading session, and the sound of the seat dropping down when he is finished (a small act that amazes her each time). Back to his room, he dresses in layers of flannel and fleece and corduroy, as if he will set off on some sort of small-animal hunting expedition. The clothes are new, she can tell—likely purchased just before this trip—and he has worn them every day thus far. He treads down the stairs, aiming to step lightly, but wide, flat-footed heels strike each step with a sharp *creak*—her husband stirs but does not wake—and then through the kitchen and out the back door. Now Han Jung-joo rises in one swift, silent motion and moves toward the window, watches him in the backyard. He stops at Bear's pen, opens the gate and pets the dog, bending down for a full embrace. He is awkward with animals, approach-avoid, but happy. He fills the food dish.

As he closes the gate behind him and heads down the driveway for a morning walk, he runs into Cho Jin-sook, who greets him enthusiastically, always making an extra-deep bow; she is eternally grateful for his having taken the dog responsibilities away from her and is noticeably less on edge this last week; even her husband has remarked on it.

Han Jung-joo observes, watches him like this. Every morning now for a week. She does so without notice, peripherally and privately. There is nothing in which she takes interest that bypasses her husband's knowledge; there has never been. But now, *this*. This is something new.

It unsettles her. She cannot name it, nor brush off its hold. It is not clear to her what it is. She does not like *unclear*; and so it is not a pleasant force, it grips her too hard. It seems to be a moving thing, a tentacled, reaching thing. Too much internal motion, a vague feeling of nausea. But she cannot free herself, this force impels her. She keeps moving, keeps watching, struggles to find her balance. *How long*, she wonders, *will he stay?*

She dresses and fixes her hair and face before joining Cho Jin-sook, who has started on the morning meal. Her husband is up now, singing old folk songs in the shower, which means he is in good temper. She finds herself carefully choosing her clothes—slimming pants, bright-colored tops—taking time to carefully pin back choice strands of her newly darkened hair, leaving large, heavy curls to rest on her shoulders. She spends an extra moment with the mirror's reflection, the image fading in and out, somehow youthful and ghostly at the same time—a remembered self and an unfamiliar self, mingling. A low vibration hums in her ears.

She keeps moving.

From the kitchen, she listens peripherally for her husband's footsteps descending the stairs as she commandeers preparation of the *guk*. She holds the large chef's knife at a forty-five-degree angle, chops the green onions into tiny diamond shapes, like confetti, counts the garlic cloves carefully, as if working out a golden mean of proportion in her mind. She is aware of Cho Jin-sook watching her these last few days, perhaps noticing a turn of attention, things off kilter. She is a rather nosy woman, in a *concerned* sort of way, and not stupid. Han Jung-joo focuses even more acutely on the efficiency of her tasks now, giving the woman minimal fodder for judgment.

Han Jae-kyu is later and later to the table each morning. He and his brother have stayed up nights, talking of old times, drinking *soju*, watching the local news. His brother's presence has warmed him, but is also taking its toll.

Over the years, through time and distance, Han Jae-kyu has come to regard his brother with a mixture of reverence, endearment, and perplexity. Concern is a recent addition to this list— with his brother's sudden arrival, without particular purpose. And alone.

They have not been in touch very often but for the occasional phone call, three or four times a year, sometimes more if there is family news to convey, such as the recent decline of their eldest brother's health. These calls are typically stilted by voice delay and the psychological pressure of cost. Under these circumstances, they inevitably have spoken to each other in a kind of small talk, further abbreviated by shorthand, awkward and familiar at once. They have often tried to use memories as a connector. "The weather here today is warm and humid . . . it reminds me of those terrible summer days on the island, when the trade winds were down and the haze stayed on for weeks" or "Hae-joo is becoming a rascal, he reminds me of our cousin, do you remember cousin Ho-sik, the one with the funny hooked nose?" They would laugh over these memories, but rarely move beyond cursory exchanges. Each brother conjured for himself who the other had become, how his life—its textures and realities—may have looked, sounded, smelled. And the picture that each held of the other in his mind resembled more the shape of his own mind, of whatever residual space existed there, like the last puzzle piece, which is already outlined after the others have fallen into place.

Now, here together, their rapport is, on the one hand, easy; it is the comfort of a shared boyhood, unspoken understanding of a certain time and place. A tiny nowhere place that only a small living few know firsthand. It is like the burden of a secret, the release of telling and hearing.

On the other hand, that affirmation is layered with the pain, a wincing guttural pain, of hard times past. It was not an easy childhood. Han Jae-kyu, seven years junior, has fewer memories of those harder times—the poorer times, before the eldest brother had established himself on the mainland and the rest of the family came to join him. And there are the memories of wartime, the surreality of it, the imprints made on the child which now haunt the grown man's memory. Han Jae-kyu is less shaped by these imprints than his older brother. Still, he inherited the familial memories of those times, by oral legend—including his two brothers' escape, their desperation to get away.

"Do you remember," Han Hyun-kyu says, "when there were only potatoes to eat, for weeks and months sometimes? *Everything* we made from those tiny, ugly potatoes." He squeezes one hand with the other, fingertips poking out over top, to show how small.

"I cannot eat potatoes to this day! My wife thinks it's funny, but they truly make me sick."

"And I can't get enough somehow. Always, I crave potatoes!"

"Well, my wife will be delighted; finally, she can make her favorite potato dishes."

"Somehow, even the terrible memories are sweet." There is something familiar in this sentiment, and yet Han Jae-kyu cannot quite apprehend it. His brother has alluded to this idea before, in one of their recent phone conversations, perhaps their most recent one, a few months ago. He sensed then his brother's nostalgia, a distinct sadness, but did not until now mark it as anything substantial. It is a strange notion to him, nonetheless—that a bad memory could also be a happy one.

"Do you know they have roads on the island now, paved ones?"

"Is that right? Incredible. I can still feel the pain in my feet from those long journeys in thin-soled shoes to Auntie's house, when she needed herbal medicines from the village."

"You carried me on your back once."

"You were a runt! That was the easiest part." They laugh; then Han Hyun-kyu's face darkens, and their laughter turns to quiet. "When the war started, we didn't know anything. What it was about. Why they would bother with our little island. At first, things were better. There was food. Rations. It was after the war when things got worse. There was shooting, up in the mountains, we could hear it at night. We never knew who was doing the shooting, who was getting killed. The Americans had left, they said it was over. But not here, not in the south, on the island. People were hiding in the hills with their guns." Han Hyun-kyu stops here. He seems to depart, to another place, remote. Han Jae-kyu has scant recollection of this time, and when he asks his brother to say more, he does not respond. It is as if the full land-scape of memory has dissipated, the remnants melded into just one vision, repeating sounds, leaving only a recurring dream. He seems both eager and reluctant to speak, words caught some-where between heart and mind.

For Han Jae-kyu, it is odd, it is a bit embarrassing, to see his *hyung*, his older brother, so vulnerable and unknowing; not even attempting to hide his discomfort, whatever frozen memories trouble him. There is memory, the difficulties of the past, yes. But then there is life, the present; there is the reality of new times and progress, the accomplished safety and prosperity of family. His brother does not seem quite *with* them in this present, his journey halted somewhere in the past. He has brought with him a burden, some unnamed trouble; this is evident. Perhaps too evident, care-lessly on display. At some point in the evening, Han Jae-kyu must say that it is late, they should sleep now, and vaguely resents hav-ing to do this. It seems to him his brother would sit up all night in this heavy silence, the rawness of emotion—out in the open for anyone to see. *He has been away a long time*, he thinks. And with that thought, another follows, like a call and response, a quiet echo: *He is lost, he has somehow lost his way.*

❖   ❖   ❖

But that first night, the night of Han Hyun-kyu's arrival, was a marvelous evening. Han Jae-kyu smiles to think of it. At first sight, the impression of his brother was one of immensity, sheer size and weight. He had always been the tallest and broadest of the three sons, but as he stepped out of the taxi, there in the dark of the driveway, headlights casting long, angled shadows, his older brother seemed to him larger than life—uncontainable, a pounding and solid presence in this dusty country town. As he embraced his brother, as they walked up the slight incline toward the house, gravel crunching like dry bones beneath their feet, Han Jae-kyu's excitement was distinctly seasoned with anxiety: he wondered, irrationally, if the structure itself was strong enough, or if it might just tip and fold, like those flimsy two-dimensional sets of old Western towns he'd seen at an American amusement park years ago.

But the anxiety passed. In the midst of family, wordless recognition of memory and affection, joy broke through. As his brother stepped over the threshold, the family descended upon him all at once, an amoeba of head-bowing, back slaps, and elbow squeezes. The women stood back as the men formed the nucleus at the center of the organism. As quickly as the energy gathered, it diffused, each figure falling away from the *joobin*, guest of honor, who stood large and full, beholding each member of this family body. Han Jae-kyu's hands gripped Han Hyun-kyu by the shoulders, soft and malleable in his grasp, even in their bearlike largeness. His face so much like his own, and yet so different.

Han Hyun-kyu slept well that first night. Exhausted from jet lag, sated in every way. The meal was delicious, the children full of energy, so much delight in the togetherness of family. He lay flat on his back on the *boryo*, absorbing the soothing warmth of heated floors. *How lucky is my brother, how well he's done for himself,* he thought. The boys are thriving. Hae-joo is perhaps a bit spoiled, but it appears he has the luxury, lucky boy. The children respect their father, this much is plain. And the household is run impeccably by his wife. *My brother is a blessed man,* he thinks. *My brother has built his life rightly, and on solid ground.*

After a few days, he settles into a rhythm. He appreciates the well-ordered routines of his brother's household, but is not made to feel constricted by them. He is free to move about as he pleases. His brother enjoys a full breakfast each morning, for which Han Hyun-kyu joins him after his morning walk. Han Jae-kyu then leaves for the day—a full slate of patients, surgery scheduled on Tuesdays and Fridays. Their daughter, Min-yung, sometimes joins them for breakfast, sometimes not. When she does, she stays only briefly, for appearances, excusing herself and returning to her room before the meal is finished. He is aware that she is an invalid of sorts but the subject is not touched upon.

It is the mountain air that is most familiar, and cherished. A mile to the east and they are at the ocean, what the locals call the East Sea. But here they are decidedly inland. Valley dwellers. The air moves—rises and falls with the contours of the land—in a way that is purifying. Han Hyun-kyu marks the ironies (if not consciously, just below conscious thought): First, there is little that happens here in the country, and yet the air *moves*, it is dynamic, taste and texture and life *happen* in the breeze. Second, absent the density of the city, there is somehow an absolute surroundedness here in the expanse of the valley. He feels *held* here as he never feels in the life he's left behind—as he has never felt before.

He awakens at dawn. He is the first to rise. Today marks one week. He enjoys the mornings for the quiet, the expansiveness.

He leaves the house before anyone has stirred, walks along the road that winds through the flats at the base of Bo-ho Ja Mountain. The road is unpaved, wide enough for one car, maybe a truck, and drops off sharply on either side into narrow gravel gulleys. But today is Saturday, the village is quiet. He walks not only right on the road, but in the dead center of it. The sensation is not so much of ownership, but togetherness. "Us," not "my." *This is our road, our town, our home*, the people of the village would say. Never *my road, my town, my home*. Never *mine*.

He picks up his pace, almost to a trot, to warm himself. Hands in pockets, head down, puffs of white breath. *Joooohhhhhhh-taaaah!* His own barbaric yawp, song of himself. His daughter once told him that he had a *Whitmanesque* quality to him. When he asked what this meant, he very much liked her answer: "Earthy," she said. "Natural, driven by appetite." For a long time, he has forgotten his own hunger, forgotten the sensation of it—most sensations, in fact. *It's good, it's good, it's very good!* he thinks. *Very good, very good. Jooooohhhhh-taah!* Sensation: hunger . . . thirst . . . fullness. Body. Mind. Soul? Soul comes later.

He drinks it in, the air and the world. A thirst so basic. Relief. Relief and recovery. Drink now, drink for your life.

He trots to the end of the dirt road, where it meets the main highway. A dirt road, a highway, one mile to town. Nature, civilization, home, work, country, town. The highways are new, within the last decade, he guesses. And the cluster of homes in the flats used to be nothing but wild rice fields and swampland. Things have changed, but in their own time, it seems. Not at the breakneck pace of the rest of the world, the so-called modern world. Only one year ago his brother began building his new Western home—a home that is considered luxurious here but is simple and modest by American standards. Before that, he and his family lived many years in the family house, the first house the eldest brother settled in when he came to the city so many years ago.

There is relief for Han Hyun-kyu, that things are not the same, and neither are they completely different. Evolution seems good and right, at the proper pace. One too easily forgets that there is a Natural Force, rhythms beyond the ones created and insisted upon by human beings. One forgets to seek harmony. One stops believing in such a thing. Right now, Han Hyun-kyu is not so much *thinking* about harmony; he is feeling the fiery tingle of nerves just below the surface of his skin, a sharp ache in a far corner of his upper lungs where cold air has ventured for the first time. He feels the wet of his eyeballs, bones hard and solid as stone. What he knows: *As it turns out, I am not dead yet.*

2

As a young man, Han Hyun-kyu drew many admirers, both male and female. As a promising medical student at Taegu University, he studied hard and was a favorite among his professors. But he also managed to enjoy himself and was often the life of the party among his peers. He was a good drinker, and, when he got to that place, of being *in the spirit*, a good storyteller.

No matter that he tended to tell the same stories over and again. His audiences changed often enough, and even when they didn't, his admirers were usually *in the spirit* as well, so they liked hearing the familiar stories—variously embellished each time. Their lives as students could be bleak and exhausting, and many of them were far from their families; Han Hyun-kyu's stories gave them a sense of home, of knowing and being known.

He often told the story of his escape from the little island where he was born. The story would start out serious—he would tell them how little there was to eat, how meager the education, how his mother sewed together scraps to make clothes for him and his brothers and sisters. He described his father and eldest brother as stern and joyless men. The climax of the story came when he got to that morning, before dawn, when he snuck away from the house to follow his brother and sister-in-law onto the ferry. He had to be extremely quiet and careful, lest he wake his father, who slept on the other side of the same room. He had packed nothing, but brought with him two books he cherished— a tattered biology textbook which he had read through at least five times, and a biography of Confucius that he'd been reading very slowly, savoring each episode of this great man's life and identifying with his struggles and persistence. He described to his enthralled audience the fear in his gut, the pounding in his chest, the adrenaline that carried him through.

It was this building suspense that engaged his listeners the most. During this part of the story, he added a detail which was not true but seemed to make the story more moving and always brought tears to the eyes of the female nursing students: that as he tiptoed out the door of his house, he turned to take one last look at his family, and there he saw his mother, awake, her eyes pleading with him to take good care but encouraging him on, promising not to tell. It was this detail that he liked to alter and embellish each time he told the story: sometimes his mother stuffed the edge of a blanket in her mouth to muffle her sobs; or she reached out to him with her hand, then turned away in anguish. In fact, his mother was an unaffectionate woman, tired from a life of serving harsh men; and if she did know of her son's departure, she likely breathed a sigh of relief: one less mouth to feed, one less male to care for.

He would tell the story with a happy, and even funny, ending: when his brother discovers him on the ferry, he jumps up and hides behind his sister-in-law. His brother is livid and ready to strike. *Are you crazy?* his brother yells. *Jaaahhh-shik!* Rascal!

Have mercy, brother, he says earnestly. *I want to go to school. I will study hard, I will be helpful around the house, I will be your slave! I am a good science student, I will help you grade papers at night. I will help care for your aging great-uncle. I will do anything you ask.* He would tell this part in a humorous voice, mimicking his own utter fright. By now, the men in his audience were raucous with laughter, the women covering their mouths and slapping each other on the arm. The story ends with his brother ordering his wife out of the way and raising his hand high to slap him. The brother's hand descends quickly and then suddenly stops—Han Hyun-kyu's sister-in-law has grabbed hold of her husband's wrist. *My great-uncle has had mercy on us and given us this opportunity. You should grant your younger brother the same. He has demonstrated resourcefulness and determination. Be kind to him, lest the kindness shown to us be cursed and revoked.*

My brother listened to his wife, Han Hyun-kyu would say, now bringing the story to its end, *who told him only what he knew in his heart. This is what a good wife will do. She does not tell her husband what to do, she only speaks to him what he already knows.* And with that, he would leave his audience moved, and satisfied. An evening of blowing off steam would come to a close, with warm feelings and a good moral.

In addition to his joviality and particular charisma, Han Hyun-kyu had physical qualities unusual and thus attractive among his peers. He was relatively tall—five foot ten inches—with wavy hair and round eyes. Being from the south, his skin was dark—normally a sign of peasant origins, but in his case also a bit exotic. He had strong, thick-fingered, skillful hands, which served him well during his surgical rotation, the most difficult year in medical school.

All these advantages notwithstanding, Han Hyun-kyu was not comfortable with women. The only women he'd ever interacted with were his mother, and his two sisters—who feared his elder brother, doted on his younger brother, and generally ignored him. In groups, women were silly creatures who giggled in one another's ears and were good for entertaining; one on one, he found them frightening, incomprehensible, and too fragile. He didn't like the way they sometimes looked at him—with a mixture of need and appetite. When a colleague of his would tell him that so-and-so from the nurses' class had taken a fancy to him, he would laugh and brush it off, as if it didn't affect him one way or another; when, in fact, it terrified and disturbed him. And whenever he would see said nurse, he would make a point of becoming suddenly very busy and absorbed in his rounds.

There was one woman whom he always cared for a great deal, and that was his sister-in-law, the wife of his elder brother, who had (in fact) defended him on the ferry those many years ago, and who had helped raise him during his school years. She was always kind to him, and when she scolded him about studying or obeying his brother or showing respect toward her great-uncle, he always knew that she did it for his good. It turned out that she was not able to have children of her own, and so over the years she grew sad and withdrawn, while relations with her husband grew colder and more distant. But Han Hyun-kyu always remained affectionate with her, and he coveted her small kindnesses.

So, many women chased him—in that coy, indirect way—but none could catch him. He was focused on his work, now the rising star in the surgery department at Taegu University. In his final year of training, he was offered a fellowship in New York, in a place called Long Island. He knew almost nothing of New York, of America, but vaguely liked the thought of returning to an island. Eight years of medical training had worn on him, and he thought a few years in a new place might do him some good. Besides, it was a great honor to be offered such a fellowship, which would be well compensated and highly esteemed by any of the major hospitals in Seoul, where he hoped to eventually launch his career; not to mention the opportunity to travel to the States—that great land, South Korea's conquering hero.

What clinched it for him was that his sister-in-law encouraged him to go. She told him about a niece of hers who had been studying in New York for a few years and who could teach him English. She had met her niece only once, when she was just a child; but her older brother, her niece's father, a wealthy man and a world traveler, said she was very smart and had grown into the spitting image of her aunt. This sounded promising to Han Hyun-kyu, who was now twenty-nine years old and thinking that the one thing he needed to progress in his life and career was to find his bride.

3

To: cms_painter@gmail.com
Fr: Mrs_Han_JJ@hanmail.com

Dear Min-suk,

I write to you on a crisp and clear autumn morning. From the desk where I am sitting I can see the sun rising over the mountains. Do you remember when I used to rouse you in the mornings for school, and you'd infuriate me by staying in bed another ten minutes, so you could watch the sun rise? You liked the colors, you liked to watch them change. How easily entranced you always were. I thought maybe you were praying, but later you told me you just liked to be still while the light broke over the world; that you wanted to make sure you weren't missed, the one little boy left in darkness.

Thank you for your postcard, which I received last week. I don't think I would care for Tokyo very much either. It is good that you have a hardworking representative who can take care of things for you there. Hopefully you will not have to travel as much, and we can see you more often. Min-yung especially always misses her Baby Uncle.

I have sent Soo-young a small birthday gift, hopefully she has received it. I addressed it to her mother's house.

A week ago we have received a special houseguest. Dr. Han's *hyung,* Han Hyun-kyu, has come from America. It was something of a rush to prepare, but we have a new *ajjummah* who is very capable, so we managed just fine. We had a wonderful feast the night of his arrival.

Dr. Han is very happy to see his brother after such a long time. The two of them are very much alike, and also very different.

Well, I just had a few moments this morning and wanted to write to you. We are all doing fine here. I hope that you are feeling better about your work and that the pressures are alleviating. You must remember always to take care of yourself.

> With warm thoughts,
> Jung-joo nu-nah

By mid-morning, once Cho Jin-sook has cleared the table and started on other household chores, Han Jung-joo finds herself alone with her brother-in-law. They make small talk on various subjects—the children, her husband's busy practice, her family in Seoul. She is careful in her line of inquiry, stays close to subjects immediate and apparent, such as his journey from America, his health, his impressions of how the village has changed. Their exchanges those first few days are formal, and even-toned. They are also brief. At the first hint of a lull in conversation, Han Jung-joo excuses herself to check on her daughter and tend to the day's chores. She listens, and watches, as he moves about the house, the yard, down the driveway for an afternoon walk.

Often he just stands with his hands clasped behind him, looking out toward the mountains.

They met for the first time many years ago. When she and her husband first began courting, just before Han Hyun-kyu left for America, the eldest brother gathered the family for a farewell. It was in fact her first Han family affair. She was nervous, and so many of the details of the event escape her now. What she remembers is the emotion in the eldest brother's voice as he spoke of Hyun-kyu, of his determination as a young boy, and now his journey to America. It was a grand sort of speech, imperious and dramatic, intended to rouse a kind of collective happiness and pride. But she remembers a strain of regret, a hint of anguish in the eldest brother's expression; and she remembers her soon-to-be husband turning to her, whispering in her ear as they listened: *"Whae gu rae?* You look as if you are at a funeral, not a celebration!" And in fact, yes, she felt a distinct mourning for the occasion, as if they were bidding someone farewell for good, as permanent as death.

But when she bowed and shook Hyun-kyu's hand, wishing him health and good fortune, and they spoke easily with each other, she was reassured that her husband must certainly be right, her own instincts overly sentimental. The man before her, setting off on his new adventure, received her wishes with utmost confidence and enthusiasm, a fire in his eyes, a firmness in his handshake. Surely this was the beginning, and not the end, of a life.

"Watch out for my brother," Hyun-kyu had said to her teasingly. "You must keep him in line! He can be a rascal."

He remembers her as slight and diffident, pleasant and accommodating; deferring in all things to her future husband. She seemed proud of Jae-kyu, and grateful for the match. Now he sees that she has become something else, something *more*: still faithful to her good husband's every need, and yet stronger, more assured, and substantial. Even physically, she strikes him as fuller, more upright in both posture and manner. She has made this life, her life in the country with the respected Dr. Han Jae-kyu and the children they've raised, her very own. She has built this respectability, she has shaped it. She has learned well the degree to which her own happiness lies in the happiness of her family. His admiration is a swelling, a royal-red balloon inside him.

He is both comforted and unsettled by her. Yet another new *sensation*. He finds himself watchful in her company. And he is unsure how to address her, this Mrs. Han, this well-heeled matron of the town. When they first met, she called him *op-pah*, he called her Jung-joo, and they spoke freely and casually. He remembers joking with her, about how she was too skinny, teasing that she could never be a good-enough cook for his brother with his enormous appetite, looking like someone who hardly ate at all. There was an ease between them back then, like true brother and sister. Now, so many years later, a lifetime passed, and they are strangers again. He has come loaded with fatigue—and shame, perhaps—he is not quite sure yet. He recognizes the freedom she allows him in asking nothing about the life he has fled so suddenly—it is a freedom to find his way to the right footing. She displays a quiet openness to him; as if all the inner rooms of her mind and soul are so neat and orderly that she has run out of chores, now restlessly looking about for the right flourish, the beauty that lies beyond perfection. It surprises him, how clearly he sees her.

He sits at the table a little longer, examining his hands. *These are old man's hands*, he thinks. Hands which were once useful, and skilled. Now; now there is tenderness, there is pain. The skin is like bark. *What is a man without the skill of his hands? A man's hands are his work, and his passion.* He folds them together, pressing hard with thumbs and fingertips, bearing down on vein and bone.

She leans over the counter, watching him. They are both still and silent. This is the moment when normally she would take leave. Today, instead, she sets water on the stove for tea.

The pain of his hands intensifies, and it's good, he thinks. It's deliberate and focused. Some men his age worry that time has passed, is passing. Han Hyun-kyu has worried lately that too much time lies ahead. Years stretching out, years of nothing in particular. *What now?* he thinks. *For* what *will I use these hands?*

He is aware of her watching, her staying. "Please, don't let me keep you," he says.

She does not answer. She is very still. One beat. Two. He looks up, they catch each other's eyes. Neither looks away, both minds are spinning. *Who? What? Why?* It is not a long moment, but a full one. It is she who looks away, straightening, turns to mind the teakettle, now blaring and yet muffled in his ears by the thick silence. She pours his cup and places it in front of him, leaves the room without a word. Han Hyun-kyu remains—now in a state of high nerves.

4

It was an early October wedding and a subdued autumn day. A small gathering of family, friends, and colleagues at a Methodist church that neither of them attended but was convenient and nearby. Han Hyun-kyu wore a fine navy blue suit and an unusual tie—bright metallic gray, not quite silver, sky blue in under-tones—that had tiny-tiny red birds on it, almost like polka dots from a distance, wings spread and all heading in the same direc-tion. He had picked it out himself; it reminded him somehow of hot summers on his island home. The bride wore a simple white dress—silk shantung, fitted and straight-skirted to mid-calf, with pearly beads around the neckline. She also wore gloves and a felt hat with a plain, smooth rim, from which hung a delicate sheer netting for a veil; and satin flats, as she was conscious of accentuating her height relative to the groom.

The bride's parents arrived from Seoul just hours before the ceremony, along with Han Hyun-kyu's elder brother and sister-in-law, who stood in for his parents, now both deceased. The bride and the groom had friends from their respective training programs stand with them at the altar—a surgeon originally from India named Parag Khorana for the groom, and a posttraumatic stress specialist from Wisconsin named Becky O'Toole for the bride. In all, the wedding party made for a strange but not unfestive mix. The bride and groom both seemed a bit distracted, and everyone in attendance sensed an uneasiness about the event, but nothing they could put their fingers on. No one noticed Lee Woo-in's frequent visits to the ladies' room or the hint of sallowness in her cheeks. Here were two handsome, accomplished individuals, well on their way to shining careers in surgery and psychiatry; an attractive couple, and seemingly well matched. Each certainly could have done worse.

The wedding took place a year and three months after Han Hyun-kyu's arrival in New York. He had been thrown headlong into the fray of competitive hospital training, working grueling hours and struggling with the language. Within a month, he was desperately homesick—for Korean food, familiar faces, a language he could speak and understand. He wasn't eating or sleeping well. He lost weight, his eyes sank behind heavy bags. The work was challenging and interesting, and once he discovered his rhythms and routines, he proved his abilities to his colleagues—while still feeling the daily humiliation of stunted communication.

His sister-in-law wrote to him and reminded him of the niece who spoke English. She included her name—Lee Woo-in—and phone number, both of which he already had, written in his address book. It was the only name in the book, in fact. He had hesitated to call, did not want to approach her primarily in need, had wanted to wait until he was a bit more acclimated and could call her for a proper meeting, man to woman. But he was desperate. His sister-in-law's letter was just what he needed to encourage him to make the call. If for no other reason, for the prospect of a home-cooked Korean meal.

That first phone call was indeed awkward. Lee Woo-in had heard that he would be coming to the States, but apparently did not expect him to contact her. After fumbling through the initial surprise and clarifying who he was, they agreed to meet for lunch on a Saturday.

It was late summer, the last hot days, and very humid. Han Hyun-kyu arrived at Lee Woo-in's apartment a few minutes early, his white button-down shirt damp with sweat, drenched around the armpits. It was over two miles between their apartments, and he had walked because he did not yet have a car. When he knocked on her door, she took a minute or two to answer—granted, he was early, but he did not appreciate being made to wait outside in the heat—and when she opened the door, it seemed an eternity before either of them spoke (in fact, it was a long five seconds).

He was not at all what she expected. Her aunt had described him as tall, but he did not seem tall (perhaps it had to do with his posture at that moment). He did indeed have a handsome face, if a bit dark, and such beautiful wavy hair. But something about his demeanor underwhelmed her. He seemed withered and worn, not at all like a confident surgeon who had just won a prestigious fellowship to study in America. Her aunt had told her the story about how he came to live with them in Kyongju, his escape from the island, his resolve and determination as a young boy. She couldn't help but smile, holding back her laughter, seeing him now so damp and soggy, as if he'd actually *swum* here from that island.

She was truly the spitting image of her aunt. Taller and thinner, her features a bit sharper and perhaps less kind, but there was no mistaking the relation. It took his breath away, as if he'd been waiting his whole life to meet her, this woman who resembled so closely the only woman he'd ever loved. Her hair was different—more modern, a puffy American bob—but her face: those eyes, those cheekbones, and especially her smile (a hint of mischief beneath it at first, battling laughter). He stared. Perhaps his jaw dropped, he couldn't have known. He was lost in the reverie.

After the five seconds passed, she spoke. *"Kuruh gat sumnik ga?* Did you walk?" He took a moment to come to himself. *"Neh, mul gi ansumnida.* It's not far. But it's very hot." He loosened his top button, revealing the border of his undershirt. *"Mian hamnida.* Sorry to make you wait, I was just straightening up a bit. Please, come in." He did, just long enough to use the bathroom and freshen up. Her apartment smelled like roses mixed with ammonia, an unusual scent, which he liked. Clean and feminine.

They went to lunch at a Korean restaurant on the main drag near Lee Woo-in's apartment. She apparently went there often; the owner and waitresses knew her. "You come here and eat by yourself?" he asked. "Sometimes," she said, "but often I take out. My studies keep me very busy." He nodded, not knowing what to say next. It was strange, sitting here with this woman, a relative of sorts, so familiar and foreign at once. He focused on her face, which continued to captivate him. The way he looked at her must have moved her, or at least flattered her; he noticed her blushing. With flushed cheeks, she struck him as even more beautiful.

Han Hyun-kyu did not say much at this first meeting, and so Lee Woo-in did most of the talking. She told him about her studies in psychiatry, how she had always been fascinated by the study of the mind, was utterly shocked and then completely taken by

Freud when she first read him in college. "A brilliant mind," she said in English, then translated when he seemed not to understand. "Like a light going on in the middle of a shadowy history," she said in Korean, "telling us who we are and why." She said this in a dreamy way, as if actually seeing this light in her mind.

He was listening, but not quite; he was too nervous. He needed something to do with his hands. He spent much of that lunch looking at his hands, in fact. She watched him, noticed his preoccupation, felt a jolt in her body, looking at them herself. She could see the skill, all his talent concentrated in the sinews of those hands—fluid but imposing, like hills of the great Sahara.

He did attempt to say something: "Your aunt, my brother's wife, are you close with her?"

"No, not at all. I've only met her once, when I was a child, and spoken on the phone with her a few times. After she married and moved to that island, my father and the rest of the family hardly ever saw her again. My father's family is very modern; they were surprised when she married your brother and moved to that remote place. According to my father, she had gone there on holiday once, fell in love with the simplicity of the place, met your brother, and married him on a romantic whim. I think after a little while she was desperate to leave there and was glad when they did."

"My brother, too, was desperate to leave."

"And you, too?"

"Yes."

"I've heard the story of your 'escape.'"

"It was long ago. I used to tell the story often. But since coming here, I've almost forgotten."

When the food came, they ate their lunch in silence, both eager for the awkward meal to be done, and yet sorry that it should end.

They did not meet again for some time, as their schedules did not allow for much socializing. It was he who again made contact, requesting this time the favor of English conversation sessions. He came again to her apartment, which no longer smelled like roses and ammonia. It was something else—kimchi and *daen jang*!

"I thought you might be missing Korean food. Hospital food isn't so good, is it?"

He was thankful, and while the food was mediocre, it was the best he'd had in a long time. This time they ate and talked at the same time. He dared to practice his English.

"The food is dee-lish-us. I am sehr-jun. My name is Doc-ter Han. You have pret-ty face." He was happy to make her blush again.

Their courtship took some time, as they both continued to focus on their studies and clocked long hours of clinical work. When they met, she did most of the talking, about psychiatry and her most interesting cases, in that same distracted way, and he continued to half listen, focusing on her face, that familiar face that struck him so deeply. She enjoyed his attentions, and felt flutters of excitement when she glimpsed his surgeon's hands, which sometimes occupied her thoughts. She cooked for him whenever he came to her apartment. His English improved little.

One evening, as they ate and exchanged playful smiles, they also allowed themselves some drink. He had brought a large bottle of *soju*. In a moment, their mood shifted. She was telling a story about a patient who thought himself from another planet, and they were laughing; but the laughter ceased abruptly. Han Hyun-kyu blinked his eyes wide and allowed a pleasant buzz to settle in his ears. In silence, with eyes lowered, Lee Woo-in stood up from the table and walked slowly—heel on toe, heel on toe—to the bedroom. It may have been the last time she'd moved with such measured, unhurried deliberation.

A new relationship began, one that would never have occurred in Korea, where they would have been surrounded by family, a culture of propriety. Here, in America, in a place called Long Island, Han Hyun-kyu and Lee Woo-in became lovers.

Two months later, Lee Woo-in discovered she was pregnant.

5

To: Mrs_Han_JJ@hanmail.com
Fr: cms_painter@gmail.com

Dear Nu-nah,

Yes, I am back from Japan, with relief. I am catching up, and I must thank you for reminding me of Soo-young's birthday. Can it be that she is now eight years old? How time goes by, like a speeding train with foggy windows. That boy who sat still for the light of sunrise is now an aging man, increasingly irritable, decreasingly of earthly use (Soo-young's mother, always these days so purposeful and positive since her remarriage to that awfully congenial art historian, would, I am sure, agree).

Nothing prepares you, dear sister, for how time whacks you hard just below the knees, so that you fold over, like a pair of old flannel trousers . . .

My work, my work. I work, but I do not paint. I produce paintings. I would like to see the light break over the world again. Instead, I see commission after commission. They say, "Paint this," so I do it. I haven't painted a true painting in too many years now. (The postcard you received shows the one painting from years ago that they allowed in the exhibit. I fought for this, and for the card. Of course no one as yet has shown any interest in buying it, which gives me secret pleasure.)

Save me your sunrise, nu-nah. Your honorable
houseguest from America will, I am sure, appreciate your
beautiful piece of country, and your always impeccable
hospitality. I will come to you when you are less engaged,
perhaps early in the new year.

My love always,
Min-suk

P.S. What is your true opinion of Min-yung's husband? Is it
improper of me to ask? (As I say, *increasingly irritable* . . .) But
you know that when it comes to my niece, I speak only from
best intentions. Dear nu-nah, forgive me, your daughter is
not the belle of the ball, but she is a special one; you know
this, I know you do.

6

Han Hyun-kyu is not surprised to hear from Ah-jin that she is
coming. It is not that he expected it, but now that he hears it, it
seems natural, and not strange at all. Of course. Of course she
would come.

As he awaits her arrival, he begins to wonder about her. How
is she, when did she return from her travels, is she healthy, is
she happy, has she seen or spoken to her brother? He feels a
pang of guilt for not having thought of her in some time. It's
strange how it used to be that every minute of every day his
thoughts were occupied with his children—worrying for them,
their well-being and happiness. But since Han-soo has stabilized
and begun recovery—one year now living on his own, holding
down a job—and Ah-jin has established her career (albeit a dangerous and unstable career that worried him for many years, but
then he had no choice but to accept it, to entrust her to her own

life, which absorbed her in a way that seemed a good thing), he has stopped worrying about them quite so much. And it was likely then, when the children were not filling his thoughts so fully, that he began to think of his own life, the long drone of unhappiness stretching out before him. What kind of existence was this, alongside this woman who did not love him and whom he did not love?

No, not "love," not what his children's generation talked about when starting up and ending affairs one after the other. Respect, basic respect. And care. Common concerns, a certain measure of comfort. *Solace.* This was all he longed for. It had occurred to him only recently—a sudden clarity, like a snowy TV screen giving way to a vivid picture after a hard smack on the side—that this was not too much to ask.

But now, hearing from Ah-jin, he remembers his father's role and the old worries return. Her letter to him, short as it was, makes him wonder. *I'm coming there to see you, just want to see that you're all right. Henry is looking after Mom.* It was a kind of joke, he recognizes—*Henry is looking after Mom*—as if Lee Woo-in could be looked after, as if either his son or his wife would ever imagine such a thing, as if her being *looked after* was of central concern right now; but also Ah-jin's way of assuring him that Han-soo is all right, and that Lee Woo-in is aware of, perhaps initiated, her journey. No matter; of course she would let the children know. He hadn't thought ahead this far—how could he have, without talking himself out of it—but yes, of course, it makes sense that Ah-jin would follow after him.

He knows so little of her life, these years she's been away, "globe-trotting," as they say. He liked to think of it that way— trotting about the globe, lighthearted and playful. He can only imagine what it's really been like, but years ago stopped trying; the thoughts that came into his head were too frightening.

Ah-jin will arrive shortly. He is relieved, at the least, that she is now back in New York and soon will be with him. For a moment, the relief of it, of knowing her whereabouts and having her near, eclipses the awkwardness, the uncertainty, of what he's done.

This morning, Ah-jin's impending arrival gives him something to talk about, in the kitchen with his brother's wife. They have kept a strained distance since the lingering moment between them the day before.

"I hope it will be no trouble—my daughter coming."

"Of course, not at all. We are happy to welcome her. We are glad that we have room for guests. This was why we built this house, after all. For family." She emphasizes *family*, her eyes fixed on the spot of counter she is scrubbing with a sponge.

"That is kind of you. Yes, family is everything." His voice trails off, as if unconvinced; or perhaps wanting to be convinced.

"Your daughter is not married?" Han Jung-joo asks.

"No, she is not."

"Women marry later in America. They are very career-oriented."

"Yes, my daughter is a photographer. For the news. She travels to places where there is war."

"That must worry you."

"Yes . . . well, only sometimes. When I think of it. I try not to think of it."

"She must be very smart."

"Yes. My daughter . . . my children . . . they are good children. My daughter . . . perhaps she takes after me. She is . . . she has always been . . . a good daughter. Responsible." His face is hot, he shifts uneasily. He knows he has said more than he should. She does not seem to notice his discomfort. But he senses a change in her manner, a loosening in her posture. She quiets, is very still, then speaks.

"It is good . . . to have a daughter." A visible sadness washes over her. In an instant, he feels an openness between them, wide and gentle. "Of course, sons are good too. They are good for their fathers. But eventually, they leave. They find wives, they get married. If they are good boys, they become devoted to their wives. This is the nature of things. But a good daughter—a good daughter never leaves her mother. The bond grows even closer as time goes on." She is speaking quite freely now. Her voice has deepened over the years, he notices. The sadness accentuates this, the timbre is warm—it reminds him of a simple Bach cello suite that Han-soo once played when he was young and which he's always loved for its alternating major and minor, hope and melancholy.

"Your daughter is a lovely young woman," he says. The statement is transparent, but proper. In fact, he has seen little of Min-yung, she has been so much withdrawn. The other day, passing her door in the morning, he thought he heard a murmuring, like a prayer tongue, and then a sudden soft "Ha!"—a devilish sort of laugh. It sent a chill through him. Later, seeing her contrite and impeccably mannered at the dinner table, he thought he must have been hearing things—but for the chill, the physical memory of which lingered, unmistakable.

Han Jung-joo struggles for words now. The motion in her stomach, the nausea, grips her again. She has been watching him, and listening, and now, here, there is something she wants to say. She feels them, the words, like stones rumbling within; nothing explicit, but as real and noisome as the material world she knows and manages with such meticulous care. "Yes, she . . . has a good heart. She is very kind. But she is . . . *passionate* as well." The word she uses here means something like "bursting" or "overflowing," usually referring to a rush, a violent force of water, like a giant wave or a storm. It is a word she has used rarely, if ever, before. She is trying to express something very singular about her daughter. And she realizes now that in fact she has been waiting a long time for just this moment of expression, this release.

He smiles faintly, but says nothing. She sees, with some embarrassment, that he does not know what to say. She has perhaps said too much, she has burdened him with her muddled thoughts. She is glad when he speaks—"Her husband, he is a good man?"—but it is an impolite question; she is taken aback by the asking. More appropriate would be to ask what sort of work he does, where his family comes from. But she does not balk; yes, she understands, this "new" thing, he is out of his element, beyond rules, and she, here right now, she is with him too, in this strange place of anything goes.

"He is good, I suppose; but not good enough." This is all she says, all that is needed. The young man's absence at the birthday celebration, the first weekend of Han Hyun-kyu's arrival, and for the two weeks since then, has spoken for itself. She continues, her words taking shape now. "You are a man of science, you know the human body. My husband as well, of course. My husband believes in Western practice, he is pure science in his ways. But something tells me . . . I wonder if, living so many years in the West, if perhaps you understand the error of such an approach . . . the body alone, apart from the mind or heart. I've listened to you, your stories, your memories, speaking with my husband. I hear that you remember, that you appreciate . . . We have raised our children a certain way, my husband likes to think of us as a modern family. But my daughter, her passion . . . her health and her mind . . ."

Anxiety rises in Han Hyun-kyu as she invokes his brother and reveals that she has been eavesdropping on their evening conversations, talks between men. He is confused, he feels somehow wronged, on the defensive.

"My brother . . ."

"My daughter is very sick."

Han Hyun-kyu's heart knocks hard in his chest, slowing to a calm. Here: this is where she is leading him; this, her declaration. There is relief now, an exhalation, for both of them. He knows now, he sees, what she wants to say, what she is trying to tell him. And there is a purity in it, an unhinged sort of desperation, which is familiar to him. The words emerge in a rush now, she seems to need to say them, but Han Hyun-kyu has already heard her: "My daughter. She is sick. Her body, her heart. She is not well. We have not . . . she is different, so different from my sons. Different from other girls. We have pushed her, she needed to be coaxed, somehow. Everything. Her marriage. Her pregnancy. I have not . . . as a mother. You sense things. I have been too close and too far." She stops, catches her breath, hand on heart. "My daughter . . . she will not survive us. She is sick, and . . . we pretend. That she is fine, that she is like other girls. Perhaps . . . we choose our shame over her." Han Jung-joo's voice as she speaks is firm now, she has found new strength with each word, forcing out timidity and the trembling with which she began. And with her last statement, she looks directly at him, as if demanding confirmation.

What she does not say, what Han Hyun-kyu hears nonetheless: *My husband does not see, he does not understand. No one understands. Please, please understand. . . .*

What Han Jung-joo does not, could not, know is that he does not exactly understand either. A mother aching for her daughter, stricken by the girl's melancholy, her soul sickness. He does not understand. He is not familiar. He feels only a coldness when he thinks of Lee Woo-in, how she is with Ah-jin, how she's always been with him. Han Jung-joo's tenderness, her raw despair, is something altogether different. But he sees. He sees, and he does not look away.

He stands and goes to her. Takes her hands—soft, warm from the blood of emotion—wraps them tightly in his, squeezing them to the point of pain, as he squeezed his own. She rests her forehead on their mass of hands, does not dare look into his eyes. He stays there with her as she feels the pain, steady hard pressure. It is the best he has to give, and in this moment a rush of feeling overwhelms him, a new and soaring elation: how good it feels to give, how good to be received.

7

Ah-jin was born just shy of eight months following the wedding. There were no concentric rings of relations, immediate or extended, to count or judge; they were alone in their new endeavor as a family. Becky O'Toole helped Lee Woo-in find someone—an overtly Pentecostal Jamaican woman named Ida, who had a four-year-old daughter of her own in tow—to help with the baby and the balance of household chores so that she could finish with her studies. Both Han Hyun-kyu and Lee Woo-in were uncomfortable at first with a nonrelative in their home every day, talking Jesus gibberish to their child, having hands in their food and clothes and private spaces; but they had no choice. Things had been thrust upon them. Everything was different now, the foreignness of their life weighed on them in a new way, its temporary lack of tethers giving way to an extended, indeterminate groping along a wide and unfamiliar path; without signposts, without the givens of everything they'd known up to that point.

How did they get here? On the one hand, it was a muddled blur; on the other, quite clear. A series of decisions: flight from one's home and family; immersion in a foreign world; disconnection from a set of rules or social expectations; an allowance, judgment compromised, the conception of a child; a rushed marriage. And now: a zealous black woman in their home singing Caribbean lullabies to their child? Anything was possible. They were flung into a roulette of forces. Survival and the basic care of the child, Ah-jin, became primary; reliance on the goodwill of the few friends they'd made required. In turn, they focused on work and study, the main thing each of them could hold as constant.

Lee Woo-in was not familiar with the ways of motherhood. Han Hyun-kyu knew only pieces of her family history: as a young girl she had traveled extensively with her parents on business trips, minded by an *ajjummah* and a tutor. By the time her family returned to Seoul and settled down, after the war, her parents were estranged from each other. Young Woo-in found herself lost in the gap between them and discovered absorption, along with an impulsive drive for superiority, in her studies. She excelled in every area. And yet now, when it came to her daughter, Lee Woo-in was largely without specific resources—either the naturally inherited instinct or learned know-how—to care for her.

Han Hyun-kyu, on the other hand, took to the child immediately. Ah-jin cried inconsolably in the arms of her mother, but calmed and cooed when nestled into the crook of her father's arm. At the celebration of the child's *dohl*, Han Hyun-kyu beamed and boasted to colleagues and friends of his daughter's ability to utter four intelligible words, while Lee Woo-in busied herself with food preparation and, as noticed by several guests, the consumption of healthy tumblersfull of rum punch.

Han-soo was born just under two years after Ah-jin. He had his mother's eyes. The children thrived, for the most part. They were healthy. They were A students. They stayed close to each other. At an early age, Ah-jin became Han Hyun-kyu's helper—learning to cook Shake 'n Bake chicken and tuna casserole by reading the packaging, and stepping in to care for the boy when needed. He came to rely on her.

Lee Woo-in opened her practice and worked out of their

home. She was always there, but never with them. By the time
the boy went to school, she had relinquished almost all day-
to-day care to Han Hyun-kyu, Ida, and Ah-jin. In the evenings,
she would join them for dinner, but eat little. Increasingly, she
lived on a steady diet of cocktails. Han Hyun-kyu never spoke
of it, but he could see his daughter growing increasingly moody
and withdrawn, especially in her mother's presence. Han-soo,
on the other hand, reveled in Lee Woo-in's flamboyance, her
wild stories—most of which had to do with her work, with the
subject of dreams.

"Everybody dreams," she would say at the dinner table, eyes
wide and bloodshot, waving her long-fingered hands in the air.
"The key is training your mind to remember, so you can engage
them." Two out of three among her audience stared back blank-
faced, quietly hostile. Turning to the third, sweetly: "What did
you dream last night, Henry?"

Circus clowns, he would say, or *A car chase, with a man-eating tiger
in the backseat*, when he was older. He would close his eyes, trying to remember. The dreams grew more and more elaborate.
Han Hyun-kyu never knew if he was making up these dreams,
but suspected he was, and worried over it. His mother, mean-
while, delighted in her son's *rich subconscious*. "You should chan-
nel your creativity," Lee Woo-in said, focused completely on
her son as if her daughter and husband were not there. Henry
(now he was *Henry*) started writing fantasy stories—involving
violent boy action-heroes with superpowers and sweet, helpless
animals—and won a contest in the fifth grade. Later, he wrote
murder mysteries, featuring a trash-talking Korean boy-sleuth
who shaved his head, listened to rap music, and dominated a
Latina girlfriend named Eva. The boy-sleuth was also a hypno-
tist, and in this way—tapping into the subconscious of victims
and witnesses—solved many of his mysteries.

Henry would sometimes read parts of his stories to his
mother at the dinner table, who clapped her hands at the end

and cried, "Bravo! Wonderful! Such colorful characters! So much suspense!" Ah-jin seemed to enjoy the stories as well; she would type them up for her brother on the Smith-Corona. Han Hyun-kyu took comfort in Ah-jin's involvement in whatever Han-soo was doing, as he felt he could trust her to make sure he was all right. But he himself did not understand these stories, the point of them—or why his wife was so excited. It seemed to Han Hyun-kyu that the two of them, his wife and his son, lived in their own strange and frivolous bubble, a deviant place.

In high school, Henry's shoulders broadened and his face grew handsome. He seemed to Han Hyun-kyu restless and without focus. At his father's urging, though with resistance, he started playing soccer and baseball. He excelled at both. Soon, he fell in with a popular crowd and began staying away from home. For most of his junior year, he dated a precocious, striking girl his sister's age named Naomi—half-Italian, half-Chinese—who was voted homecoming queen. Han Hyun-kyu did not think it a good idea to get too serious about a girl at such a young age and grew concerned when he saw Henry's increasing obsessiveness—long late-night phone calls, moodiness, extravagant gifts—and secrecy. He only knew what he knew through Ah-jin; Henry never talked about the girl or brought her around to meet the family. He did ask his father for money to buy a sports car, which Han Hyun-kyu refused, and this became a silent war between them.

The summer after she graduated, Naomi went to Italy with her family and wrote to Henry that she'd fallen for a college freshman, a boy from Boston named Campbell who was studying sculpture in Florence and would be back at Wesleyan in the fall—where she'd be attending as well. (Ah-jin had given her father the letter to read.)

It was then that Henry's fierce recklessness began in earnest. Han Hyun-kyu took cues from his daughter, who noticed everything about her brother.

"Henry hasn't been to work in two weeks," she said at dinner one night. They were both working at a restaurant in the city, she as a waitress and he as a busboy. Lee Woo-in was gorging herself on the meal that Ah-jin had prepared. It was one of Lee Woo-in's dry seasons, when she'd white-knuckle a week or two weeks without anything to drink, a test of her own will, when her work wasn't going well and she felt blurry and fed up. During these seasons, she would eat in crazed binges.

In his customary even tone, Han Hyun-kyu replied, "Han-soo is doing fine. His SAT practice scores top-notch, did he show you?" But his voice shook. He knew that his daughter was not one to sound false alarms.

She rarely saw him, Ah-jin told her father—speaking directly to him and emulating his tactic of ignoring her mother. When she did see him, usually out with friends, he always had a beer or liquor bottle in hand. What she didn't say, what Han Hyun-kyu sensed she wanted to say, was that she had forgotten the look of his eyes when they were clear and bright and alive. That she could feel him slipping away.

Or, perhaps, this was what he himself wanted to say.

"Henry is brilliant," Lee Woo-in said, throwing her hand up in the air. "You don't need to worry about him. It's difficult, having his kind of talent. There has to be room for volatility. You crowd him, both of you." Han Hyun-kyu winced at his wife's words. When she wasn't self-absorbed and muddled by her own drunken fog, she was sharp and coarse like this. So unequivocal, as if she had any right. He could feel something inflame inside his chest, the pressure throbbing.

"Shut up, Mother." Ah-jin was quick and dispassionate. She stood up from the table, gathered all the dishes, and left the room. He'd never seen his daughter like this before; she was normally one to draw inward from conflict, like himself. Perhaps she'd gathered her courage, knowing she'd be leaving for college in a few weeks. A moment passed, of shock and airlessness; Ah-jin had taken all the oxygen with her.

Han Hyun-kyu then came to himself. He stood up and left the room, following his daughter's lead. Something had changed in an instant; they could not change the past, but the future would be different. They would walk out of rooms. They would not merely ignore, they would refuse. His daughter would show him how. They would help each other—to more than just survive.

8

Min-yung lies in bed, in the half-waking, half-sleeping state to which she has grudgingly grown accustomed as of late. She feels both warm and cold always—too warm to stay awake, too cold to fall asleep. She feels her mind slipping into the same confusion, the same doubleness. *I'm tired of this, I want to be well*, says one voice inside her head. *Let it be over, what is to be hoped for*, says another. She is drained, from all the battling. Soon she will give in. Soon one voice will prevail.

Moments of clarity—so vivid they are nearly blinding—come over her, and she sits up, short of breath, eyes stinging and blurry. It is not a nightmare, it is waking terror. She rocks herself, muttering, wishing away the image before her: her child, a boy, dead. No violence, no blood, just her beautiful baby boy, without breath, a bright light drawing the child into itself, swallowing him completely. In the darkness, in the absence, she feels the skin of her forearms, cold now and tingly—longing, longing like actual fervent hunger. She did not have a chance to hold her child. She never felt his living body in her arms.

Your child is safe, your child is well, a voice says. What voice is it? It is not familiar, it is an impersonal voice, it does not know her. *Ha!* She refuses the voice. *Liar. Who are you? Prove it. Make me well, then.*

She lies down again. Now sleep comes, warmth wins out.

Talk of another visitor, arriving soon, has filled the house; she has listened but not heard, and yet something quickens in her memory. She has been returning to childhood frequently, not so much as thought, but as transport; as if, in illness, in confusion, there were no boundaries of time, no *now* or *then*, only what is most real to the senses, what comes clear and true. Who, after all, demands adulthood from her now?

Empire State Building, fall 1979. She is wearing a pink velour sweat suit with white faux-fur lining, her mother's favorite out-fit. She liked to please her mother by wearing it, felt somehow, even at three years old, that certain things must be worn for her mother's pleasure. The elevator is packed with other mothers and children, the fathers seem to have all gone ahead. They are preparing for something, bracing, but she doesn't know what is to come.

"*Ee ruh keh heh,*" her mother says, standing behind and leaning over to show her the fake chewing motion, exaggerated jaws. "Do like this." She doesn't understand. She shakes her head and frowns, *No, not hungry.* Her mother sighs, smiles a nervous smile in the direction of the others. Then the elevator takes off, and it seems as if someone reaches inside her head, pushes outward with tight fists, pressure building. Tears pour, she cries out and turns to bury her face in her mother's hip. "*Gwen chan ha.* It's all right," her mother whispers, an edge in her tone.

When the elevator stops, the pack pours out. Min-yung keeps her face firmly nestled until she can feel the jostling all done. Someone takes her hand and leads her out, walks her to the nearest bench, sits her down. It is Ah-jin, her cousin, whose face is familiar to her now, part of their group these past days, their "family"—these people who look out for her, who know things, who bring her what she needs and respond when she cries out.

Ah-jin takes Min-yung's hand and opens it, palm up, places something in it—a white square, smooth and cold. "Ahhh," Ah-jin the helper says, opening her mouth and pointing inside, then doing the same thing her mother was doing, the chewing motion. "Chiclet," she says. Obediently, Min-yung puts the white square in her mouth, bites down, again, then again, and again. It's hard work, but she is getting the point now, the pressure in her ears pops; feels good, like a sneeze. Ah-jin has an easy face, calm and straight. Min-yung keeps chewing, chomp-chomp, grin and grimace. Maybe the calm face will laugh.

But no, she is not laughing. She nods, matter of fact, glad to be of service; takes Min-yung by the hand and leads her back to her mother. Quickly, she turns her attention to the next assignment, the next problem to solve: there is a ruckus among the boys. The three of them are punching and kicking. But they are laughing too, they are pretending to be Ninja Turtles.

The third boy's face, the one who is not one of her brothers—Min-yung doesn't like it. It is not a helpful face, not like Ah-jin's. It upsets her, and once already—as he bent down to her level, making elastic faces, trying to win her over—she fell to tears. The boys laughed and praised his humor, even her mother encouraged her to polite affection. "Han-soo *op-pah*," her mother said, nudging her. Min-yung turned away. Something loud on the surface of his expression, something that seemed to emanate from under his skin—an unruly tremoring—variable, unlasting. Her brothers, though older, were reduced to followers in his magnetic presence, but he repelled her, like the wrong ends of magnets forced together.

The day is windy, even on the ground. On the observation deck, people are snapping photos of messy-haired families, scarves flapping. One of the boys, Hae-joo, hits the ground. They are all still laughing, but a pant leg has been torn at the knee, and there is blood. Min-yung's mother and Ah-jin run over, on the scene in an instant.

Min-yung is left alone. It is just for a moment, but long enough, for her to baby-step toward the railing. As she approaches—open sky, edge of the unseen—she feels an inner tremor of her own.

Ah-jin is behind her now, hands on her shoulders, pulling gently back and away.

Ah-jin. Helpful Ah-jin. Another visitor, arriving soon, they say. She listens to their talk but hears only fragments. *Arriving soon, your cousin from America, Ah-jin.*

Her face is calm and straight.

Soon, one voice will prevail.

In sleep, in transport, Min-yung is able now to welcome the relief, her cousin's steady and simple assurance. *Ah-jin is coming, coming to help. Relief, like a sneeze. Hands on my shoulders, gently pulling back.* For once in a long time, dreaming of Ah-jin, she sleeps soundly.

9

Henry's nine months in rehab ended on a cloudy, muggy day in August, an hour upriver from the city, in a town he'd never before heard of and would never see again. Three months previously, Marvin, his psychiatrist, broke the news that he didn't think he was ready, even though his two buddies who'd checked in at the same time were cleared to go. "Cleared" just meant with Marvin's blessing. The program was 100 percent voluntary. You could leave the Center without "clearance" at any time, it just meant you couldn't come back. No readmittances for AWOLs; no exceptions. A kind of paternal "as long as you're under my roof" policy. On the other hand, those who left with clearance were welcomed back if they relapsed; in case they needed just a little reinforcement time, sit-ins at meetings, a shot in the arm of support, so to speak. *Inside.*

It was a *humiture* day, the sort of day one would say felt tropical—except for the absence of lush greenness, white sand beaches, anything colorful. A more apt descriptor was oppressive. Henry thus reentered the world on that first day heavy on his feet, soggy and uncertain.

Marvin's strongest suggestion was *structure*. "Find meetings, go often, go daily if possible. You'll need the voices of recovery in your head. Not forever, it won't be a crutch. You'll find your way back, but don't be a hero. Take it slow. Use your sponsor. Each. Step. Matters. Take as long as it takes."

Sponsor. Structure. Slow. All right, then. All right.

He carried only a single duffel bag, his wallet (no credit cards: all canceled, a fresh start), and an e-mail printout with an address. A friend—one of Jane's friends, actually—another photojournalist whom he sort of dated a few years ago, kept a place in the city but was away on assignment and would be long-term, working for the China bureau at least six more months, in Beijing. He could stay at her place as long as he needed, as long as she was away. Possible periodic drop-ins by her stepbrother when he was in town on business, but there were two rooms, enough beds. No problem.

A Gramercy address, nice 'hood. Nicer than he could ever afford on his own. When he arrived he surveyed the place—sparsely furnished, clean, good light, electricity working—and collapsed on the couch, sneakers on. It was four in the afternoon; he slept until morning.

The next day he made himself a list (another Marvin suggestion: *There will be a flood of things, it will feel impossible: take a breath, make a list; do one thing at a time*). Groceries. Want ads (the *Times*, *The Village Voice*). Phone. Internet? There was a laptop on the desk. He turned it on; it was working, cables all hooked up. He was able to check his e-mail.

Talk about a flood of things: he'd stayed on top of it the first few months, but then went off the grid altogether. The last dated e-mail was from three months ago; the mailbox must have gotten full, most of it spam.

Something from his mother, leedoctorofmind@aol.com.

Henry, you haven't been answering, we don't know how you are. But I understand. Your father worries like a woman; but I understand. You are getting well, you will be better than before, strong and successful, when you come out. Realization, of all things, is costly. Don't loose heart. They won't let me speak to your doctors, so I can only hope they are well trained and have right views. Paul keeps us informed. Love you, your mom.

A *loose heart.* Ha. *Maybe that's it,* he thought. What other diagnosis made sense?

Paul was the only one who visited regularly. Jane had been mostly out of the country; Dr. Lee never requested to visit; his father came a few times, an hour or so of near-wordless awkwardness, nothing monumental. They left him alone, mostly because he'd asked them to. Paul came about every other week, even after the split with Jane. They'd watch sports on TV, talk about coaches and draft picks, the latest doping scandals. Like regular guys. Paul would always find a way to bring things around to the obvious, though; a subtle opening, in case Henry wanted to talk about it.

They treating you okay here?

Yeah, it's pretty good. They leave you alone mostly. It works, you know, that reverse-psychology crap: not a lot of rules, responsibility is in your hands, make your own choices. Everyone's in the same boat, so the peer pressure, you know. It's in the right direction.

You making friends? Some good guys?

Yeah, a couple of guys. Mostly older. They're all telling me I'm smart to do this now, before it gets too late, or too hard. Before I have more to lose.

You look good, man, you look beefy. Food's good?

Paul would stay through the game, maybe just until halftime, depending on what he had going on. He was always upbeat, had that look of freshly showered and ready-to-go, like next he'd be heading out to help a little old lady with her groceries cross the street. Henry loved Paul, loved him in that particular way that a man loves another man who is in no way—could never be—his rival. Paul was somehow absolutely solid, and all *give*, at the same time. There was nothing Paul couldn't receive, absorb, accept. You couldn't knock him down; but then there was nothing to knock *against*. After the break with Jane (neither of them ever spoke to Henry about what actually happened) he seemed a little strange to Henry, like he'd had the wind knocked out of him, or seen a ghost—all scooped out and hollowed. But after a time—not so soon after but not too long either—that vacancy started to seem less like an emptiness and more like a capacity, an expectancy. *Ready-to-go.*

Henry could only marvel at that kind of always-game resiliency. Infinite serenity and forbearance. It made him laugh out loud and shake his head when he thought of it, which was just what he did when he talked about it with Marvin. "Man," he said. He had started that day in a good mood, but something turned in a moment, a dark cloud passing. "What?" Marvin asked, hand on chin in rapt attention as always. "Just . . . I don't know. Man." He was feeling something, a dis-ease; the urge to get out of there, be alone. He didn't want to talk about Paul anymore, or about anything. He wanted to hit a wall, and hit it hard. He wanted the wall to be solid all the way through, *no give*.

A loose heart. He'd have to tell Marvin about that one.

In fact, the nine months were all about *no give*. At the Center there were walls, walls everywhere, literal and otherwise. Hard edges. Fixed barriers. Bang bang bang up against them. Keep banging until you wear yourself out, until you no longer have to jam full force every which way to know where you are. You just know. You learn where the walls are from a safe distance, save yourself the bruising and shattering. You start to feel things in your body—things other than bruising and shattering—for the first time in a long time. The feeling of hunger, for example. *I want a burger, medium-rare, cheese and bacon*, Henry thought. He felt it everywhere in his body, the craving was strong, and specific.

He told Marvin, and Marvin smiled. *Your eyes*, Marvin said. *What? What about them?* Henry asked. *I can see them. I think you're ready. Ready to be cleared.*

First day out. Back to the list. *Cigarettes. Call Jordan.* He looked at the list and sighed. It felt like a lot. It felt like plenty. He thought of adding *Call Paul*, but decided he'd wait, maybe another day or two, get some kind of rhythm going first, feel his way around. He'd call Jordan, his sponsor; that would be enough for today.

He went for the cigarettes first, picked up the *Voice*. At a sidewalk café he ordered a Coke, sat down at a table next to a couple arguing in loud whispers (which was somehow soothing), scanned the classifieds. It wasn't as hot or as muggy as the day before. The sun was out. A slight breeze.

He finished his Coke, lit up a cigarette. Leaned back in his chair. He'd circled a few things in the want ads with a bright blue Sharpie. Mostly entry-level desk work, a couple of restaurant jobs, a messenger service. Dog walker—which sounded the most appealing, being out and around, moving, moving. He liked animals. He wasn't qualified for much, had spent most of his postcollege years drifting, borrowing money from his parents, odd jobs, some acting auditions.

But anything was possible now; he felt good. He was out, and he was okay, and he had a list, and he would call Jordan. He thought about his last session with Marvin before he left. "We'll need to talk more about your mother," he'd said. "She'll probably always be a looming figure for you. We have to start with that, really *get* it at the *acceptance* level." At first, Henry thought it was a joke. His mother was all they talked about, it seemed, how much more could there be; and how much more cliché could they get? At the same time, he couldn't think of one insight, one revelation about her or how he felt about her or anything she'd done or not done, or what any of it—his mother, his father,

Jane, Paul—what any of it had to do with his nine months. He drank too much, he lost control, he stopped drinking; and then he was hungry. And now he was here, sitting at a table on a sidewalk, smoking a cigarette and already imagining his new life as the neighborhood's friendly, *ready-to-go* dog walker (Henry's Hounds—in his mind he was already onto his own brand). He laughed to himself (or maybe out loud, the arguing couple was too engrossed to notice), fully convinced that he most certainly did *not* need to talk more about his mother.

No, he was done with all that. Nothing was wrong, nothing was missing, nothing was broken or needed fixing. He was on top of the world, at a towering height, he had a list, and a phone number, and nothing could hurt him, not with his list and his phone number. He was dizzy with vertigo, the world at his feet. He got up, tucked the newspaper under his arm, left a generous tip; then smiled and winked, happily, cruelly, at the mascara-smudged woman at the next table.

No, nothing could hold him now, nothing would keep him down. Not even a loose heart.

Women and Children

1

I received Clayton's e-mail with the news about Sarah just before leaving for Baghdad. I was in Paris for what was supposed to be a good long break but was really only four days, five if you counted travel time. I had few friends left in Paris anymore. The Parisians I knew had moved—to their family's country villages, where they had rent-free homes to inhabit and inherit, or else to New York to pursue (I tried to tell them) the ultimate grass-is-greener illusion. The Americans I knew were all journalists and had either signed on as permanent staff writers and photographers for magazines (weeklies and monthlies, for a slower pace) in other cities, or quit altogether. The life got old, and so did we.

Clayton had written a few days after the attack. He would be flying her body back to Raleigh. If I had jumped right back on a plane, I could have made it for the service. But I didn't. It was not a serious consideration.

I had already spoken to Julien—my one contact still in town, not likely to light out for the frontier, nor the farm, any time soon. Over the years I'd come to consider him a friend, a *grand frère* of sorts; he'd been my home base for over a decade. I made him swear that this lag in assignments was actual, that he wasn't pulling some protective paternal bullshit on me—he'd already suggested once that I take a break, that I'd been pushing too hard.

"*Chérie*, trust me. I'm really not that thoughtful, who do you think you're talking to? Come back before Baghdad; it's lovely here, the leaves are turning, everyone's in a good mood, we'll do something, you know, amusing."

"What happened to the Julien I used to know and hate, the one who worked us all like slaves and bullied us until we made money for you? And that oh-so-endearing sexual harassment thing you had perfected . . . ?"

"No, no, no, my dear. Listen. Let's clear this up now and for all. All these years, I've seen something. You poor girls, you misunderstand. The French, we *love* women. *C'est tout.* On so many things, yes, we think ourselves more sophisticated than you and your McNuggets of everything. But on this, we are hopelessly simple, uncomplicated. Be sexy, be matronly, be aggressive, *sois coquette.* It's good, all of it! Your 'harassment' is our pleasure, our adoration. And you were so adorable in the beginning, of course I couldn't resist."

"Yeah, okay. I get it, it was all in my head." He sighed, a strangely sober sigh.

"I feel sorry for you American girls, always seeing something ugly or vulgar in your sex. Such a waste. And now, my dear, you are no longer . . . you have become . . ."

"*Une femme d'un certain âge.* Yes, yes. *Je sais, je sais.* Save it, *mon ami.* I'm coming back now, I'll see you soon."

"Good, good." His sobriety brightened up. *Yes,* I thought, *you are a simple man.* "I am having some people together, for my fiftieth. You will come? Yes. Guess who is in town. Our dear lady, Madame Martine."

"Really? Eloise? God, it's been . . . I don't know, a long time."

"She has a show. Finally, after all these years, the Parisian establishment is recognizing her. It's at the Beaubourg! Didn't you read about it?"

"I haven't honestly looked at a newspaper in weeks."

"So ironic. What is it you say? The cobbler's children with torn soles?"

"Something like that."

"Hurry back. I'll catch you up."

My flat was in the Marais, 14 rue de Picardie. It was the closest thing I had to a physical home, which wasn't saying much.
Even our place in New York, Paul's and mine, felt less like home
to me, more like a place to visit; he used to get at me for leaving
my clothes in a duffel bag—one week, two weeks. I'd had the
place at number 14 since I first arrived in Paris . . . over ten years
ago. I even had a plant—a flowering cactus—which I found mildly
reassuring.

It wasn't until I first took the flat that I learned of Dr. Lee's stint
in Paris. I knew something of her childhood travels, but Paris
had never before been mentioned. I had just signed a lease and
called my parents to let them know where they could reach me,
expecting to get my father. Dr. Lee had her own phone line for
clients and rarely answered the home line. But everyone was
out, and whatever restlessness had seized her at the moment
prompted her to answer.

"My God, Jane, you must be just a few steps from our hotel. I
wish I could remember the name. It might still be there. It must
have been six months, nine months . . . we stayed for quite some
time." She stopped talking, and I thought maybe it was something in the connection.

"Hello?"

"Sometimes I'd find a way to get away from the *ajjummah* and
just wander on my own. I was . . . I don't know, fourteen or
fifteen. Yes, fifteen. I remember now. I didn't even mind the people staring . . . a young Oriental girl wandering alone the streets
of Paris. It was like a dream for me . . . and I guess a little dangerous. Anything could have happened." She laughed and trailed
off. I heard the clink of ice and understood now the silence. She
spoke so rarely of her past, I should have known. "I would love

to visit you there sometime! It's been so long. To wander those streets again."

"I'll be here so infrequently. It's mostly just a pit stop. One room, barely furnished."

"Oh, I know. It was just a thought. It was a good time. My mother loved Paris. She was happy, I remember her . . . smiling a lot. She took me shopping. . . ." She was drifting off now. I could picture her: sheer silk blouse with a high pearl-buttoned neck, something in a light peach or lavender; pencil skirt, her long legs curled up underneath her in an impossible feat of flexibility; hair in a swooped bun, a little loose, maybe a strand or two falling forward; her eyes a little red, a little larger and sunken because maybe she hadn't been sleeping. "But anyway . . . I wanted to say to you . . . don't neglect Paul, he won't wait forever. A man is a man, after all. And . . ." another pause, another clink ". . . invite Henry sometime. Henry, I'm sure, would enjoy it. He hasn't traveled much, he stays close to home, close to me, maybe too much; it would do him good, I think."

"Sure. Right. I'll invite Henry." My sarcasm was juvenile, but I knew it didn't matter, she wasn't paying attention. To me, to Henry. He was in his sixth year of college, struggling to finish, switching majors like socks, showing up and disappearing in fits and spurts. From what Paul told me, he was sleeping at our place more than he was at home, and rarely sober.

"Well, be safe, Jane. Don't do anything foolish out there. I'm all for women professionals, of course; but don't forget you are a *woman*, after all. There is a *difference*, especially in that man's world. Trust me, I know." I had nothing but more sarcasm welling up in response, so I said nothing. I couldn't deny the effort of something like earnestness, but . . . with Dr. Lee, it was always the same. Even with the effort, you couldn't receive it, because Dr. Lee spoke in loops: from herself, about herself, to herself.

❦   ❦   ❦

I avoided funerals; that's the short of it. Julien had caught wind of the incident in Gereida—it wasn't a big story, but he knew I'd been there and remembered Clayton—so he noticed it, tucked in a corner on page 11 of the *Tribune*.

"You've stayed in touch at all?" We were in his office, my first stop when I arrived.

"Not really. Not until this."

"It's terrible." He frowned, almost a pout.

"It happens."

"Jane. You're okay? She was a friend, no?"

"This is our work, Julien. She was a subject. It happens." I could hear my own overinsistence. Julien's silence confirmed it. "If I went to every funeral, every time . . ."

"My God, Jane . . ." I braced myself for a lecture I sensed coming. But then he sat back, he retreated, hands clasped behind his head. "Do you remember the first one?"

"The first one what?"

"The first loss. The first *death*."

"I don't know. I'd have to think about it."

"Well, I do. My first photographer, just three months in. I took over, you know, when my uncle died, suddenly, from a heart attack. I was . . . thirty? Twenty-nine, maybe? Anyway, this guy, mid-career guy, lots of promise, you know, good instincts. Committed. And I was . . . well, I was just starting out, so what did I know? He had gotten in, a deep inside contact with Nicaraguan cocaine . . . right in the middle of Iran-contra. It was big, and I thought, *What a break, I can make the family proud, show them what I can do.* Well . . . it was horrible. He and two reporters. Shot many more times than necessary. I had to call his wife. I remember it upset me much more than my uncle's death; and I loved that old man."

"You don't blame yourself, do you?"

"What, you mean would I have done different with more experience? No, probably not. He was going in, I don't think I could have stopped him. But I would not have been so excited about it. I am never so excited now, not like I was then." After a few moments, he looked up at me, smiling a tired smile.

"I don't remember," I said.

"Say again?"

"I don't remember. The first one. It's all sort of . . . mixed together. In my mind."

"How old are you, dear?"

"Are you kidding? *Cher* Julien, in America, we don't . . ."

"Thirty-eight, thirty-nine? Jane, listen to me, you need to know, maybe you don't see it yourself . . . you have gotten old. I have noticed this in you. And I don't mean your *ass* is sagging. I mean your soul, *l'esprit*. Which is to say that you have stopped living and started on . . . the other thing. This is inevitable, perhaps; but not necessary. *La mort, la mort*, it's everywhere, and then it's nowhere, and then . . . it's inside you, you become *de bons amis*, too chummy. You are *closing up*." He said all this with such intent, boring into me, zero irony.

"You know, you're becoming awfully grave in your old age. . . ." I was attempting to lighten things, but he wasn't letting the bone out of his teeth.

"Are you insulted? Well, good. *C'est ça.* You should hear this."

"And do what exactly? Jesus, Julien . . ."

"*Arrête!* Take a goddamn break. Your life, Jane. This is your friend speaking, not your boss. Tell me. What the hell happened? Before Gereida?"

Dr. Lee's father was a wealthy businessman. He ran a bridge-and-roads engineering company, with contracts all over the world. Fluent in Japanese and English, a little bit of French and Arabic. His father was a chief adviser to the governor-general during the Japanese occupation. They were essentially yes-men to the Japanese, shop managers for the bosses. My grandfather did not think much of Korean political leaders when it came time for him to choose a profession. He wanted to get out. One war had ended, another was imminent. He wanted to travel and live well. At this, he succeeded.

They were cut off from the family, which was what my grandfather wanted. He married my grandmother, the daughter of a poor Christian minister, eager as her new husband to escape the confines of her predestined fate. This finalized the estrangement on both sides. The two of them became world travelers, with young Woo-in as their pet in tow—their only child, minded mostly by a series of tutors and *ajjummah dul*.

All this I learned from my father. Some of it he'd gleaned from Dr. Lee herself—her version of her past, anyway—some of it from Dr. Lee's aunt, my father's elder brother's wife, who introduced them in the first place and was the only family member to stay in touch with my grandfather, her younger brother.

That's all we really know; but here's what I imagine, what I piece together . . .

Dr. Lee's mother—a shrewd, elegant woman of great value to her husband's business affairs, having well learned the art of wifely charm and poise from observing her own mother, a minister's wife. A strain of Russian blood—they were northerners—somewhere in her family line, thus explaining their unusual height, long noses, touch of red hair; and stubborn passion, survivor's strength. My grandmother serving her husband's professional purposes faithfully, but also taking liberty to do as she pleased, with whomever she pleased—my grandfather's success earning her a free pass to the worldly existence she craved.

Often she left young Woo-in in the hands of an ajjummah, *once the girl's daily lessons were completed (the tutors were often attractive young men). On occasion, she would bring Woo-in along for a museum or garden tour, or a lunch out with the wives of her husband's colleagues, and my mother would observe her mother with awe: her facility with the basics of new languages (Japanese, French, Russian); her ease with foreign fashions,* somehow made unique and native to her when she donned them; her ability to both modestly demur and somehow overpower her various companions with sharp opinions about anything from politics to art to the proper way to cook a fish (if it was to be cooked at all).

Woo-in also feeling a sadness toward her mother, who seemed to move about in a protective bubble, barely brushing shoulders with the warm bodies around her. Pecks on the cheek, feather-light handshakes with a bow—these were the limits of her mother's (ostensible) physical connections. In this way, Woo-in learned an immunity to loneliness: she saw that her mother, too, was essentially solitary, and yet never bereft, or without inner resources. Always radiant and appealing and admired. Sometimes she craved closeness to her mother and would have, unchecked, burst into the protective bubble to nestle at her breast, feel her warm breath on her hair; but such opportunities did not arise, and to forge ahead with such heedless acts of expression was simply impossible. Instead, Woo-in channeled that hunger into fierce adoration, from a distance; and in this way idealized her mother, who was in fact a listless and deeply unhappy woman, indulging in reckless, fleeting affairs with many men.

"So where and when is this party?" I hadn't answered Julien's question. Luckily, I didn't have to.

"Ah, it's late," he said, looking out the window, the sun beginning to set. "I have to get over there, my wife, she will . . ."

"Your wife?"

"My wife. You remember Sophie?"

"Yes, of course, Sophie, mother of your children, your neither-of-us-are-the-marrying-type longtime partner?"

"Oh, didn't I mention it? We decided what the hell. The laws, you know, they are getting worse. It was the children, really, their idea. So conservative, the young kids now. I think Jean-Paul, the older one, has found religion. God help us all. Anyway, they wanted us to do it. They spent a fortune on one of those obnoxious cakes and everything. But Sophie wore *blood red* silk, it was fantastic. Don't worry, there were no invitations, just the four of us."

"Unbelievable."

"Yes, well. There you have it. Now. Tonight, nine o'clock, you remember Café Gamin? We have the garden for the evening. There will be small portions of terrible food and a lot of liquor. I told Madame Martine that you were coming; she will monopolize you all evening I'm sure."

"I'm sure there will be others to monopolize *her*."

"Yes, well, you know her. She is very . . ."

". . . fast."

"Yes. She knows how to get away when she needs to. Although, I tell you, I sense that she is slowing down. If you can believe it. But you, you she will want to see. She claims you, you know. Her discovery. And you've been good, always giving her proper reverence. That's why you stay in her good graces. Now go home, have a nap or something, pinch your cheeks and brighten up, okay? For your friend, who is *truly* old. You are not upset. By what I said?"

"Of course I am."

"Ah, well. My work here is done. I will see you tonight!"

I shared my imaginings, a version of them, with Henry once. This was before he hit bottom, when he was doing the denial thing with both me and Paul; and when he was more staunch in his defenses of Dr. Lee. I thought he might appreciate it, my efforts to understand her better. Not so.

"Sounds like some kind of made-for-TV miniseries to me. I mean, the Russian thing? What is this, *Anna Karenina*?" He put the back of his hand to his forehead, swooning.

"The greatest book ever. The greatest *story* ever."

"Our grandmother died of lung cancer, not train tracks."

"There's some drama there."

"Says who? Most of life is pretty damn boring, you know. The music doesn't always crescendo when bad things happen. Shit goes down. People survive. You overdo it with Mom sometimes."

"Maybe."

"Give her a break."

"Sure, Henry."

"I mean, really. What's she ever done to you?"

Eventually, when Woo-in reached high school age, they sent her back to Seoul, where she boarded at Kyong-gi Girls School. She saw less and less of her parents (who saw less and less of each other) and threw herself headlong into her studies.

The rest is pretty reliable, the story of her steep professional rise. This she spoke of freely and abundantly, her most favored subject, really. Her award-winning high school senior thesis, "Dreams and the Psychological Terrain of Childhood." Her continuing research at university, lauded as bold and uniquely rigorous (aside from the occasional vitriolic naysayer, mostly academic rivals), as she drew from across disciplines and cultures—Nietzsche, Rousseau, the Abstract Expressionists, archaic symbolism, Korean shamanism, Emerson, and, of course, Freud. In an early article, she would quote the painter Agnes Martin— "We are all born 100 percent ego. The rest of our lives is the ongoing tragedy of learned adjustment and waning percentage"—and later chose as the title of her first book *Born Ego: Recovering the Self*, whose first titillating sentence read: "You were born a genius; you are capable of returning to that state."

The book was published in the early seventies, when Freud and psychology were falling out of fashion in favor of the random, the psychotropic, and long before the advent of Dr. Ruth, Oprah, and the mass self-help industry. *Born Ego* sent ripples through the psychiatric community, and even became a general-reading hit among a certain influential readership—middle-aged parents, artists and professionals, emerging from hippiedom, growing weary of *whatever feels good* as a life philosophy. Dr. Lee had become a kind of celebrity guru on the inner workings of the mind; American feminism and multiculturalism had worked to her advantage in opening the few key doors she needed to move ahead. And as a wife and mother of two, she was thought by many of her colleagues, men and women alike, to be the Woman Who Had It All. It was a lot to maintain, I suppose—both the career, and the image.

What the hell happened?

You can be aware of your own remoteness—an inner disconnect—without too much struggle. You can live like this a long time; a whole life, really. You can count it an asset, exploit it as such. In your work, for example.

Don't forget you are a woman, after all. There is a difference. Trust me, I know.

A lot happens in a woman's body. I understand this. In my mind, I understand. But you can be aware, you can live a long time. . . .

First, a child: a life of some sort, not quite human, and not quite *yours*, but a life, growing, undeniably. Then, after the bleeding, after the *flushing out*, substance and soul—which is not painful, exactly, but something louder than pain and completely silent— after the completion of all that, then: your mother's words (your mother who has done nothing really to harm you, nothing to speak of), her words rumbling in there, a ruthless aftershock. *Don't forget.*

There was nothing I could do—about the bleeding and the noise and the silence. About Dr. Lee being dead right. It is, I think, impossible—the impossibility at some point takes charge—to maintain, to keep the struggle at bay. It is not sustainable. This remoteness. From things that live and move in your own belly. Your very center.

A life comes into being in the dark small space, a sadness, between two people. Drains away in a pool of black blood.

Someone flushes it down with one hand.

And then it's over. There are no bystanders.

2

She was there before I arrived, which surprised me. Eloise was the sort to make grand entrances. I did not even notice her right away. I chatted with some other agency photographers for a few minutes by the bar before seeing her, sitting at a corner table with Sophie. Immediately I could see that she was changed: her posture contained and quiet; the subtle, almost submissive, style of her hair, pulled back by barrettes on either side; the way she held her glass, with both hands wrapped around and fingertips loosely entwined. There was no throng, no radius of charisma; just Eloise, talking with an old friend.

As I approached the table, she looked toward me and smiled, reaching out her hand. It was a kind of underwelcome, as if we'd just seen each other yesterday. Maybe Julien had misread her, maybe she didn't "claim" me. Maybe I was one of the ones she would get away from.

"It's you, Jeanne. Come sit. Sophie is telling stories about Julien."

"I'm making things up," Sophie mock-whispered as I sat down, taking Eloise's hand, whose grip was soft, but not unaffectionate. "Just for fun. Eloise likes stories, and I like to make her happy." Sophie was a journalist for *Le Monde* years ago, but gave it up after her daughter was born. She looked fresh—slightly tanned and freckled, her strawberry-blond hair bright with sun—

but also gave off a tautness of energy, too much water welling up
at the dam. I looked at the wineglasses on the table; she was on
her third, at least.

"Sophie dear, come, say hello to Etienne, he is here all the
way from Marseille." Julien's arm arched over my head, taking
Sophie's hand and escorting her away. Leaning over to kiss my
cheek, he said, "You just arrived? Look at you, a new woman. I
can see you had a good sleep. You ladies should have seen her
earlier today. The walking dead. Eloise, talk some sense with her.
She is overworked. *Chérie*, make sure you get some of that *tarte au
chocolat*, now *that's* deadly."

"He is crazy. I love that man. To me, he is always young, that
young boy who took over the family business," she said. "I knew
his uncle, you know." She winked.

"It's good to see you, madame. How are you? It's been . . . ?"

"You lose track, right? I know. I was trying to remember too.
It doesn't matter in some ways. The years go by. But I see your
work. I see it in important places. I am always happy to see your
work. You've been doing well. You've been working hard."

"I just arrived last night. I plan to see your show tomorrow. I'm
looking forward to it." This was in fact true. I had never stopped
admiring Eloise's work. Her later work especially became less
sensational, less frequently in the thick of violence in action,
and yet somehow reflected even more her determination to get
to the nut, the most stark and incriminating symbols of whatever wrongdoing she saw. And there was always mystery at the
heart of her photographs; whether beautiful or horrifying, always
essentially unfamiliar.

"Tomorrow is closed. But even better, I will call Charles,
he will meet you there and let you in. It's terrible with all the
tourists, anyway. I would go with you myself, but the funeral is
tomorrow."

"Funeral? I'm so sorry, who . . . ?"

"My father. That's why I am here. He was not sick for too

long, that's the good thing. He was ninety, you know. I go to Champagne tomorrow."

"I'm sorry, I didn't know. I thought you were here for the show."

"I would not have come just for the show, it does not interest me all that much. 'Too little, too late,' as they say. But it's a full retrospective, that I am happy about. My early work, it's all there. And now they are calling me, they want me to teach—seminars at the Beaubourg and the Sorbonne. It will bore me a little, I think I am tired of talking talking talking, you know? But I'll do it, most likely. For Christine. Which may also be 'too little, too late.' " She laughed, took a drink. "But . . . we do what we can."

"Christine?"

"You have not met? She is somewhere here." She looked around the room, then motioned toward someone. A young girl, about sixteen or seventeen, with slouchy posture and porcelain skin, came and stood by Eloise, who clasped the girl's hand. It was immediately clear who she was. "My daughter. Isn't she beautiful?"

"*Bonsoir*," I said, reaching for Christine's other hand. Eloise grabbed my wrist and squeezed, and for a moment, the three of us were joined, as if we might bow our heads in prayer.

"*Bonsoir*," she said. Her voice was tiny, like a child's.

"She has just started her final year at *lycée*. Who were you talking to, dear?"

"*Sais pas*. Somebody. Somebody who recognized me as your daughter and wanted to know about you."

"And did you tell them that there is really nothing to know about me?" Christine shrugged, and Eloise laughed, stroking her long red hair. "Don't worry, we'll dye your hair black and get you sunglasses, like Audrey Hepburn, and no one will ever know." Christine did not laugh. She began twisting her torso around, swinging her arm and, with it, the hand that Eloise held—again, like a small child—restless to get away.

"I am going outside to smoke."

"You can smoke in here, *chouette*."

"I am going outside anyway. *Fait chaud*." Christine fanned herself with her newly freed hand and stuck out her tongue.

"Say good-bye to Jeanne, Christine."

"Nice to meet you," she said, pronouncing each word like an English lesson.

"And you," I said.

"Wait, I have an idea. Christine, you have not seen the show yet. I am arranging for Jeanne to go tomorrow, when the museum is closed. Why don't you go together? I'll be back from Champagne by evening. You don't want to go to the funeral anyway, I know. How about that?" Christine looked to me, then to her mother, considering, weighing the two less-than-appealing options. Apparently, a complete stranger seemed less torturous to her than a dead grandfather and a slew of relatives. She shrugged, an assenting kind of shrug.

"*Bon*. I will tell Charles *à midi*. At the entrance. I think you two will have a nice time." Christine shrugged again, this time with a genuine smile in my direction, and off she went.

"Her father has remarried. A second time. The new wife is unbearable. So unbearable that she wrote to me, after many years of silence, of hating me. She has not forgiven me, but she is finding her way now. I am the lesser of two evils. With any luck, it will grow into something better. I think maybe I can be of use to her now."

"So you will stay?"

"I will try it out. We will try it out. My daughter is very attached to Paris, she is not a traveling type. I offered to have her with me, but she did not care for that. She gets violently airsick." I laughed, louder than I meant to. Eloise did not at first think this funny, but then she seemed to see what I saw. We both laughed, a hearty, cleansing laugh. "You are well? I am sorry for not asking until now. Somehow it is like no time has passed."

She was searching me now, tuning her attention in the way I remembered, sensing with her instincts. I felt somehow like I didn't really have to answer.

"I've been working long and hard. Maybe Julien told you. This is my first break in some time. There is something in Baghdad next week, so I'll be leaving again."

"You are in Paris now, it is your home base?"

"More or less." We were searching each other. Circling. There was a new parity between us, both of us vaguely uncomfortable with it. I had a fleeting urge to say more, to tell Eloise about Paul, and the pregnancy; suddenly I wanted to talk about it. But she looked away for a moment, distracted by a ruckus across the room—the waitress dropping a glass—and the urge passed as quickly as it came.

"I hope you don't mind. I do think you will enjoy Christine. But I understand, you are doing me this favor, she was grouchy about coming with me to Champagne. So I thank you."

"A private showing at the Beaubourg? The pleasure is mine. Will your family miss her?"

"They've never met her. I have kept her from them, or them from her, I don't know which exactly, or why. In fact, they didn't know she existed until she was five or six. She is raised mostly by her father, you know." I did not know. Eloise had a way of speaking as if everyone knew everything about her. Or maybe, I wondered, it was just with me. "I am regretting it now, that she never knew my father. My mother died before she was born, but my father . . . he would have loved her. He was like that. He loved females, all females. Nothing lurid, nothing like that, he just . . . the smell, the touch, the *details* of femininity, you know. After my mother, he had so many women, but never settled down. In a way I admired him for that, he never pretended, never acted the faithful husband. Maybe he failed my mother when she was alive, I don't know, I was too young, but it wouldn't surprise me; and maybe that was enough deception for a lifetime. Anyway, Chris-

tine, she is a girlish girl, much more than me. He would have
adored her. It was a mistake, keeping them apart." She paused
here, pushed her fingers through her hair and looked up. She was
pulling at the tip of an outer eyelash. Was it a tear she was fighting? "You learn things—many of them too late, you know." She
was sad, genuinely sad. And surprisingly. Regret was not something I would have expected from her. My impulse to divulge,
to tell, returned; it seemed I might be able to somehow walk
through the open gate into her field of sadness. It was not a place
to which I would have requested entry, necessarily; but while
the gate was open . . .

"Les jolies femmes!" Julien was quite drunk, a happy drunk. He'd
spilled red wine on the front of his shirt, and Sophie was trying
to get it out with a napkin, clumsy and drunk as well. "What are
we talking about? No war talk tonight, no politics. We are cel-
ebrating the beginning of my turn downhill. Jane, tell me, why
do the Americans say that? *It's all downhill from here*, as if it's a bad
thing? Downhill is fast, it's exhilarating, it's effortless! No?"

"Because . . . there is no more challenge, no more mountain
to conquer. And at the bottom of the hill . . ."

"There you are, at the bottom." It was Eloise who finished
the thought, exactly as I would have. Except she spoke without
irony, and without bitterness. She said it in a way that made it
sound quite peaceful.

3

When Julien asked me—about the first one, the first death—he
had no way of knowing what would happen in Baghdad just two
weeks later. He didn't know that there would be more to come,
and so soon. He didn't know that I myself would come close to
being the *last* one. And he didn't know that the blast would liter-

ally quiet the external world around me; that the inside stuff, brain and heart, would begin to ring, to sound off.

On the flight to Korea, I write a postcard to Christine. I'd been thinking about her—even with all that's happened, it feels like yesterday, it feels somehow close, our time together—and I told her I'd stay in touch; something I rarely say, because it's something I rarely do. As I'm writing, *How is school going? Are you keeping up with the piano?* I am also recalling our visit to the Pompidou, our private viewing of Eloise's show; and then it hits me. The first one.

Why didn't it come to me then, in the gallery? I can see the image, one of Eloise's most lauded, from the early eighties. Christine had never seen it before—she'd not seen much of her mother's work—and was clearly struck by it. It was a young Kenyan girl, about Christine's age, who'd undergone female genital mutilation, just moments before the photograph was taken (we know this from the accompanying text). The girl was seated in a chair, looking directly at the camera, like a portrait. She wore a smocklike dress, her arms and legs skinny branches stemming from a shapeless center. The girl sat straight and still. She was not weeping, she did not have a look of torment. Rather, she was a blank; she was a ghost of herself. Her skin was black and smooth, the whites of her eyes a stark, solitary brightness. In the background, seated to the far left, the draping dress of an older woman, hands and feet peeking out, but seen only from the neck down. The title of the photograph indicates it is her mother.

Recalling the photo, and the moment of seeing it with Christine, I stop writing; I remember it so clearly now: the Syrian girl whose sister's wedding I'd photographed for a culture piece in a travel magazine. The girl was two years younger and next in line for marriage. A husband had just been identified for her; the wedding would take place one year after her sister's. Shortly, she would undergo FGM. After the wedding, a weeklong affair, as I

was getting ready to leave, news spread throughout the village:
the girl had drowned herself in the river. Her mother made a
formal announcement to the family (I was present but not per-
mitted to take photographs). I remember her speaking in a tone
I'd never heard nor imagined; it was almost bestial, a fantastic mixture of staunch resolve and desolation. She said that her
daughter had confessed to her she was not a virgin; she regretted
the dishonor that had been brought on the family. That was it,
nothing more was said.

Together—I learned afterward, from a close cousin—the
mother and daughter had gone down to the river, where the
mother filled the pockets of her daughter's dress with stones.
She stood on the shore as the girl waded into the deep, not once
looking back. I asked the cousin how she knew this, had she
witnessed the drowning herself. She said, simply, "This is how it
happens." It was one of my first feature assignments, and at the
time I couldn't quite grasp the full meaning of the act. The community accepted it—the women especially—with utter solem-
nity. And I didn't have time to think much about it; I was off
again to Paris, then the next assignment, hours later.

But now, I see; in my gut, I feel it. The daughter's fidelity to
her mother's honor, the mother's unflinching love in the form
of an awful courage. Together, they enacted the girl's fate—
privately, defiantly. They would not simply await a husband's
wrathful judgment.

As we toured the galleries, I was sensitive to how Christine
might be feeling. In the beginning, I tried to gauge her reac-
tions, but she spoke little, and betrayed even less in her facial
expression. Mostly, we wandered separately. But she did stop for
a good while in front of the Kenyan girl's portrait, and there I
rejoined her.

"It's something, isn't it?"

"People *like* this one?"

"I wouldn't say they *like* it, so much as they admire it. It's very well known." She continued to stare at it.

"It is strange . . . I know I am probably supposed to feel out-raged or something. Like at the world, or whoever it is that did this to her. But . . . it's *her* I feel angry at. I mean, it's like you want her to fucking *do* something, or *feel* something, not just sit there and *pose*. It's like this terrible thing has just happened to her and she's just like *obeying* everybody all the way up to the end, including . . . including my mother."

"Hmm . . ." I noticed Christine's chest moving up and down, her face flushed, as if what she was feeling, what she'd just expressed, had been rigorous exercise, had gotten her blood pumping. "I never really saw it that way."

"Do *you* like it?"

"I don't know, to tell you the truth. But it does move me. I always thought of her as brave. *Because* she's posing. She knows something has just been taken away from her—or I think she does—and she's sitting there, looking at us, composing herself for people to see, and she's saying something just by being seen. And I always kind of imagined that the woman in the back-ground, the mother, she really didn't want to be in the picture at all, which is why she's cut off—but that the girl, the daughter, she ordered her mother to be in the picture. Like, you're responsible too, this is about you, so *sit down*, you're *in this*." She seemed to consider this for a moment.

"I guess . . . we could just *ask* my mother, what it was like, what really happened."

"You *could*. But that would sort of defeat the purpose. You know?"

"Yes, right. And she would see it that way too, I'm sure, so she probably wouldn't tell me anyway."

"Have you studied or tried photography? Does it interest you?"

"No, not really. My father is a musician, you know. I think I take after him mostly."

"And you have brothers or sisters?" Eloise hadn't mentioned any other children; but then, she hadn't mentioned this one either.

"I have a half brother. He's seven. And my stepmother, the new one, she is pregnant now."

"That's kind of a big family. An interesting family."

"Not really. It feels quite lonely, actually. And not interesting at all. More like . . . pathetic."

"How do you mean?"

"Like no one can keep it together enough to just make *one good thing*. It's just lots of . . . *half-ass*." I laughed. As much as the French like to condescend to English-speakers, they do love to swipe our expressions. Or maybe what they love is to mock us by using them. Ironically, *half-ass* sounded not so crude, kind of lovely, coming out of Christine's mouth.

"You should go sometime. With your mother, on assignment. See what it's like." It wasn't like me at all, this advice-giving. And I felt not so much qualified, as perhaps . . . obligated.

"*Why?*"

"I don't know. Maybe you'll get a sense . . . of why she does it. Why we do it. There is nothing *half-ass* about it. They are not your stories, your lives . . . your families. But they are so real, you can't believe it. I've never said this to anyone before—it's one of those things you're not supposed to say—but there are times when you come to envy them. The people, the ones who are suffering. There is nothing fake out there. There is, in fact, an unbearable amount of truth. And there is nothing *pathetic*, only very very sad." I had a sense that I should stop talking, but the momentum—of the confessional—propelled me. "And you become . . . addicted . . . like a high, a hyperclarity. Because your own life, your own family, your own *half-ass* stuff . . . It's just a whole different . . . ." What? A whole different *what*?

"You make it sound noble. Like this, this kind of thing"—
she turns to the Kenyan girl—"is, like, *redeeming* or something.
Like some kind of higher state, when really it's just horrific. My
friends and I, we talk about this, about why we dislike America.
Your George Bush especially. It's these stupid ennobling ideas,
saving the world, making statements, such bullshit. All these
words, like *free* and *liberated* and *God-fearing*. I mean, Jesus Christ.
I'm a Catholic, my father is too, and we actually like believe in
God and faith and something, you know, good and spiritual . . .
but you guys, you Americans, I'm sorry, it's not *you* specifically
or anything, but you like *ruin* it all; you like fuck it up into something really . . . *pathetic.*"

She said all this while looking at the photograph, her voice
trembling slightly. She was lost in her speech, and I could tell
that she really wasn't directing all of it at me (or at George Bush,
either); that she was mad about a lot of things. A lot of other
things.

And when she was done—her indictments so final, so sure—an
urge rose up in me, a red-hot flash, to slap her. It was so intense,
and unexpected, I found myself blinking hard a few times; and
for a second, I thought, I feared, with no one in the gallery but
the two of us, that I might just do it.

The intensity kept burning, deeper and hotter; but as it
burned through, it started to turn into something else—a kind of
supercalm, a generosity. I saw Christine in that moment for the
unhappy girl she was, too much left to fend for herself, but doing
pretty well, all things considered. I felt the tension in my arm
and hand relax. She turned to me. I took a deep breath.

"So, do you play an instrument?"

"The piano."

"And do you love it?"

"Oh, yes. At my father's house, I have a room, my practice
room, with my baby grand. But my stepmother is turning it into
a nursery."

"So you'll live with Eloise?" She shrugged.

"We'll try it out. She said she'd get a housekeeper. And I'm bringing my piano."

"Well, good luck with that. I mean, I understand, a little bit . . . that she might not be an easy person to live with. But what I meant to say, before . . . if you have a chance, if you see a chance, to know her, if she lets you—you might be glad for it, later on." She turned back to the Kenyan girl. We both did. I think we each started to see her just a bit differently.

On the postcard, I write: *I hope everything is working out. Say hello to Eloise. Remember, don't ask about the Kenyan girl. That would be* half-ass. *Make her your own.*

Book Three

Civilians

Force Depletion

1

Ah-jin did not send her precise travel information. They fretted over her arrival, but Han Hyun-kyu assured them that his daughter was an adept traveler, she traveled for her living and would have no trouble finding her way. Of this he was quite sure.

It is late afternoon when the dog begins to howl. Han Hyun-kyu sits in the family room half watching a soap opera and half reading the daily paper. He is in a state of repose, his legs stretched out to rest on the coffee table, a heavy *tampyuh* covering them. He enjoys the largeness of the room with its high, pitched ceilings and immense windows, the late-autumn sun gently warming the air through the glass, as in a greenhouse. He is about to doze off when he hears the dog.

She arrives with nothing more than a backpack and a camera bag. When she enters the house, greets her relatives with a deep, stiff bow, she strikes him as both familiar and strange. He embraces her, relieved by the mere fact of her existence, but feels that beneath the bulk of her layers of clothing, she has become very thin. Worry follows swiftly on the heels of relief. He tries to catch her glimpse in the midst of formalities and reintroduction; to see her eyes. She is avoiding this for the moment, but he thinks he sees in her posture, her manner, something of what she's brought with her: his daughter has suffered something, perhaps many things. She is changed.

He sees something else, briefly: with her short haircut and tall, thin figure, she resembles even more strikingly Lee Woo-in. She is beautiful, this daughter of his; which perhaps he has never quite seen before, not in this particular way. It seems an indulgent thought, and yet he understands at this moment what people mean when they say, in English, "She is quite *becoming.*" Ah-jin seems to be *becoming*—something, someone.

On Han Jung-joo's instruction, Cho Jin-sook sweeps Ah-jin off to settle in before she has had much chance to speak—to tell him of her journey, of anything that has happened since his departure. She must wash and rest before dinner; her aunt has declared it. He entrusts her to the women—these women who seem to know all that is required for a weary traveler in a foreign land—and notes the return of relief. She is in good hands now. Yes, she is safe.

At dinner, he learns of her recent activities through the family's inquiries. She is careful to share only generalities—her rusty Korean conveniently lends itself to imprecision—and relates a minor incident on her latest assignment, which she describes as *heem du ruh*—exhausting. She has decided to take a rest from her work and hopes to return shortly. Han Jung-joo expresses the proper amazement at Ah-jin's agility for such difficult work; Han Jae-kyu nods in assent: "This is too much for a woman!" he says jovially, directing the comment toward his brother. "Women do everything now," Han Hyun-kyu responds, with some pride. "Ah-jin, tell your uncle and aunt where else you've been."

She starts to list places, but fights back a yawn. Min-yung, who has sat quietly next to her cousin throughout the meal, now takes hold of Ah-jin's arm: "She is worn out from the long trip. We should let my cousin sleep," she says. Han Hyun-kyu marks the girl's enthusiasm, the first sign of initiative he has seen in her since his arrival. (Han Jung-joo, who has stood to clear the table, pauses for a moment, noting the same.) The two young women leave the table together, and Han Hyun-kyu feels happy now, he has almost forgotten the strangeness of everything. Buoyed by the warmth of alcohol rush, he is amazed that it could be like this, so effortless. And he imagines that the two of them could stay forever, resting in the peace and comfort of his brother's household.

But a flash of soberness breaks through as he watches Min-yung move away slowly, with heavy steps and drooping shoulders. The two young women leave the room, arm-in-arm, and it is unclear who is supporting whom. He knows that Han Jung-joo is noticing the same, her daughter's lassitude returning like a black mouth, swallowing any signs of revival. Both their faces must fall visibly, as Han Jae-kyu speaks, rather abruptly: "We are all tired. Today, I had patient after patient; I have a full day tomorrow. *Ajjummah*, we are done here, you may clear the table."

Next morning, the kitchen is filled with the bustle and heat of Cho Jin-sook rushing around, preparing breakfast, adjusting to an additional guest. She mumbles to herself as she moves from task to task, reminding herself so she doesn't miss anything, and enlivening the room with the cheerful chatter of work. Min-yung is again animated, coming to the table with Ah-jin, her attentions quickened and focused. That first day, Min-yung monopolizes Ah-jin, insisting they go for a walk after breakfast. Ah-jin agrees, out of politeness, no doubt, as her father can see that Min-yung's attentions are a bit much for her. Han Jae-kyu has left for the office. Han Hyun-kyu and his sister-in-law once again remain.

"Ah-jin is very beautiful," Han Jung-joo says. "Like a swan."

"She is too thin, I think."

"She just needs rest. And nourishment."

"I am grateful to you for providing both."

"She is family. She always has a place here." Han Jung-joo says this somewhat absentmindedly; an automated statement, not insincere, but neither particularly earnest.

"Yes, family. Family is everything." He wants to say something to her about Min-yung. About her illness. He wants to ask but recognizes this would not be proper, certainly not in front of the *ajjummah*. "Min-yung can be a good friend to Ah-jin. She has never made friends easily. As she got older, she buried herself in school. And then taking pictures, all the time."

"Your daughter must be very brave." Han Hyun-kyu considers this. It has never occurred to him that his daughter is *brave*. He has always seen her work as something like an obsession, something that takes her *away* from things. Something not quite normal. And he takes it as a matter of course that his daughter would find something to do with her life which takes her *away*. But he marvels now at how everything takes on a different cast here. How everything seems kinder. *Ah-jin is brave.* Yes, that is most certainly true. Han Jung-joo continues. "Min-yung was always quiet and lonely as well. The boys dominated everything. She got lost in their aggression. They were wild. And always fighting each other." Han Jung-joo laughs, remembering something far off, then fades to silence; as if a page has turned, a new image replacing the other.

Cho Jin-sook is finishing up the breakfast dishes. Something in Han Jung-joo's voice, an unfamiliar softness, gives her pause; this does not go unnoticed. "Auntie Cho, did you remember to close the dog's gate?" The question is more teasing than scolding.

"Big Uncle has done it," she says, and they all laugh, knowing that this has been the case for the last two weeks.

"What will we do, Auntie Cho, when Big Uncle is no longer with us?"

Min-yung and Ah-jin walk in silence. They could not be more different—in appearance, in carriage—and yet they form the image of a couple, a kind of match. Next to Ah-jin's long, thin face, Min-yung's fleshy cheeks and flat nose seem a caricature, an

Oriental doll face, but a sad and sickly one, without the smiling eyes. Min-yung holds Ah-jin's arm tightly with two hands, as if she is leading her somewhere. And yet she walks slowly, with effort, as if all her strength is in the holding.

It is a chilly morning. Min-yung is wearing an odd layered outfit of formal Korean dress, wool sweater and sweatpants, thick rag socks, and slippers—like a street woman who happened upon the castoffs of the wealthy. She is not wearing a hat or gloves, her hair is tangled into a braid that falls off-center down her back. It is cold enough that they can see their white breath in front of them.

"You must be freezing, cousin. We should go back, you will catch cold." Ah-jin speaks to her cousin in Korean. They both speak slowly and carefully at first, they communicate at the level of children to be understood.

"No, no," Min-yung says. She grips Ah-jin's arm even tighter. "I am inside all the time. I want to be out. I am so glad to have company." They walk on in silence, covering little ground; the slow pace is both trying and reassuring to Ah-jin. A few times, she looks back toward the house.

"Shall we go back? Perhaps your mother needs some help with chores."

"No, no. Let's stay a little longer. I want to speak with you now for a bit." Underneath a tall tree on the side of the road, a large stump has served as a sitting place. There, the two cousins rest, Min-yung pulling Ah-jin down next to her with unlikely force. "You have just arrived, but I feel as if we are good friends, for a long time. Do you feel that? We are like sisters."

"I have no sisters," Ah-jin says. "So I can't really say."

"And neither have I, so it is perfect! We've met before, a long time ago, I remember it, it is very clear. Do you remember?" She does not wait for Ah-jin to answer. "I feel I can confide in you. I feel you are here for a reason. Do you feel the same?" Ah-jin shifts a little, loosens herself from Min-yung's too-hard grip. But Min-yung holds firm, she is not prepared to let go.

"I am not sure what you mean." Ah-jin feigns difficulty understanding. In fact, she does not quite understand. The words she comprehends, but her cousin's behavior, her intensity of attention, is unsettling.

"There is no one to talk to. We have lived in this town for always, and yet we have lived apart from everyone. I am very lonely."

"Apart? What do you mean? Your family seems very well established. . . ."

"My family is so good. So sufficient. They have need of nothing, and so we live like this, alone. There are people around, of course, it is a small town; but we are alone, in our hearts, in our souls. They like it this way." Min-yung seems to Ah-jin somehow both restless and sunken at the same time, unable to either be still or move. Ah-jin struggles to listen, to indulge her cousin's talk. She is captive for the moment and senses an instability, possibly danger. If she was out in the field, if this was an assignment, an interview, she'd end it now, she'd cut her losses and move on.

"My mother, she frightens me," Min-yung says, apropos of nothing. And yet her timing is dead-on, she has found a foothold in Ah-jin's attentions. "Do you know what it is to be frightened by your own mother?" Ah-jin looks now into her cousin's eyes, sees something alarming: the terror of a child. Her cousin, a grown woman, speaking as if she's seen a monster under the bed. The question should be easy—too easy—for Ah-jin to answer, and yet she hesitates, detects a stormy dissonance between her cousin's words and her mind; which renders any possible answer irrelevant.

"Don't tell her, please don't ever tell her! But she is so *good*. And everyone is *good* . . . for *her*. My brothers have made their own good lives now, they have done well. Everything is just right, just so. Her standards must be satisfied, at all cost. Do you understand? Somehow, I think you will understand."

"I have only just arrived. . . . I am not sure. . . ."

"You are a world traveler! You live on your own, you are like those women we read about in school . . . like Jane Austen and Emily Dickinson. . . . People thought they were unnatural, but I don't think so. They were just unusual, and they were lonely, and they were *free*. Like you. You're like that woman, the photographer in that movie, *Gandhi*. . . ."

"You mean . . . Margaret Bourke-White?"

"Yes! That one. Just like her. You will be famous like her." Ah-jin laughs, a gentle laugh; she is amused by her cousin's references, women so far from her reality. She sees that her cousin is a romantic, a fierce one. Ah-jin observes her cousin's eagerness, her abandon, and for a moment relinquishes her own fear, her instinct of danger, to feel a mixture of pity and kindness. But the moment passes, and all is eclipsed by a stronger wave of discomfort. What does she *want* from me?

Min-yung does not take offense at Ah-jin's laughter, she is not sensitive to condescension. She is too focused, her mission too pressing. "You must see it, you must feel it. How small, how unchanging, how *perfect* everything is here. . . ."

"Min-yung *ah* . . ." Ah-jin speaks in the diminutive form now, as if to a child. "You have a very nice home and family. I am . . . myself, I am worn out. I am just starting to rest. There has been some difficulty for me recently. I am enjoying your family's kindness. It is good, this kind of . . . this . . . warmth. This peace. And you, you are expecting a child. All this is good for you, isn't it? A place to rest, to be taken care of?"

"You are tired, of course. I can see that. You must work so hard. What would it be like to work so hard at something, to be so devoted ? . . . Tell me, cousin. I wonder. I wonder about a lot of things."

"Of course you will travel someday. You and your family, your husband, your children. There is no reason you can't see the

world yourself." Min-yung slumps deeply and frowns. She is a
different person, completely, from the stoic specter who sits at
table with her parents. Even in her dejection, she is alive, her
eyes are wild.

"*Ah-nee*. This is not true, I am afraid." There is a dim absolute-
ness in Min-yung's statement, a sobriety that takes Ah-jin aback.
Up until this moment, Ah-jin has doubted Min-yung's stability,
her mental clarity. But now, this pronouncement, she speaks it
with resolve; a mature woman takes the place of the child from
moments before. An image comes to Ah-jin's mind, of a little girl
in pink, solemn-faced and composed, gazing out into the New
York sky—lowering her eyes to the depths below. The memory
chills her; and with this shift in her cousin's demeanor, this
unexpected lucidity, Ah-jin understands that she cannot dismiss
her cousin too easily. *We are like sisters.* She has only just arrived,
and yet something—past, present, future—*ties* them. Min-yung
has decided this.

"What is it, cousin? Forgive me, but you do seem unwell. Is
there something . . . ?"

"I am thinking about my child. It is a boy, you know. We've
just found out. Woo-sung does not even know yet. But he is not
much interested anyway." She looks away now, pulls her sleeves
over her hands, restless again. "He does not love me. It was all
arranged, by my parents, my mother mostly. Probably some sum
of money, a promise of a large house or other 'gift.' Maybe you
think me shameless, that I allowed them to do this for me. It
is true, I did not protest; I did not see any point. It is not so
unusual, anyway. Often it works out, the couple lives happily
together, when it is a good match. I thought perhaps I would be
one of these, they call it 'after-love,' what develops once they
are married. But in my heart, I knew better. My parents knew
better. We all knew. But we pretended. We pretend. That I am
not 'funny,' that all is as it should be." She pouts. Ah-jin struggles
to keep up with her cousin's abrupt shifts in mood, in personal-

ity. Now Min-yung's pout disappears, and again she is clear, she is forthright as she continues to speak. "But I don't care about all that now. Yes, I am sick. When Woo-sung found out, that was it for him. No one says it—not him, not my parents—but he is gone now. He will probably seek to remarry as soon as he can. And I have to think about the child. If he survives. I will not, but he might . . . it's all I think about. It's all I have now."

"I am sure you will be fine." Ah-jin is now determined to end their talk. She wonders if her father—her uncle, and her aunt—are aware of Min-yung's pronouncements, her mental state. "Your father, he is a doctor. . . ."

"Yes, my father watches my health, and he is not a foolish man. But he is slow. To see. And he keeps up the pretense, he needs more than anything for all to be good and well. He does it for *her*, I think." Ah-jin stands now, looks back toward the house, toward her father—who will explain, surely, who will be her ally, as always.

"We should turn back now. It is very cold. . . ."

"Cousin, I do not have a lot of time." Min-yung holds Ah-jin's arm with both hands. She seems to concentrate all that she is, all that she must say, into the strength of her hands and the piercing focus of her eyes. "The doctors say it is uncertain—my prospects—and so everyone chooses to believe that once the baby is born, all will be fine. But I know. I know different. A woman knows—what is happening, in her center, in her body. Please. Cousin. Do not think I am crazy. Or if I am crazy, then no matter, I will do what must be done, ask what I must ask. You could . . . *Ah-jin uhn-ni*, big sister . . . you could take him? You could take my son? You would like to have a child? You could raise him, he could have the kind of life you have?"

Ah-jin lies awake, listening. It is daytime in her body, dark night all around her. She hears everything now, everything inside her head, the sound of thoughts as they form, like the slow creaking of an old house; her body's humming and beating, which is a kind of music, not unpleasant, a soothing rhythm. She hears everything from the inside out now—now that what she hears externally is muted, and less trustworthy.

She lies awake, vigilant. Jet lag, partly, but something else. She is out of her element here, purposes unclear. No assignment, no subject.

I'll try to come back with something that makes sense.

Running toward the danger.

You would like to have a child?

In sleep, the noises grow loud and chaotic, full-body. She hears the blast, over and again, vibrations coursing through vein and muscle. She hears her mother's voice, somewhere in her belly. Deep in her chest, she hears Sarah's southern *y'all*; a Syrian woman's deep-throated sorrow; Christine's defiant certainties and veiled longings.

In the cleft between day and night, sound and silence, Ah-jin lies awake, eyes wide open. Without her camera, her vision has become multiple, this place a house of mirrors. *Ah-jin uhn-ni . . . you could take him? . . . You could raise him, he could have the kind of life you have?*

As if she knew. They held each other's gaze, two daughters, two would-be mothers, wordless, suspended. Dual madnesses, perfectly refracted in a moment. Everything happens in a moment.

Breathe. Blink hard, pull yourself back. She sees in Min-yung's eyes a recognition—which she does not refuse. Min-yung smiles, rests her head on Ah-jin's shoulder. *It's time to go back now, cousin. It's getting cold, the rain is coming. I'd like to see my father now, I should find him. Let's go now. You are unwell, and you should rest.*

2

Han Jae-kyu has begun to notice something different in his wife lately. The change is subtle, but marked. The first change he noticed was in her sleeping habits; she comes to bed later, rises earlier. He attributed this to the added work of minding houseguests, and thought no more of it. But there is something else. Tonight they are having dinner at the home of a longtime patient of his. At the table, there is talk of grandchildren. Their hosts inquire about Min-yung, about her latest ultrasound and whether there is knowledge yet of the baby's gender. Han Jung-joo answers that it is too early, they do not know yet—which is untrue. The child is a boy, they know this. It is not that Han Jung-joo would want to keep this information private that strikes him as strange; of course they would, they do not generally share with friends and acquaintances the details of family matters, which they have always held sacred. What surprises him is that she answered so quickly, without first allowing him to answer on their behalf. Without either looking to him out of the corner of her eye, or tapping his knee as she sometimes does to signal for him to pay attention; when something in the conversation requires his collusion.

He suspects that their hosts, whom they've known for many years, may also have noticed this minor breach: they would expect Dr. Han to answer questions related to their daughter's medical status and would also likely see through the lie, as they know full well that Min-yung is already five months along. But he is not concerned with the perception held by these friends just now.

There was that moment, the other night. When the two of them—his brother and his wife—seemed somehow in sync. Their moods shifted in tandem. At first, it struck him as uncanny.

But then a different sensation arose, one that he cared not to indulge. He dismissed it immediately, diffusing any unease and exercising his right and privilege as head of household: he sent everyone to bed. It's what he used to do with the children when he sensed them conspiring mild rebellions with their knowing glances and under-table communiqués. It was important, he felt, to show them zero tolerance for acts of disrespect, however subtle or implicit. To abide such behavior opened the door to what he believed was a slippery slope; the beginning leads to the end, and each downward step is both detectable and significant. He and Han Jung-joo agreed completely on these matters and, ultimately, built their lives and their family upon this principle— that to cultivate a large happiness, one tends to the smallest of details.

But he is grappling with an awkwardness now as the insight of that moment returns, and the small evidences of his wife's change mount in his mind. How strange, the rise of an authoritative instinct, and the swift exercising of it; there are at present no children in his house, after all. But all is altered since his brother's arrival.

And it appears that Han Hyun-kyu will stay longer than any-one anticipated. There is still no talk of his reasons for com-ing, nor his intentions for departing. He seems to be settling into a repose of sorts—no, not repose, Han Jae-kyu senses too much agitation to call it that—but a routine, and a familiarity. He finds it strange that his brother expresses no remorse (however falsely contrived) for his sudden arrival and now-extended stay. Of course it is in truth no real imposition—there is both room and time enough for an addition to their household—but his brother seems to have lost, during his years in America, an intui-tive sense for the humbled "I"; *juh*, instead of *nah*; the manners of apology, overstated in good measure, and self-effacement.

Three weeks since the enormous shadow of his brother's figure cast itself upon their home's pathway in the dark of the

night. Han Jae-kyu, aware of his own restiveness, the roots of
which elude him, reflects on how one takes for granted a baseline of orderliness, patterns of being. How these patterns come
into relief only upon arrival of an aberration—as with, in this
case, a foreign guest.

Foreign? He surprises himself with the thought. Is his own
brother in fact a *foreigner*? The idea disturbs him—especially so
when he thinks again of that moment, that *synchronicity* between
his brother and his wife.

Han Hyun-kyu sees that Ah-jin is faring well here. She is settling
into her own routine. Only a week she's been with them, but
it feels to him like she's been here always, the two of them at
home together. They speak little to each other, beyond the daily
summary of activity, and neither feels particularly pressed to do
so. She is different, he thinks; *becoming*. Quieter in her skin, not
so anxious to *go* as she's been all these years. Her color is deep-
ening, she is getting on well with her aunt and her cousin. Once,
after returning from a walk with Min-yung, she seemed agitated,
seeking him out with her eyes. But the moment passed. Whatever it was that may have disturbed her seemed to settle, like a
cup of hot tea cooling to a soothing warmth as it goes down.

He sees her sometimes chatting with Han Jung-joo and the
ajjummah, in her childlike Korean, which grows more fluent and
easy with each conversation. He takes comfort somehow in seeing her among women. He begins to see her as perhaps they see
her: *a swan, a brave swan*.

Evenings, Han Hyun-kyu sits with his brother and enjoys a
pipe, reads the paper, listening with one ear to local news on TV,
while the women tend to leisurely preparations in the kitchen
for meals later in the week. Sometimes, his mind interrupts
his repose, and panic overtakes him: thoughts come and go at
breakneck pace—thoughts of the past mostly, everything jum-

bled together in no particular sequence, images and memories of two countries and two families, his own childhood and that of his children, words and experiences and feelings. A barrage. Giant waves.

At these moments he will put down his paper, frozen. Sometimes he will move his lips. Words come to him, strange words, words he was not aware lived in his consciousness—like tongues of fire, coming from heaven, or hell, or somewhere in between. He makes no sound, the movement of his lips subtle as his mind heaves and turns; yet he is aware that these moments, these violent interruptions, do not go unnoticed by his brother, his host . . . who asks no questions and makes no comment.

Han Hyun-kyu might, under other circumstances, be self-conscious about his younger brother's observations of him. But here, now, he resists nothing. Let the waves come—the strangeness, the upheaval. There is no other choice now, he has opened the floodgates, he has *done it*. He is vaguely aware that what is happening to him is an exorcism.

Shame on you. He can hear her even now, Lee Woo-in, her shrill chastisement; the concentrated contempt of a lifetime. *You are ridiculous, running off like this. What kind of man runs away from his life to live with his younger brother? You are an embarrassment, a disgrace.*

Your daughter is very beautiful. Like a swan.

The shooting, up in the mountains . . .

Henry is slipping away. . . .

She is passionate as well. . . .

Be kind to him . . . be kind to him. . . .

What kind of man . . . ?

She remembered, it was very kind of her. . . .

There has to be room for volatility.

Please, please understand. . . .

It's good, it's very good!

We should call them Jane and Henry.

Please, please understand. . . .

❦   ❦   ❦

As Han Hyun-kyu gives greater and greater permission to the voices, battles them out quietly, Han Jae-kyu begins to wonder with new impatience how long his brother and niece will stay. He does not like this position he is in, of realizing that he will have to be the one to say something. He will have to make something up. It is a terrible thing to do, he feels it as a conflict; his brother must be suffering something, but what can he do for him, now, at this late stage? Han Hyun-kyu has money enough, this he knows—or at least as far as he knows. He can manage things, everything can be made just so in America, there is always freedom to do as one pleases. It is not as if his brother is destitute or without possibility. His brother must manage his own affairs, whatever they may entail. Perhaps he is having trouble with his wife (likely so, from what he has deduced of her temperament), but they must smooth it over. It is not for brothers to talk of marital matters or get involved, and Han Jae-kyu nearly shudders to think of such a conversation arising. Yes, he must find some excuse for suggesting their departure. He must think first and always of his own family.

But then his wife anticipates him perfectly. At dinner one evening, Han Jung-joo announces the impending arrival of her younger brother, the painter Chae Min-suk. This, also, she has not discussed beforehand with her husband—they have spoken of it, undecidedly, months before, with regard to a project he had proposed to them—but Han Jae-kyu is not vexed, as he thinks he understands her plan: with the arrival of this additional family member, surely his brother and niece will volunteer to depart shortly. Han Jae-kyu generally enjoys a rapport with his brother-in-law and so relaxes into this news—the familiarity of his wife's impeccable planning and caretaking a soothing balm.

3

Min-yung lies flat on the *boryo*, knees up, arms akimbo, palms up to the heavens. Mind whirling. Every morning, every evening, she pulls the thin, satin-covered mattress from the closet (a wedding gift from her in-laws), unrolls it, then rerolls it and returns it to the closet—because of her parents, who insist she sleep on the bed. She does not like beds—their middling height, cold squeak of metal springs, boundaries of width and length. The floor is warm and hard and expansive. From here, she can see the sky out her window—stars on clear nights. From here she can spread her arms like an angel, or reach for the ceiling with her fingertips and never get close.

She smiles to herself. Hands on her belly now, she begins to sing, softly.

> *Flowers bloom in the hills*
> *Fall, spring, summer*
> *Flowers bloom in the hills*
> *Far off in the hills, all alone*

A lullaby, something she heard the *ajjummah* singing the other day. "What is that?" she asked Cho Jin-sook. "You don't know that one? Old, old song. My grandmother taught it to me. Peasant song, from the old days. Good luck and good health for babies."

> *Little birds sing in the hills*
> *Dwell together with flowers*
> *Bloom and sing, like orphan sprites*
> *Far off in the hills, all alone*

Min-yung stretches her arms straight up, fingertips reaching. The floor is warm and hard and expansive.

There is a knock at the door: *Min-yung ah*. Her mother's voice, unnaturally timorous; she cringes. Too much in that voice— anger, guilt, fear. *Cowardice*, she sometimes thinks. *Min-yung ah, pob mok ja*. Let's eat. Min-yung rolls to one side, silently, holds herself, her child, around the middle, tight and tighter, holds her breath, wills their beings into concealment. Her mother stands outside the door another few seconds, is about to knock once more, she can sense it (sees her mother's slender arm raised but paralyzed in mid-motion); but then relents, slippered footsteps receding.

She exhales. Feels the adrenaline of escape, an urgency to now think fast, execute her plans. She reaches for a pen and a piece of paper, sits up halfway, leans on one elbow, writes for her life, writes, finally, what she means to say. A few sentences are all that is required.

It is a clear night, the darkest blue, blacker than black. It is the color of the body becoming the soul. Lying flat again, eyes to the heavens . . . she is nearly ready. There is one star, the brightest, on which she focuses all her being. The star is her child, the boy who will survive her. He will. He must.

She should feel shortchanged, but tonight, now, she feels she has lived longer and deeper than anyone could hope for. She has lived the lives of a thousand women—Emily Dickinson, Jane Austen, *Margaret . . . Bourke . . . White*.

She is giddy, light-headed. She lies still, breathing slowly, deeply, for minutes, hours. A pleasant warmth fills her mind as her fingers, her toes, go cold. Her left side begins to tingle. A sharp pain shoots up her leg, lightning-fire. The pain is intoxicating, she feels powerful, electrified, like a god.

Her mission accomplished. Ah-jin is her ally now, she is sure of it; her savior sent from above. No further words were exchanged between them, after their talk by the tree, but she is certain: her cousin understands, she *sees*. And she will ensure everything. Min-yung remembers so clearly: the helpful face, the one who took care of things. The one who saw her as she moved toward the railing, held her by the shoulders as she peered out over the edge.

She is floating now, up, up, she reaches toward the window. She is a lightning bolt, she is aglow. The blue-black pulls her into itself, gathers her up, the sky her true mother, true father, ever-longed-for beloved. She feels herself letting go, letting let, farewell to the body, to the pain, shame and uselessness of sluggish organs, cells dying, losing pace minute by minute. No more. No more falling behind, no more misfitting. Farewell, good day, good night.

Yes, everything will be all right. My son will be all right. All is ready now. I am ready.

Deployed

To: cms_painter@gmail.com
Fr: Mrs_Han_JJ@hanmail.com

Dear Min-suk,

You mustn't wait so long to come and see us. Do not consider our convenience, we enjoy a houseful of visitors. My brother-in-law's daughter, a world traveler, has recently arrived. You will enjoy their company and help us to keep them occupied and entertained. We are not, I fear, sufficiently interesting company with our small-town ways.

My husband is eager to hear your ideas for your work studio. We will look forward to seeing you straightaway, if you are not otherwise occupied.

> Yours,
> Jung-joo nu-nah

Chae Min-suk is a man nearing fifty, but his sister still thinks of him as a boy. His looks are indeed boyish—he is fit and his face is round and handsome—though streaks of gray have begun to compromise his teenager's hang-dog hairstyle. He and his wife are for the most part estranged; he sees his daughter, Soo-young, infrequently.

He is the last born, the *mangnae*. Always he enjoyed freedom from family responsibility, his sister took care of most things. His freedom was what allowed him to become an artist, to focus his energies on drawing and painting; to fall in love with Beauty. From a young age, before he knew anything, he daydreamed, enraptured by the natural world. He drew and he painted.

Briefly, he considered a vocation in the clergy. As a child, he felt sure of an afterlife, a life of the spirit, and of a benevolent creator of the world's wonders; he had a vague and youthful hope in the idea of devotion to the good. At seventeen, he submitted an application to the seminary and sat for an interview with the Presbyterian minister who was an old classmate of his father's. The minister spoke to him of life on earth and life in heaven, how a man of God is clear about the difference between the temporal and the eternal. He asked young Min-suk if he was prepared to commit himself, from that moment forward, to renouncing all things temporal, choosing always the eternal. Struggling to absorb the full meaning of the minister's question, Min-suk barely breathed, his heart racing; he wanted more than anything to say yes—*Yes, teacher, yes, I will.* It was hours, it seemed, before he spoke, and when he did, finally, his guilelessness got the better of him. *Moht hamnida,* he said, eyes lowered, his voice a bare trembling whisper. *I cannot.*

He thinks back on that moment from time to time, recognizing that he knew nothing of what the old minister spoke, the question like a heavy stone tossed onto concrete, landing with a thud. He understands now that what he wanted, what he really wanted at that moment, was to say yes—*yes, yes.* To something. To anything. To be *required,* and to meet his life, eye to eye.

Such *earnestness,* he thinks when he recalls that moment. Such *sincerity.*

⚐   ⚐   ⚐

In art school, he kept close to tradition. The politics of the day—he was nearing graduation during the massive student uprisings that ended in the Kwangju Massacre—drew many of his cohorts into abstract experimentation and socially driven narratives. He made a painting once, in an attempt to follow the current, depicting a man and a woman, laborers hunched over in a vast and lonely field—the sun setting large and heavy over the hills, many more fields to hoe than had yet been worked—which won him accolades among his classmates and the more radical teachers. But he hated this painting. To him it reeked of dishonesty, of sentimentality. He turned his focus back to nature paintings and calligraphy.

When he painted, he saw everything. Love and hate, beauty and ugliness, heaven and earth. When he painted, his sight became exalted, his soul a vessel of Nature. In those days he painted with passion and purity. He received everything and gave back everything. When he painted, he knew he was complete. For a brief time, in those early years, he felt that he had become a kind of priest after all.

He had many women but was not the settling-down sort. He was neither inattentive nor cruel, only distracted and restless. He had no particular position on romantic love, he assumed that all things of lasting truth and authenticity would make themselves known—with solemn joy, without fanfare. He was young then, time had yet become real.

He always stayed close to his sister. As often as he was able, he paid visits to her and her family in the country, especially when he was a student. In particular, he enjoyed the company of his young niece, who was often left in his charge; it was the one service he could pay, an offering for the kind care he received. The girl was curious—in both senses—a budding toddler, and he found in her a fellow pilgrim on a parallel path of exploration. She was eager to express herself, grabbing for wordlike sounds, pointing, insisting, scrunching her face in frustration when the world failed to understand what was so perfectly clear to her. She struggled more than she succeeded, and it concerned her mother greatly, who, in his quiet opinion, overcompensated by dressing the girl up, covering her oddness with precious frill.

He learned from his niece something he's never forgotten: that sometimes you work to dislodge your expressive roadblock; other times, you abandon it, you move on. She did this—chose between the two—seemingly willy-nilly. But perhaps not, he sometimes thought (and still thinks). Perhaps not.

As he approached the age of forty, he hit a crisis. He had become famous by this time, a highly commissioned gentleman artist whose work hung in the presidential Blue House. He worked very hard, he produced hundreds and hundreds of paintings, in accordance with the expectation that a serious artist be prolific—quantity mattered as much as quality. He was exhausted, he no longer enjoyed his work, and he began to wonder what it was all for. He could not remember whether he had once known the meaning of his work and since forgotten, or if he had never known at all; like when a woman would ask, at the time of his leaving, "Did you ever love me?" and he would rack his brain, but would have no answer.

At forty, he decided to get married. Soo-young was born shortly after. His wife was an ambitious arts manager, second in command at the National Museum of Contemporary Art in Seoul; the daughter of a well-respected ceramicist and sister of a young painter, one of his own protégés—which was how they met.

Three years later, he had another crisis. He had an affair; he left his wife and child. (Soon he abandoned his mistress.) He wondered at the time whether he would be able to live with himself, leaving his child like that. He rationalized at first, that the child would always be well provided for, her mother's fierce love and social connections a wall of protection that had rendered him superfluous anyway. But then he asked the question again, he needed for himself a true answer. And the answer came back: *Yes, of course.* He would be able to live with himself. He had lived with himself this long, he had always been this same man after all.

This was five years ago now.

He receives the e-mail from his sister as a gift. He has been thinking about the studio, this place in the country where he can disappear, where he can work in a new and different way. His work has all but come to a standstill; he produces (his assistants produce as he looks on) but he no longer creates. He is a bystander in his own career. There is pressure, from his wife's family especially, to sell work, to provide amply for the family he has abandoned.

He proposed the idea of building a studio to his *hyung-nim*, his brother-in-law Dr. Han Jae-kyu, some time ago, when he first learned of their plans to build a house in the valley flats. The two men are ostensibly as different as could be, but share at a baseline a respect for, an absorption in, work. Most people in his *hyung-nim*'s hometown do not know him, by face or reputation, and so he can be anonymous, presenting no threat to the family's position. It is the only way such an arrangement could work.

But he is surprised to hear his sister write that Han Jae-kyu is *eager to hear his ideas.* It is clear to him that his sister is overstating. In fact, the whole of the note is strange, and strained; she is all but insisting on his visit, and in short order. How unlike her to betray such impatience.

He has been summoned. Something, it seems, has happened. Is happening.

He welcomes the summons, along with the shroud of mystery. He welcomes it as a mission, a kind of adventure. He receives the note as a reprieve—like an itch scratched, or the nicotine of a cigarette—the calming of irritated nerves. He is happy at this moment to say yes—*yes, yes*—to be *required*. To meet the challenge, eye to eye.

2

The journey by train from Seoul to Kyongju, three hours and many stops, is pleasant enough. From the train station, he will take the bus, which leaves every two hours—a forty-five-minute ride—and drops him at the lake. From there, it's a mile and a quarter walk to his sister's home. He chooses these modes, rather than airplanes and taxis, because he prefers to arrive in his own time, by his own feet. The complex arrangements of meeting times and pickups vex him at some fundamental level, strike him as cluttered and unbeautiful—a kind of unnecessary pollution. He does not carry a cell phone.

The route runs through four different provinces and ten stops. He studies the map on his ticket envelope. Each province is shaded a different pastel, each rail line a bold, bright color. He notes that the map artist did not attempt an accurate rendering, but rather an abstract one—the curved outlines of the landmass smooth and undulating, the peninsula solitary, like an amoeba floating in plasmic fluid. He appreciates the combination of whimsy and science—a view of the country as an organism, dynamic and alive. He tucks the envelope neatly into his billfold, like a treasure.

At Wonju, vendors board the train selling *hodo kwaja*, walnut cakes. He buys a box for his sister's family. When they were children, his father would bring these home when he returned from Seoul. In those days, the cakes were handmade and sold in small cloth bags, tied up with a piece of rough twine which the old women coiled tightly around the bag's opening to keep the cakes fresh. For the children, in those days, they were like drops of heaven. It occurs to him now, as an absentee father, the wisdom of this ritual—his father's associating his return with sweetness.

At Jecheon, where several rail lines intersect (blue, pink, purple, green), people embark and disembark, trade places, layers of movement and transition. He is reminded of one of Soo-young's toys, the Spirograph—an American product, given to her by her uncle, the young painter, who'd found it at a junk shop in Los Angeles when traveling. An ingenious creation, he thinks: the child inserts a colored pen into one of several holes in a toothed wheel and moves the pen and wheel in even motions, back and forth, up and down, corner to corner, around another wheel or other shape, on a sheet of paper. The wheel turns, the pen moves in rhythm, and magically, the child has created elaborate geometrical shapes, layered atop one another—like atoms in motion, magnificent in their ordered complexity. He remembers how Soo-young loved the toy, it was her obsession, for months; and then, of course, she tired of it and moved on.

The train arrives at Kyongju. He has slept. In his dream, his daughter is a grown woman, she is an artist. She asks him to pose for her, he tells her she should not waste time on portraits. She shows him her canvas, she has already started. He strains to see what she's done, but the lighting is strange, somehow too bright and too dark at the same time, so he sees nothing. "Don't you like it?" she asks him. She waits, she is waiting for his response. But he is wordless, he cannot speak.

The old bus driver recognizes him from another visit, many years ago. Seeing the same faces every day, a visitor's face must stick in his mind. "Oh, it's you," the driver says, a gentle smile fading in, like curtains drawn slowly. The driver asks about his wife and child. He says they are well, thank you, smiles and nods. The driver asks nothing more. In the rearview mirror, the two men catch each other's eyes. In the driver's face he sees weariness and loss; though not the sort one feels responsible for, like his own. No, the old man has lost something, or someone. Someone precious to him. Perhaps by cruel chance.

He remembers now. The driver's wife was a regular patient of his *hyung-nim*'s. She was chronically suffering—from what exactly he never knew. The two men look away now; they allow the hum and rumble of the bus to cover a multitude.

The bus slows to a stop, he bows his respects and gratitude to the driver, the driver nods in return. He steps off the bus, but not before marking the driver's face in his mind—another treasure from the journey.

As he approaches the house on foot, he admires its quiet preeminence—how it rises up from the valley, not daring to compete with the commanding granite tops of the surrounding mountains, yet gesturing its own measured dignity. Sitting on a low hill, just above the other surrounding homes, it is the only two-story structure outside of town. He feels something like happiness as he walks toward it.

It is midday. There are no cars parked in the drive. Knowing his sister, she is in town, gathering sundries and provisions for his visit and the guests. No doubt she is minding their every need, providing every comfort, large and small. He peers through a window, just to the side of the front door, and sees no one. Perhaps his sister has taken the *ajjummah* and his niece along with her. Perhaps the American relatives are out sight-seeing.

He walks toward the backyard, and as he begins to unlatch the gate, the shepherd barks sharply, startling him. "Oh, it's you," he says, remembering the dog's temper. "Be calm, be calm, it's just me, Baby Uncle, you remember." He lays down his bag and the box of walnut cakes. "It's all right . . . you remember . . . be calm." He feels somehow free to speak aloud here in the country, as he never would in Seoul. The dog continues to bark, and he then does something he also would never do in the city: he walks toward the threat. "Calm, calm," he says, stepping into the yard but leaving the gate open.

The shepherd maintains its guarded stance, a low growl now building to an eruption. He continues speaking to the dog in friendly tones until he is just in front of the pen. The growl deepens. Seeing that the animal will not be charmed, he tries a different tack: standing tall, hovering as large as he can, he looks the dog hard in the eyes, asserts dominance.

Pandemonium ensues. And suddenly there is nothing in the world but open air and the wild howl of the beast. He is struck by the magnificence of it and begins now to laugh, as wildly as the dog howls.

They continue to laugh and howl, he and the shepherd, for some time.

When he sees her, it is as if she has always been there; and, in fact, he thinks that he *felt* her there before actually perceiving her by peripheral vision. Initially, the presence he felt was that of a child—a boy child—and his first instinct when he realizes that he and the shepherd have been discovered is to cover the boy with his coat, shield him from the scene. Instead, he freezes. The shepherd, too, relents, as if it is no fun at all without him; as if the descending stranger is obviously more menace to himself than anyone on the property.

The girl (he can see that she is a girl, she is narrow in the shoulders and has small feet) stands outside the fence, some thirty feet away. With each second that passes, he seems to recognize something new about her. First, she is somewhat tall, nearly his own height, which is not terribly tall, only five foot eight, but unusually so for a Korean female. Second, she is not a child, nor a girl, but a grown woman. This he deduces not based on her appearance, strictly, but by her stance, her posture, which has a kind of aggression to it—somehow erect and forward-leaning at once. Third, she is not Korean, not native, it is clear by the way she is dressed: more masculine than feminine in dark, heavy denim and thick-soled black boots.

He takes a few steps toward her, almost to the fence, and can now see that she holds a camera in her hands, a rather large one with a hefty zoom lens. As he steps again, she raises the camera to her face and points the lens at him, twisting to focus. She click-clicks rapidly, and he lunges at her, instinctively grabbing for the lens. But she is already halfway down the drive, below him on the incline. The movements are quick, like a single fluid motion. It is as if she, akin to the shepherd, is a creature of the wild, preying and protecting simultaneously.

They pause—he at the top of the hill by the house, she down below, halfway to the road. He catches his breath, pleasantly bewildered. She lets her camera hang from its strap, stands with hands on hips, leans back on her downhill leg. A truce. She starts up the hill, elbows wide, walking a cowboyish walk. He starts down toward her.

"You don't like photographs?" she says. They are still at a distance, a proper one for a man and a woman who are not acquainted. But he can see her face more clearly now and under-stands who she is: the American niece his sister wrote about. She has his *hyung-nim*'s high, rounded forehead, and her skin is dark and freckled, unlike the porcelain white faces (chalky as they grow older) of Korean women. He should have realized right away, but somehow she is nothing like what he had in mind. Or perhaps it is the surprise of the encounter that confused his expectations. She speaks in Korean with some confidence, though her American accent is marked.

"No, I don't like them," he says in English, which he has learned well enough through his travels and collaborations. "Not for me." She looks down for a moment, deciding, he suspects, what language should come next.

"I take photographs always," she says, continuing on in

Korean. By this, he takes her to mean that picture-taking is a habit of hers, perhaps even her profession, judging by the quality of camera she carries—and he takes it as a kind of apology.

He waves his hand and smiles, a signal of surrender and good-will. "I will speak English," he says. "I will explain."

"All right," she says.

"I am Chae Min-suk," he says, bowing his head slightly, keeping eye contact. She watches him closely. "I am younger brother to Mrs. Han. Baby Uncle." She nods, a bit gravely; the information changes her stance, her attitude toward him closes, deflates. "Well . . . what I want to say is . . . eh . . . I am sorry for . . . trying to take your camera. I do not meaning to . . . take . . . eh . . . steal." She opens to him again just slightly, amused by the apology, or perhaps by the phrasing. He is not deterred but rather challenged to prove his prowess, or at least his boldness, in English. "And did you . . . take picture of dog?" he asks. At this, she drops her head and looks to the side. He thinks she may be holding back laughter.

"Yes," she says, standing tall and facing him with eyes both bright and tired. "Yes, I did."

3

She tells him how it happened. She watches his face turn, the awful way in which her words extinguish the wondrous delight that she happened upon, and captured on film, just moments before.

She tells him that her aunt and uncle have gone to see Min-yung's in-laws, to speak to them face-to-face, and pay their respects for likely the last time. That they will return to the hospital to sign away whatever must be signed away, and arrange for everything which must be arranged. That her father has gone to the eldest brother's house to break the terrible, bad-luck news. That the *ajjummah* has gone home for the day, to recover from the shock of finding Min-yung early this morning, still and lifeless on the *boryo*.

"Kidney failure," she says, the words sounding foreign, even in English, and leaving a cold metallic taste on her tongue.

She can see that he is taking in each piece of information in line, like pulling up an anchor, hand over fist. "And the child?" At the end of the rope, there is nothing; his question is a grasping, empty-handed and confused.

She concentrates now, gathers strength to answer, but cannot. The silence becomes a tense intimacy between them. Confusion dissipates. "No," he whispers. "There would not have been any real chance."

"No," she says, speaking now inwardly. A hint of chastisement in her voice. "No, there wouldn't."

He considers that he should do something, but he does not know what. Check on Min-yung's room, perhaps, straighten things up a bit. But no, he would not want to disturb anything, not in his sister's home. He must quiet his agitation. He must wait.

They stand together awkwardly in the kitchen. She fills the kettle and places it on the stove, opens and closes cupboard doors gingerly, as if there were someone who might be awakened by the noise. He sits, and when the water is ready, just before it boils, she serves him, then turns to leave.

"Where are you going?" he asks.

"I am walking about, taking a few photos. I am not very useful here." She feels she should leave him to some time alone, to his grief, before they all return.

"But no; you have made this tea, as a comfort." He smiles a sad smile, is somehow fully present to both the weight and the levity of the live wire between them.

"It is a certain time of day; the quality of light. Perhaps I have an hour. I'd like to climb the mountain path, just over there to the west."

"May I join you? I will not disturb you. Your work. You will see." He does not wait for her to answer. He sips his tea, seems to bow into it, like a prayer. When he looks up again, she sees something; his comprehension of what has happened visibly seeping down, from head to heart, into the blood. His face flushes, in anger and embarrassment; his confidence turned to vulnerability in a flash. "She was a special one," he says, to no one, to anyone. "She was a good girl."

From where they are they can see for miles, to the East Sea. The climb was short but steep, they moved quickly and are both winded. They climbed as if running away, vaguely running toward. Both welcome the deep breathing, the pain in their chests.

They move away from each other. With her panoramic lens, she can capture a long stretch of the coastline, a near-twilight shot. She holds focus there for a few moments, is aware at the back of her mind of the sentimentality in the composition, the orange-brown light; it is the stuff of coffee-table books. She drops the lens, the blur of her boots fills the viewfinder. When she lifts the lens again—two, three seconds pass—the light has changed just slightly, brown swallowing orange, a gray cast. *Click click*, she snaps.

She descends along a different path a short ways. Her window is now very short, the light will change again soon. He is sitting on a large rock, facing west. With a long lens now, quick and quiet hands, she frames his profile, not straight on, from a rear angle. His eyes are closed, his chin raised. A single silver streak in his hair catches the light of a just-rising moon. She can see that he is not alone in his thoughts; he is, rather, in conversation . . . with his heavens, his gods, whomever he counts responsible for irrevocable loss. He breathes smoke into the cold, like a shaman. His jaw is soft, his face expressive, in motion, just under the surface. It is as if he is speaking with a friend, talking it through: *Why? Why this blackness? Why sorrow and loss? Why are some souls hard and enduring; why others fragile, not long for this world?* She is touched by a childlike quality in his mourning, a simple self-forgetting; distant from the commonness of both self-drama and stoicism. *She was a special one; she was a good girl.* She holds him in focus; then drops the black box from her face.

They descend with the darkness, follow the sun into the valley. Midway down they see Han Jae-kyu's car pulling up the drive. It seems a long time before any of the doors open.

4

The work on the studio goes quickly. Chae Min-suk supervises and stays close. Mr. Song, the builder, has a short window of time between jobs and is motivated to start and finish within two weeks.

His *hyung-nim* followed up and arranged everything. And while neighbors and friends of the family who stopped by to bring containers of food and monetary gifts found it odd—that the family would be taking on a construction project at such a time—Chae Min-suk was relieved, and thankful, to Han Jae-kyu. For deciding to act, providing a new focus. For sparing them one more day of this heavy, aimless grief.

The wake and the funeral were executed with all due care and diligence, the service efficient and spare. They spoke little during those days. His sister took care of everything, made it clear by her focused activity that she did not require, nor wish, for assistance. Once or twice he saw her and her husband in consultation; other than that, there was little talk or interaction.

Woo-sung was like a phantom and did not participate, except of course to attend. After that night at the hospital, he went to stay with his own parents in the next town. They saw him at the services and nodded their heads, recognizing that he would no longer be part of the family. He would quickly fade into a closed chapter, more remote as the years went on. Soon enough, they all knew, he would remarry, and disappear from their lives. These parts of the story were already written. There was perhaps even some comfort in it.

Han Hyun-kyu offered to leave immediately. "We will travel to Seoul and perhaps return to you in a few weeks," he said. But Han Jung-joo would not hear of it and seemed even a bit angered by the suggestion. Chae Min-suk could only wonder why his sister fixed herself so obstinately, especially as her husband was silent on the matter. But he did not think on it much; he was preoccupied and wished, too, for them to stay.

He saw Ah-jin, observed her. She seemed lost, at times like an old woman who'd wandered into a strange place and couldn't remember how she'd gotten there. There was a gentleness to her grief, a kind of light fragrance, even as she subsumed it to boyish energy, hiking off into the mountains daily with her camera.

He'd not seen the two cousins together, but in his mind's eye he could imagine it, the vision he would have beheld had he arrived even just a day earlier: the women together in the kitchen, warm with the smells of ginger and fish broth; his sister and the *ajjummah* bustling about, Min-yung and Ah-jin seated side-by-side at table folding *mandu*, laying the dumplings out on trays in identical rows, a rhythmic duet. Ah-jin absorbed in her task, tentative, but also somehow perfectly at home.

He wished Ah-jin could see what he saw, the uncanniness of it, and the beauty. Surely she would find something in it to photograph.

♣　♣　♣

One night, he had a sudden and desperate desire to see his daughter. He wept alone in his room. His grief became confused: he was certain that Soo-young had been lost to him, or that she'd always been lost to him, or that if he were to see her or speak to her, she would no longer be Soo-young, she would be unrecognizable. He was haunted by these thoughts, and he wished for the first time that Soo-young's mother was with him, to reassure him and be by his side. He felt an intense aloneness. Untethered.

It was like that for a full week, seven days that felt like a thousand. Silence and weight. They lived together like this—each of them bottled and airless and alone—because death, when it came, seemed to demand it.

Finally, the call to the builder was made; the stalemate of their days came to an end.

The day before Mr. Song arrives, Han Jae-kyu and Chae Min-suk map out the site, confer on plans and drawings. They are focused and lively, they embrace the release afforded by distraction. Han Hyun-kyu joins them in the yard but stands at a distance, hands clasped behind his back, face up to the mountains. Chae Min-suk is struck by how large a man his *hyung-nim*'s brother is; or, perhaps, how large he *seems*. At least a foot taller than himself and his *hyung-nim*. But that, of course, cannot be accurate.

The two men discuss the parameters of the structure. They agree on a basic shape and size, nothing more elaborate than a simple box with a slant roof and skylight. They disagree on materials—Han Jae-kyu in favor of wood siding and asphalt shingles, Chae Min-suk preferring a more liberal use of metals. He argues the cost efficiency of aluminum, the durability of tin. He describes to his *hyung-nim* manufacturers who these days make sheets in colors and textures that have a less metallic look to them—warmer, softer—and argues that it is important, for his work, that the space have a distinct separateness from the house, that it not match but that it needn't clash either. Han Jae-kyu, the elder, indulges him his argument, while Chae Min-suk, the expert, silently acknowledges his *hyung-nim*'s generosity—a welcome moment of rest and implicit relational balance, the first either has had since Chae Min-suk's arrival.

The surface of the lake shimmers in the distance; Han Jae-kyu shields his eyes using his right hand as a visor. Several feet away, Han Hyun-kyu clears his throat, begins humming an old folk tune.

"*Ku reh*," Han Jae-kyu says. "I understand."

Chae Min-suk bows slightly to his *hyung-nim*, says that he will make sketches, specify materials, and see if the builder can find the right suppliers. Han Jae-kyu nods his head, looks in the direction of his brother, squinting, then again lowers his eyes. "You will have windows," he says. "You must have light, to see? Which way will the windows face?" Chae Min-suk steps toward Han Jae-kyu and turns the palm of his hand so that it is oriented as the studio will be, and he draws an invisible sketch with his finger: *here, and here*. A small window on each of the long sides of the rectangular box, but not directly opposite each other, and close but not identical in dimensions.

"One should not be able to see directly through the structure. The inner and outer light, the space, must be dynamic. There must be movement, the kinetic flow of ideas. Not like a tunnel, where thoughts rush through in a linear manner, only to be lost." Han Jae-kyu nods again. Then he looks up and calls to his brother.

"*Hyung!* Come now, then. Help Min-suk with his measurements." His tone is energetic, positive. He hastens back to the house, like a man running toward, and away, simultaneously. It is strange, Chae Min-suk thinks, and sad; seeing his even-mannered *hyung-nim* in this nervous state.

Han Hyun-kyu approaches with swift, heavy steps. The ground rises and falls just slightly between them, and so he seems to grow larger, then smaller as he traverses. Standing now face-to-face, he sees that Han Hyun-kyu is a man who always stands with his shoulders back and chest forward, yet with his weight still centered and even. Not a giant, no. But a man with a kind of inner vigor—mounting, perhaps ready to burst—the source of which eludes him.

"I am at your service," he says, with something like good-naturedness. There is, almost instantly, a kind of peace between them; an absence of vying or positioning, nothing material at stake.

"Many thanks for your assistance. We should not be long, just a few measurements. I am sure you would like to get on with your plans for the day."

"Not at all, not at all. I am enjoying the spaciousness of my days here. There is . . . forgiveness here, to move about without a plan." Han Hyun-kyu fishes for this word—*forgiveness*—and seems pleased with his choice. It is a good word, Chae Min-suk thinks. When Han Hyun-kyu says it, the peace between them opens up even wider.

The two men work for a few minutes more. Han Hyun-kyu holds the end of the tape measure, exactly as Chae Min-suk indicates, motioning and nodding. He makes notations on a small notepad, and for a moment he forgets Han Hyun-kyu's presence. He can see the structure taking shape, feel the materials in his own hands. His mind begins to work, a quietness comes over him, an unformed image of the new work captures his inner eye, foments like a tiny, powerful tornado, somewhere just below the surface of consciousness.

A slight movement by Han Hyun-kyu, perhaps a shifting of weight, or the rustling of his jacket, and he is brought back to the surface, the task at hand. He apologizes for daydreaming, perhaps just a minute if that, and they finish the last of the measurements. He beholds Han Hyun-kyu and sees that he is a man at once looming and receding; and pleasant company. He finds that he has nothing in particular to say to him, and yet here, in the crisp open air of the morning, away from the strangeness of their motley assembly, this household of anxiety and grief, he decides, rather impulsively, that Han Hyun-kyu is someone to be admired. Whatever his secrets—his past, his flaws—he seems to Chae Min-suk simply, and fully, *a man*. A man of flesh and matter, a man whose blood pulses purposefully. A man in search of something. Perhaps . . . forgiveness.

Chae Min-suk is gratified, now especially, to see the realization of his vision. There is only one thing for him that could displace the despair of the last week, so immediately and completely, and that is his work, in process, fleshing out from idea and sense to substance. Han Jae-kyu deferred to him in all respects, and so they build in metals—flat aluminum sheets for the exterior walls, corrugated tin for the roof.

He has chosen a dark amber color for the aluminum; the tin is a matte silver. It is a small, modest structure, and elegant in its not-quite-square proportions. It draws to itself the early winter light, absorbing and reflecting in measure at different times of the day, gleaming faintly like a jewel in the rough. And there is beauty beneath the surface as well: the builder has found an ultrathin, highly effective insulation material for the walls, floors, and ceiling. Tomorrow, the builder will bring in a concrete contractor to pour the finished floor, which he imagines will be stunning in its lusterless simplicity.

Han Jae-kyu seems to him also energized by the progress. He feels the two of them now share in his vision and sense of satisfaction. This morning they stand together in the yard, blowing warmth into their cupped hands, discussing how the scale of the structure suggests both an enlarged playhouse and a small schoolhouse; a place of youthful release and focused learning. These are pleasing observations.

But he is also aware of a new tension mounting. His sister

does not share their pride. She keeps at a distance, she continues on in silence. Reproachful, he suspects. Perhaps he and his *hyung-nim* have gone too far, too fast, in engaging themselves, finding a new focus. The two men are peculiarly allied; they have witnessed the mercilessness of existence—the unfairness of fate—and their betrayal is to live, shamelessly. They leave the dying to the dead.

Ah-jin lingers on the margins to observe the construction. It seems she has decided to make some kind of work out of their project, a photo-documentation. She directs her restless energy into the camera, always into the camera. He feels he has hardly seen her face this last week, so persistently does she position herself behind the black box with its probing nose, its all-seeing eye.

And the camera is more than just her tool. When she holds it up, he has a sense that she is no longer with them. As if she sees something other than what appears in her viewfinder, something within, some essential truth or incisive view of what goes on at the surface. Or perhaps she is lost to some reverie, or memory, something exceedingly beautiful, or horrifying. When she drops the apparatus from her face, squints or stares at the subject for a moment, she seems to do so sightlessly, looking elsewhere, beyond or behind the vision of the living. And whatever it is she sees, it is very faint, growing fainter. It draws her down, and away.

5

It is Han Jung-joo who suggests that she and Ah-jin go to the baths.

Three weeks have passed since the tragedy. Ah-jin and her father have attempted once again to insist that they leave them, but to no avail. "You are a comfort to us," Han Jung-joo says. "Of course, if other obligations call you back, we will understand. But otherwise, you must stay, please." She speaks authoritatively. Ah-jin and Han Hyun-kyu do not consult on this point, and neither do they protest.

"The men are busy with their building project, we should go and occupy ourselves as well," she says to Ah-jin. Her tone is congenial at the same time it is declarative; she is not to be refused. "I have not been to the *oncheon* in a long time. Ah-jin, you will enjoy it, Korean hot springs are very good. We will go tomorrow morning, early, which is the best time."

They depart for the large complex outside of Kyongju at dawn. In the car they are silent most of the way, until Han Jung-joo speaks. "*Bap beun-dae* . . . you are busy? We are keeping you from your work?"

"No," Ah-jin says. "My agency, they know I am taking some time off." She adds, "I have been taking photos in the valley, and in the surrounding area. Some of you and Uncle as well."

Han Jung-joo makes a face and shakes her head. "No, no. I don't like pictures." Ah-jin laughs. She suspected as much, which was why she took them stealthily. "Did you . . . take . . . picture . . . of . . . Min-yung?" Han Jung-joo asks this question in halting English, which surprises Ah-jin; her aunt has spoken only in Korean.

"Yes. A few. They are nice ones."

"I would . . . like see."

"Of course."

In the women's dressing room, Ah-jin follows her aunt's lead, undressing completely and leaving all her things in an unlocked locker. She walks on tiptoe, bare feet on cold tiles, wraps her arms across her naked chest. They enter the bath area, and she is amazed to see how full the place is, at just before seven a.m. "The grandmothers come early, with their grandchildren," Han Jung-joo says. "Korean women live a *loooong* time; the old women come here for reinvigoration, every morning, muscles and joints and skin. Hot water from deepest earth here, best thing for circulation, digestion, even heart trouble." She looks at Ah-jin, head to toe. "So skinny!" she says, squeezing Ah-jin's elbow.

The warmth and the moisture blanket them gradually. Ah-jin lets go her arms, her shoulders still slightly hunched. Han Jungjoo carries a small plastic pail with soap, shampoo, two scrub cloths, a pumice stone. She leads them to adjacent shower stations, where they sit on low stools. Han Jung-joo turns Ah-jin's hand-held shower to full pressure, very hot, and hands it to her. "Here," she says, handing her also a pink scrub cloth. "Scrub *very* hard, make the blood flow. Like this." She takes Ah-jin's arm, scrubs until the skin turns bright red. Ah-jin flinches. "Good, it should hurt like that. Use the soap so you can scrub away all the dead skin. Scrub the feet, especially, very important." She holds out a small bottle. "Use this one for your hair."

Ah-jin remembers. Baths when she and Henry were young. The pink scrub cloth, almost identical to the one she holds now. Lee Woo-in scrubbing, harder and harder, until the children cried out.

Han Jung-joo washes her hair first, then sets to work on her own feet, arms, shoulders. Ah-jin resists staring, but can't help noticing the seriousness, the *respect*, with which her aunt tends to every inch of her own body—with which all the women here, young and old, smooth and wrinkled, tend to their bodies. At one point, Han Jung-joo reaches over to scrub Ah-jin's back. "You needed this," she says, scrubbing and rinsing, then scrubbing harder. Ah-jin braces her upper body with her stomach muscles, plants her feet against the tile ledge, and uses her legs to push against her aunt's fierce pressure.

When they are done at the showers, Ah-jin is exhausted, shiny and red. Han Jung-joo is also flushed, and looks invigorated; vaguely determined. They wrap small white towels around their heads and walk into the main baths area, where there are pools of all shapes and sizes and temperature ranges, with different medicinal and herbal additives. A few young girls swim around in the larger pools while their mothers and grandmothers sit or recline. Overhead, the skylights are blasted glass, the quality of light muted, like a cloudy day in the late afternoon. "Let's start here," Han Jung-joo says, pointing to a large pool in the center. "Not too hot. Over here, there is jet massage." (These last two words she speaks in Korean-accented English; the language of luxury products, fully appropriated.) They slip into the pool up to their armpits. Han Jung-joo leans back, rests her neck on the ledge, closes her eyes. Ah-jin follows suit, but keeps her eyes open.

After some time, Han Jung-joo stands and walks to another pool. She does not mind Ah-jin anymore, she leaves her to her own. They wander and drift into private worlds, each with its particular smells and temperatures—elixirs applied to aches and knots and scars, known and unknown, which ail each body. To Ah-jin, this room full of naked women, each body exposed and yet intensely private, is like a dream. In the pools, her arms and legs float to the surface, weightless. Walking from pool to pool, everything falls—breasts, buttocks, shoulders—like a cloud releasing its moisture in a downpour. The air is wet and heavy, the sounds slow and slushy, matching the faint muffledness of her hearing these last months. As an hour goes by, close to two, she disappears into the white noise of water streaming, begins to feel groggy, a pleasant buzz filling her head.

"Come, over here," Han Jung-joo says, tapping Ah-jin on the shoulder as she is nearly drifting into sleep. She leads them to a sliding door which opens onto a small outdoor terrace, a lone pool bordered by a wall of large stones. They stand in the warm water up to their waists, the cool air awakening Ah-jin's skin, clearing her head. She lifts her arms and holds them straight out, fingers dangling, breasts lifting as she breathes deeply, neck to the sky.

"You like it?" Han Jung-joo asks.

"It's . . . strange," she says, dropping her arms, lowering herself now, the tops of her collarbones just showing, "and familiar. Both."

"How it can be both?" Han Jung-joo floats now on her back, speaking to the sky. She flips over and swims toward the deeper end of the pool, where she treads for a moment, her upper body very still, as if her suspension were effortless. Answering her own question, she says, "American women, so complicated. Everything pulling in different directions." She uses her hands to illustrate, as if pulling a rope tightly from both ends.

"Yes," Ah-jin says.

"You needed this." Han Jung-joo smiles an opaque smile, then lays back again to float. She is inscrutable, Ah-jin thinks. Even here, even now. "You will return to your work, after you leave here?" she asks.

"It's hard to say. I have no other plans, but . . . it's hard to say."

"Your father is very proud of you."

"That is good to know."

"We don't always say what we mean, what we want to say, to our children. Maybe we should say things more often. But it is difficult . . . it's not so easy for us." This also is familiar to Ah-jin. Her father has said these very words to her before. It was the first time they'd spoken to each other after Henry went into rehab. An international phone call, halted by voice delay and anguish both. *It's not easy for us. We feel from you children, that you need to hear something, and that makes us feel terrible. But it is difficult.*

"I understand."

"Your mother must be proud as well."

"I don't know, really."

"She is. Of course she is. I met her once, briefly. Our one trip to America. You children were all young. Your mother was very busy. She is . . . an impressive woman."

"Yes." Ah-jin senses her aunt's control of the moment, waits for her to steer the conversation as she intends.

"I am glad that Min-yung found a friend in you. She needed that. You two seemed to come together, so naturally."

"She told me that we could be like sisters. She was very warm, she embraced me."

"I could see that. I am glad. She seemed very happy, all of a sudden, when you came."

"Was she unhappy? Before?" This is a mistake, Ah-jin feels it right away. She has underestimated her aunt. The question is transparent, and an insult. Han Jung-joo stands now, slowly, rising up in one smooth motion, as if from a baptism. Her eyes change.

"Let's go in now," she says. "Time to go."

On the ride home, Han Jung-joo speaks again, continues an unfinished thought. "Min-yung was always different. She had a hard time of it. Maybe pulling in different directions, too. I never could understand. It is difficult to know . . . what to do. You want your child to be happy, like other children. She always had our attention. I was always there, I tried to understand. . . ." She stops here. She seems to consider her next words, then decides that there will be none. Her lips tighten into a forced smile, which makes Ah-jin uneasy. Something has closed between her and her aunt. In an instant the door shuts, without an echo, like an ax in wood.

They drive the rest of the way in silence, having each shed a layer of skin and left it behind.

Book Four

Proportional
Response

Border Crossings

1

He is both exotic and familiar. And here, in this place, where we are all somehow captive, this seems to be everything there is to desire. There is a simplicity to this desire, and a kind of agreement between us.

It is still morning when my aunt and I return from the baths. My uncle has gone to the clinic, my father lingers at the kitchen table with a cup of tea and the newspaper. Chae Min-suk stands at the window, beholding his studio, which is nearly finished except for the floor. While my father asks about our outing, Chae Min-suk seems absorbed in his thoughts, whatever has captured his mind's eye.

"We had a good time," my aunt says. "Ah-jin had an experience." Chae Min-suk turns now toward his sister, a look of curiosity on his face, as if having heard something notable in her tone.

"You enjoyed it?" he asks me.

"Yes, very much. Such an indulgence."

"Here it is not considered a luxury," my father says. "Rich people, poor people. Everybody goes to the *oncheon*. Like . . . the YMCA, in America. Men with night jobs go there for napping, in the heated sleep rooms. Did you go there?"

"Not this time," my aunt says.

"I don't like that part," Chae Min-suk says. "The sleeping. I think sleeping is very private, and sacred. Not for everyone to look on."

"It's like the old days, when we had to sleep all of us in one room," my father says. "We advance, we buy a bigger house; but still, funny isn't it, some people, they miss it." I imagine this place, I see it, this sleeping place; I frame it in my mind from different vantage points, in varying light: naked women, young and old, lying on their sides in semifetal positions, eyes closed and faces calm, the warmth of the *ondol* against their pink cheeks. It's an idyll, this vision; but something is off about it, something that tells me I must be missing something.

"Do they . . . are there blankets?" I ask. They are all silent for a moment, confused. Chae Min-suk is first to understand.

"Yes, yes, of course," he laughs. "After the baths, you dry off, and a cotton robe or loose pajamas are provided for you. A small pillow if you like. Men and women in the same room." They all laugh now, seeing now what I was seeing. He smiles at me, he likes my vision.

In the afternoon, there is a knock at my door. I have dumped film canisters all over the bed, attempting to sort and label them. "Come in," I say, and there he is in the doorway, hesitant at first, which I find charming given his obvious natural confidence.

"I'm sorry, you are busy. Perhaps I should . . ."

"No, no, it's fine. Is there something . . . ?"

"I've come to ask you to join me. On a short excursion to Pohang. I am in need of art supplies, there is a place near the university. By the sea, about an hour's drive from here. If you are not too worn out from your morning journey. There is a dark-room in the photographic department, they know me there. You can use the facilities if you like."

We leave together. There is a kind of rebellion in our leaving. He tells my aunt, "I will show Ah-jin the museum there, at the university. And the darkroom, so she can develop some of her pictures." My aunt hands him her car keys. She is distracted, she has not put herself together today, no makeup, her hair pulled back just as it was after the baths. Her mood has darkened. She does not look either of us in the eye, though I think I can sense her gaze behind me as we walk out the door.

He asks me if I would like to drive, and I say yes, just tell me where to. "We'll go to the main road, and then follow the highway all the way east. It will take us to the water."

"And how do you know I am a good driver?"

"I do not. But I know that it has been a long time since I have driven myself anywhere. You will likely do better than I will." He speaks in English, he seems to do so with intention. It tells me that he prefers to speak directly, without the encumbrance of proprieties, the proper forms inherent in his own language.

We drive in silence for some time. I mark peripherally his shape, the outlines of his figure, his face in a different light now, a different temper, from when we climbed the mountain. He is broad and full, not exactly handsome; his face has a typicality to it, an everyman quality, like someone I've seen in a Korean magazine ad. His hair is long, slightly wavy, just graying; he tucks it neatly behind his ears. His gravity is in his chin, cleft in the middle, and to which he often holds his hand; it is a gesture of self-protection, I think. From what, I do not know. For the most part he carries himself as one who is confident in his immunity to things petty or undeserved, the small and large tragedies that befall the average person. And yet . . . the hand, the chin. Today, I feel him watching me with an eye for possession. It is a challenge. I can't explain it, but I feel somehow a worthy opponent.

"I've gone through so much film," I say, "it will be good to see what I have. Thank you for bringing me with you."

"I thank *you* . . . for agreeing to come along. And for driving." He leans away from me, looks toward the sky.

"Are you thinking of Min-yung?"

"Just now? Oh, no . . . not really. I mean, she is of course there, she is in all my thoughts in a way. Her absence is every-where. That is how it is . . . with death. Don't you think?"

"I would not have said so, before now. Before this. I've seen a lot of death, but . . ."

"Of course. In your work. You must. It's different for you, I am sure." I roll up the windows, the wind is making it hard to hear. But now, without the noise, it seems harder to speak, more aggressive somehow.

We come to the end of the major road, he points me left, then right, and we pull into the parking lot of the art supply store, at the end of a mini-mall. The sky is bright, and the reflec-tion of the sun off the water hits the windshield, a harsh yellow. I turn off the ignition and squint, look toward the sea.

"There is a beach, it's very close. We can walk there from here," he says. "It will be windy, but quite beautiful." Neither of us moves; the moment is full, and breathless.

We lean in at the same moment. Our mouths are warm and open. We begin gently, but then hunger takes over. We con-sume, pull at each other's clothing, hands and mouths. The car's console becomes an obstacle. "There is a hotel nearby," he says. Or I think this is what he says, I'm not sure. He holds my face between his hands, we are both now quieted. "I know a place, it is not far from here."

The hotel is a high-end establishment, apparently where visiting lecturers and scholars from the university are hosted. We move through the check-in process quickly, eyes averted, then find our way to a room on the ground floor. We are both, I think, thankful for the avoidance of elevator awkwardness. In the room, there are two queen-size beds, elaborately dressed in cream and forest-green quilts and frilled sheets, and the room smells of the kind of vigilant clean that implies something unsavory preceding. The bathroom is enormous, lights buzzing. The room is cold.

Deflation, all at once. Any remnants of intimacy, the cramped intensity of passion, have dissipated. We remove our shoes and sit on the edge of the far bed. He reaches over to turn on the heater.

"Are you all right?" he asks.

"I'm tired, actually. It's been a long day."

It's a strange thing we do now. Unexpected, anyway. He pulls back the covers, and together we slip in like a knife, a single tidy motion. We lie there, bodies nested, fully clothed. The sun is low but not yet set. Within seconds, we both fall asleep. . . .

I open my eyes to darkness. The light from the bathroom is a narrow wedge slicing the carpet in the corner of my eye. The room has warmed. I stir, he stirs. Half asleep, we remove each other's clothes. He wraps his arm tightly around my middle, and we resume our position, share the full heat of our bodies. I turn toward him, he kisses my forehead. We relax again and sleep, sleep longer and deeper, until somewhere, sometime in the night, in our waking sleep, conscious unconscious, we find each other in the dark and make love.

In the darkness, a winding road. The brush falls back behind me. The road is long but effortless, I carry nothing in my hands. At the end, a clearing . . .

A tiny life fights, a baby boy, my cousin's bright star. It's a burst, almost imperceptible. The child sees daylight, knows that life, this world—looming and luminous—is on the other side. There is no such thing, really, as a stillbirth.

A life comes into being in a dark small space, a sadness, between two people. Drains away in a pool of black blood. Louder than pain, completely silent.

Some are not long for this world. I am here. We are here. I long, and I long. . . .

❧   ❧   ❧

We lie here now, day has not yet come, both of us (I think, yes) alive to our senses. My whole body is raw and throbbing, layer after layer peeling away. We are in the sleeping room now, the only ones. We are the vision itself, dream and reality. We are the image in the telescope.

But he betrays himself just now, a lapse, a moment of earthly familiarity; he falls into unconsciousness, snoring an unseemly snore on the way. He rouses himself with the sound of it. I mock him with my eyes, and he seems to like this. He burrows his head into the pillow like a boy, and I seem to like that.

It all feels so easy, so good, right now. I can see, I can breathe deeply again. A space inside has been hollowed out, it is airy and bright. I think: *What's next?* It seems to me that this is all that constitutes contentment. This readiness. This weightlessness. Nothing behind and nothing before. Everything happening in this moment. Some of us, we are here, we are still standing. *What's next . . . ?*

As I descend again into this peace, this sleeping place, I am thinking about that day, that night, when Henry was lost—the perfect peace of it. It was Dr. Lee who found Henry. She went looking, she found him. For that hour, calling Henry's name in the woods, Dr. Lee was completely focused on him, and he was everything, she was nothing. Love came into relief. Did I know? Was it this love, this vision of it somewhere in my mind, that drove me to abandon Henry in the first place? Everything was fine, everything was at peace. Next morning we were all clear, and ready, all of us, just this once, together; for whatever was next.

2

I open my eyes, and he is gone. The curtains are pulled shut, but still the light comes through, and the awful sterility of the room blares.

It's late. Almost eleven. My clothes are folded neatly on a chair. I get up and dress quickly. I finish up in the bathroom and am surprised when he returns. A little disappointed. Here, in the light of day, in this hotel room, the poetry of the night before seems impossible and false.

"There is nothing good to eat downstairs," he says, a cheerful complaint. "Come, I know a better place. Are you ready?" I nod and follow him down the corridor, out a back exit, to the parking lot. The brightness is masked by a layer of dark clouds, but still I feel rudely awakened. "I will drive," he says. "You look like you are still waking up." He tells me that he has spoken with his sister, he assured her that everything was all right, that we had run into some old friends of his and that it grew late, we had been drinking, we decided to stay the night. His efficiency with this story does not, somehow, surprise me.

Over breakfast, he asks me questions—about my family, my work, travels. He is very direct and seems genuinely interested, speaks to me like we are old friends, catching up. But he must sense my reticence, and he says this: "You are wondering, what kind of a man is this? At another time, a different time, I might find some way to fool you. So you don't think I am some kind of *male pig*. Is that how you say? Anyway, today, somehow, with you, I have no apologies, no stories. I am an artist, you know this. I am a painter, successful, you could say. My daughter and my wife live in Seoul, but I do not live with them. My parents are no longer alive, my sister is my closest relative." He stops, to think, apparently. "I think that is all there is, really. And I like how it sounds, telling it to you. So simple. Nothing else." He smiles, his eyes nearly disappearing; he seems to want to kick up his heels. He is different today. Somehow, we both are. "And you?"

"Yes?"

"Your history. Your loves, your . . . heartbreaks?"

"I . . . my . . ."

"It's all right. Don't worry. I am a little bit . . . kidding with you. You are not ready. You are figuring some things out maybe. You will . . . take your time."

"Yes. But I think, too . . . all this figuring out. It can become a burden. And maybe unnecessary. Last night, lying awake, I thought, I felt something. . . ."

"I watched you, sleeping . . . for a long time this morning. You were sleeping . . . so deeply. You looked like someone unburdened. You looked lost in your dreams." I hang on his words, I listen to him tell me what I feel to be true.

"Maybe, I wonder, it *was* a dream. Maybe that feeling—it was like . . . a happiness—maybe it's only real in my dreams. God . . . maybe Dr. Lee is fucking right." I say this last part in a half-mumble, which he either does not hear or politely ignores.

"Well, I don't know, Han Ah-jin." He takes my hand in both of his. "But you look well. You look . . . better. Than the last week. Than when I arrived. I will not take any credit for that, myself. But it's . . . something."

"I needed a break, I guess. I've been working a lot."

"You are very devoted to your work?"

"*Devoted* . . . ?"

"Devoted . . . uh . . . serious? It is your . . . passion?"

"It is . . . my *work*. It is . . . what comes naturally. Easily, I guess."

"Easily. What you do—running in dangerous places, violence and death all around you—this is easy?"

"I give . . . just a little, to what I do. The rest . . . comes. It comes from somewhere else. It's *given*. There is a kind of tailwind. . . ."

"Ah," he says. "Yes. This I understand. This is what I mean. *Devotion*. It is like prayer. For me, painting is like this. I give myself, my true self, to the work. The work rewards you, it joins you, you are not alone in the execution. *Tailwind*, yes. You become most *yourself* in this process. It used to be like this for me."

"Used to?"

He nods. "Not anymore," he says, matter-of-factly. "But maybe again. Today is another day."

"I don't know if I can say I am most *myself* when I am working. But I am most free from that question."

"The question of . . . who you are?" I nod. "Yes," he says.

"Why . . . like prayer?" I ask.

"Another kind of devotion. You bring your full being, your soul and body and mind, to the foot of God, and there, He meets you. But God, like painting, like your work, like love, too . . . they are each singular, and jealous. You have to choose. You can have only one devotion, one all-absorbing love."

"Yes. I suppose that's right."

"Do you believe in God?" I smile. These questions. So free, and straight. There is a tailwind as we speak.

"When I was a child. I think so. My brother, Henry, and I, we used to pray. For *things*. Like a new bicycle, that sort of thing. It was silly, but we did imagine someone was listening."

"Childhood is like that, so full of treasures. I've tried to bring as many of those treasures with me, into adulthood, as possible. Otherwise, what is it to be grown? It is learning to die, one day at a time."

"I didn't have much of a childhood. I mean, there was a lot to manage . . . difficulties, responsibilities . . ." I pause, he is looking at me but says nothing. I wait another moment, I think maybe he will say something, something kind or comforting. But he waits for me to continue. "I don't suppose I'll ever get it back. My childhood, that is."

"No," he says, drily. "That is the miracle of childhood. It is only once, it cannot be re-created. It is too bad; the worst tragedy." I feel somehow bludgeoned by this, by the finality of his pronouncement—as if I expected something like sympathy from him. And yet, at the same time, I am relieved—by his certainty, so simple and true. *It is too bad.*

"And your daughter?" I ask.

"My daughter . . . may be more like you. A little adult, her childhood drenched in this kind of sophistication. Her mother prefers to raise her this way. I am not entitled to interfere. I love my daughter, no one can dispute that. But I cannot say that I have been devoted to her. I made a different choice."

"And do you . . . do you ever . . ."

"Regret?"

"Yes." My instinct, my hesitation, was right. He does not like this question. He sighs.

"You would be surprised. What you discover when you have a child. What you have, what you never knew you had inside you. It is very profound. It is good to find this, to see something so pure lives in you. No matter the circumstances, the failures, that thing you find, it is pure, it is absolute. I am not a good father, but this is one thing I can claim, without doubt—that I love my daughter. As I think of it, this is something which settles me. To know something. Absolutely. We need these private truths, I think, just a small few."

"I wonder . . . how you know. So absolutely."

"I think it is somehow related to . . . terror." He pauses. "Terror? Deeper than fear, stronger than fear?" I nod. "In love—the love of a father, a mother, a lover—there must be a feeling of terror. For the other person's being. Like a vigilance. You lose yourself in it, you lose your *self*. It is not effortful, it is a wave that overcomes you. That is . . . how you know. In false love, in . . . lust, you do not have this terror. You have a sense of power, of control. It is the opposite." I am stunned, I wonder if I've heard him correctly. *Love and lust.* For a moment, we are both unable to maintain eye contact. Then: "It is mysterious, I think—it is not knowable, truly—how these things affect us. Childhood, fatherhood, devotion to this or to that, God's hand, choosing the left road or the right road. Difficulties and traumas, I can see you've had your share. . . . What is interesting to me, what makes it all meaningful is *that* we are so affected. One way or another. For joy or for pain, for beauty or for ugliness. We shape, we are shaped. Remarkably. Everything, every moment. Now." Eye to eye, we each take a breath. "You and I, we shape each other, we make our impressions, our bodies, souls, minds. For good, for bad. I am certain of it. Your impression on me, that is . . . Han Ah-jin . . . *whoever* you are."

3

To: HenryHansoo@yahoo.com
Fr: JaneintheJungle@hotmail.com

Dear Henry,

I'm sorry I haven't written sooner. I tried, a few times, but I haven't had any words. I don't know. So much to say, and yet nothing to say. It will come, I think, when I see you.

We should be home soon. Dad is all right. He's doing all right.

Don't worry about anything. We're ok, we'll be ok. You be ok, too.

—J.

4

Four-thirty a.m. The glowing red numbers are not as bright or sharp as they used to be. Or maybe it's his eyes, who knows. He's had the clock radio for twenty years, remembers the Christmas when he and Jane opened the identical packages, rolled their eyes at each other; it was never a good sign when their parents got them the same thing. But this one wasn't a bad call. It meant that they could listen to music at night in bed when their parents thought they were sleeping. Or, sometimes, they'd tune in to Dr. Ruth Westheimer and giggle at the call-ins, the desperate men and women who divulged their most embarrassing sex questions and problems. What was it about private biology that was so damn funny back then? It was all of it—the vee-haf-vays-uf-making-you-talk accent, the froggy voice, the utter lack of irony when saying things like *Is the penis ver-ry soft, or is there just a lit-tle-beet-uf-hardness?* They developed a knocking system between their rooms: Two knocks—hilarious! Three knocks—gross! One knock—huh?

The buttons are sticky now, it takes forever to reset. The radio dials still work, the display continues to glow. But fuzzier, definitely. It's definitely the clock.

Four-thirty-eight. Deep breath in, big sigh out. Roll over this way, roll over that. Masturbate? Nah, not the thing. Not now. God, he feels ancient.

Jane's been gone almost a month now. He's thought of her every day, wondering about each step. Who knew how long it had taken her to get to their uncle's house in the sticks. But then again, it was Jane. This was her life, what she did: finding her way to unfindable places. So unlike him, who was always lost. Forty-eight hours she'd been gone when it already started to feel like centuries.

He was doing all right. Before she came back. He'd reached

his one-year mark, living on his own, sober. Consecutive days. Holding down a job. The clutter and tangle in his head had started to break.

He had made himself a routine that felt good, felt doable. Awake at 7:00; shower; coffee at 7:15; read the paper, eat a donut; ride his bike downtown along the FDR path (rain or shine); at his desk at the local public TV station (low-level production assistance, easy stuff) by 8:45. The workday was the easiest part—the structure was there, he didn't have to think about it. People buzzed about—sit, stand, type, talk—worked through their in-boxes. Things churned, everything like clockwork. This was all just fine with him. It was warm milk after years of castor oil.

Nights were harder. He called Jordan, his sponsor, every evening at 9:00. Every night, something to do, a number to dial. Every night, the same voice on the other end.

When Jane came back he was in a decent state. She volunteered to find a sublet, and he considered it, but figured he'd at least give it a try. She'd been there for him; and it would only be temporary. He was embarrassed by the smallness of his life next to hers, world traveler, published in *The New York Times* and *National Geographic*. They'd been out of touch, since the break with Paul, since she left for Africa and fell off the grid for a while. But he was in a decent state. He'd give it a try.

It was rough at first, making the adjustment, his routines and schedules thrown. But he managed, and felt accomplished for it. Thankfully, she slept a lot and had little interest in conversation. Sometimes they'd sit on the couch together watching TV, they'd joke and laugh and revel in their smarter-than-thou cynicism like old times, and she'd fall asleep on his shoulder, balled up and twitching as she crossed into unconsciousness. Her haggard presence had a strangely cheering effect on him: he was not the Only Fuck-Up in the World, other people had their mess of troubles, even Jane. For a time, he got to feel like the big brother, taking care of his invalid sister, going to work each day and coming home with groceries or takeout or a DVD. It felt good. Day at a time. Day. At. A. Time.

He'd learned this, the hard way. Everyone told him so, to beware of the creeping invincibility that would surge every so often. He'd felt it right away, when he first got out—like a high. But it didn't last long. He wasn't who he used to be. He was thirty-six years old. He was over the castor oil, but still only drinking milk. He made lists. He lived like a child.

All of them did, the hundreds of anonymous faces he'd seen at meetings, story after story. The gratitude of just waking up in the morning so sickeningly sweet, the humility of it a daily reminder of fundamental weakness. No one else seemed to let on how much they hated it, hated all the gratitude and low expectations. But he did. Living to get to the phone call. Living like a machine. Any day now, life would break through, they all said. You'll see, it will dawn on you. Stick with it. We love you, Henry.

But it was good to have Jane around again. Maybe it was good timing; he was ready to revisit some of his old self. He was someone's brother, they shared things no one else shared. She was a little out of it, but still Jane, and she needed him, and it felt good. Maybe he'd start to think and say things he used to think and say—witty things, interesting things. Maybe he'd try acting again. Maybe he'd fall in love. . . . Jane reminded him of the old Henry. It felt good.

But now she's gone. Those two months feel like a dream. Remote, and unreal.

Four-fifty-two. Christ. *Christ!*

It is the *unexpected* part that is most distressing. He'd managed, he was managing. When she came, he let down his fortifying structures. The new repose was barely perceptible, even to himself. But now, now he feels the consequences of the lapse.

He was prepared for the One Change, but not the second. The letting in was one thing; the letting out, letting go, was an Altogether Different Thing.

One too many things.

For two months, he was not alone.

Now he is alone. Alone again.

Again? No, new alone. Most most alone.

Five-ten. He is up, the sun loiters too long in yesterday. Across the air shaft someone else is awake, a dim table lamp through beige curtains. Or is it a candle. A candle . . . Somewhere. Jane had brought candles into the apartment. Vanilla scent, sweet and rich. Part of the new repose. How could he be so careless, to not notice the advent of pleasures, of appetite, of . . . slack and slake. If he could just find those candles . . .

Christ!

The spare room is nearly empty. Just big enough for a twin bed and a desk, he'd used it as a junk room, a gadgets room, some books and magazines; but cleaned it out for her. Now he opens desk drawers to find baby-sized hotel lotions and shampoos, empty film canisters, empty manila folders. No candles. A melted-down stub on a saucer by the bed. He holds it up to his nose, can still smell the sweet and the rich.

Ice cream.

Within a five-block radius: the Puerto Rican bodega; the Indian-owned smoke shop–newsstand; the Korean produce and flower shop. Lately he's been avoiding the Koreans. The *ajjummah* always gives him something extra, charges him for two apples instead of three, puts her hand out to signal *Don't worry* when he fishes in his pockets for change. He smiles and bows in appreciation but secretly resents what he knows will obligate him in the long run. He tried to refuse once, forcing the money on her, which she clearly took as an offense . . . come to think of it, that was the last time he'd been there.

Sunday. It's early, and the *ajjummah* and *ajjushi* don't work

Sundays, they go to church. The Egyptians will be manning the counter. He is at this moment sincerely glad he lives in a city where it is not strange to be buying ice cream at six in the morning on a Sunday in the middle of winter.

"Will that be all?" The bespectacled Egyptian with the round face is a monument to manners and consistency. Henry eyes hungrily the Marlboros above the Egyptian's head, then notices a new section, just to the left: cigars. Would be *just the thing* to go with his vanilla caramel swirl.

He pays the Egyptian for the ice cream, all the while eyeing the cigars. He barely hears him say *Kamsahamnida* as he hands him the change, and most definitely does not hear her the first time she says his name.

"Henry?"

The second time he hears her; this time more of a statement, a demand. *HENry.* His instinct is to flee, he feels cornered between the cashier and the voice behind him. There is no time to think, to trace the voice back through history, his blurry mind. The no-time no-space is an ambush, and he is heavy on his feet, stuck in the mud. He turns his head, just his head, to identify the enemy.

"God, Henry. I *knew* it was you."

Naomi.

I knew it was you. The sounds float up, away from both their bodies. Two lumps of flesh, now both stuck in the mud. Or one lump of flesh and one shiny doll, smooth and just-out-of-the-box. *Naomi.* Six in the morning on a Sunday, in line at the Korean grocer on Second Avenue. *Christ.*

God, Henry. I knew it was you. The words mean something, they're up there, waiting.

He once was a charming conversationalist, like a featherweight boxer, dancing and shadowing, light and fast. This former Henry, junior-year-in-high-school Henry, appears beside him now, an apparition—mean and taunting in front of Naomi.

Naomi . . . wow, he manages to say, clearing his throat (Apparition Henry has him by the balls, so it comes out high-pitched).

God, wow . . . how are you? This is so weird. . . . The words keep floating away, he has to concentrate to catch them before they disappear, pop like a bubble. He hasn't slept, the store seems to be on a slant, everything impossibly too small or too large, a house of mirrors.

Alone, alone.

"Yeah, God . . . Naomi . . . what are you, uh . . . do you live uhm . . ." His hands go up, twirling, nothing in particular, something about *around here. . . .*

"Yeah, I'm . . . just a block from here." Her hands are up now too (something on her hand catches the light, a tiny sharp sparkle), gesturing in the direction of an apartment building, presumably.

"Wow, God, small world. I'm just uhm . . . yeah, a few blocks up. . . ."

She's talking fast now, something about how crazy it is they haven't run into each other before. Her words phase in and out, like radio static. Jane had lost some of her hearing, she'd said, in the accident, and it occurs to him only now how disorienting that must be . . . how closely she must have to pay attention. He can't seem to listen to Naomi's words and observe her at the same time, which is a problem, because he sees her, suddenly, sees her face and her figure, sees her small, thin frame, her Chinese–northern Italian skin, so light, like skim milk, her hair that baby-light-soft. He remembers now, her smell, her touch, how she seemed to have come into the world not-quite-fully cooked, a bit too tender inside and out. How he wanted to protect her, wanted to love her, always, wanted to share all his heat, too much heat, she the perfect vessel, the perfect cool complement, settling him, emptying him.

And now he remembers that summer, her letter from Flor-

ence. He'd crumpled the letter and punched the wall, the one
between his room and Jane's, waking her from a nap. She'd
worked the late shift at the restaurant the night before and covered for him, lied to the boss, when he didn't show up to bus.
She asked him, through the wall, if he was all right, and he didn't
answer. She said his name again, this time his Korean name—
Han-soo *ya?*—and he started to weep. They were not tears of
sorrow, but rather of relief—relief from the torment of wondering, imagining; hoping and waiting. The pain of Naomi's betrayal
not nearly as bad as all that anticipation, full-frontal exposure.
Jane knocked on the door, he told her to go away. She knocked
again. He retrieved the crumpled letter and stuffed it in the crack
beneath the door. She took it and went away. It's what she did for
him, always, back then—took away the ugly things, as far away
from him as possible, never telling him where or how.

He snaps back to the present. Naomi is still talking. He interrupts her, words flying out, divorced from will: "So, what are
you doing here? It's six a.m." Naomi's face goes gray-green, her
words fall back behind a veil, but not without a girlish flutter, a
faint, self-knowing smile on her lips. Her eyes open wide and
she raises her eyebrows, gesturing *up there, over your head,* and he
turns to follow her sight line to the shelf of cigarettes.

"A very bad, very good habit," she says. "A pack of Marlboro
Lights," now speaking to the Egyptian.

A ghost. That's what she's been for a long time. Not consciously on his mind, but *there* somehow, always. He realizes this
now, face-to-face with the incarnation. There is something . . .
surreal about it. His mother would surely approve of this assess-
ment, apprehending this mysterious moment of convergence
between a subconscious force and a material, objective reality.
Naomi . . . Naomi with a pack of Marlboro Lights . . . here, now.
She's like the apple in the Magritte painting, floating. Or Dalí's
rose; a pocket watch; a butterfly.

"I really shouldn't," she says, and now she is looking down at herself, and Henry is looking down with her. Naomi's belly—a beautiful, perfect little globe, taut beneath her T-shirt, the whole world in that tiny body—looks back up at him. "But it helps with the endless nausea," she says, rolling her eyes. "I had to sneak out, Stephen would kill me if he knew. . . ."

The sun is up—way up, and way bright. He follows it, the brightness, into the direction he can't see, stumbles along a block or two. He smells bread baking, hears a small dog yapping. Walks into a row of newspaper boxes. "Hey, whoa, you okay, man?" Someone is holding his elbow. "Yes, fine, yes, thanks." He continues walking east, toward his apartment. His steps are brisk but not rushed, he finds a kind of rhythm. He's okay. He's okay now. That was weird, that was hard, but he's okay now, he's okay. Fuck her, fuck that bitch with her fucking pretty face and pretty belly.

God, she was really glowing, that brown-yellow-white skin of hers, and there was a new tint to it now, a fresh pink. . . .

Fuck her, can't think about her right now. It's not her, it's not her. Stephen? Wasn't the asshole's name Campbell? Whatever. Doesn't matter. Fuck her, it's nothing, it's not her.

He's walking east. It's quiet. A few people are out walking their dogs. The morning is crisp, the trees lining the streets hang on to their last few leaves, and the morning light catches them— *ta-da!*—the last survivors, flaunting resilience. It's a fucking beautiful morning, he thinks, and I'm fucking lucky to be alive. *I'm lucky to be alive.* He incants it, it's something Jordan says almost every time they talk.

He feels for his phone in his pocket. He feels good, he's okay, but he feels for his phone. No, it's too early, he doesn't want Jordan to think he's in crisis. *Dr. Lee.* Yes, he'll try her, just to check in, like he's checking in on *her*, making sure she's okay; the two of them, left behind, they need to look out for each other. *I'm up early, getting some breakfast, thought I'd just check in.* It rings and rings, six times. He knows the voice mail will pick up on the seventh. He hangs up.

"*Joooohhhh-taa!*" Walking and talking, he says this out loud to the beat of his stride. Not too loud, but enough to hear himself. Where is it coming from? His father's *beautiful morning!* exclamation, what always seemed incongruous given the sodden woe that hung over the man for as long as he could remember. *Joooohhhh-taaa! It's good!*

He meant it, though. His father did. His father was claiming something, and not just for himself. He claimed it for everyone, it seemed. Does he, his father's son, claim it now in the same resounding way? Does he know it to be true, this *goodness*?

Click-click. He starts. Someone is shooting a camera at him. He looks around. No one. No one is there. Whatever. He thought he heard something, felt someone focusing on him. Whatever. Back to his steps, back to his rhythm.

It was Jane. Jane had pointed her camera at him, she was messing around, the day before she left. "Put that thing away," he had said. But he didn't fight hard, he let her. He let her focus on him, let her look and see. *Here I am.*

Who is looking now? No one is there.

None of them are here anymore—Jane, Paul, his father, Dr. Lee. Naomi. They all have something else to look at now. But he, he has nothing. Nothing to look at but this, this, now, his feet, step step step step step. . . . Black sneakers on gray pavement, still going east, and now a solid yellow line—freshly painted, thick and bright.

Crossing over. Into the highway, not many cars at this hour, but a few, he feels them. He feels the one.

Step, step, step.

The car is coming, full speed, someone is in a rush, needs to get north, one-track mind.

Joohhh-taa!

I am walking, I am doing something, too, I am doing this. Look and see.

See me. Here I am. A rush, a blinding light, as he turns to see. He sees nothing but bright white, his head full of his own voice—*It's good, it's good!*

Before impact, before reflexes kick in—break, swerve, *Jesus!*— before everything collapses together, body, machine, light, dark, sound, silence . . . the driver sees his face. Remembers, even now, will always remember, Henry, looking up, a faint smile breaking. *Here I am.*

Casus Belli

"Are we having breakfast this morning?"

Han Jung-joo focuses her eyes hard on Cho Jin-sook, but does not respond—as if she hears the words but does not quite understand.

Cho Jin-sook is struck by this look and remembers it from years ago—yes, it was that same look, how strange, how uncanny—from when one of her uncles, having just caught his wife with another man, came to her father's house, stumbling and laughing and stinking of *sul*. The children all got up out of bed to see what the ruckus was about, and before their mother could shoo them back to their room, the uncle looked them all over one by one with those piercing eyes, bloodshot and yet sharper and clearer than any sober eyes she'd seen. They were eyes that seemed to be seeing for the very first time. Han Jung-joo looks at her with those eyes now, and for a moment she is frightened.

"Yes, yes, of course," she says now, breaking the gaze abruptly and standing up to smooth down her skirt, her blouse, her hair. She is thin, very thin, Cho Jin-sook notices. In her long skirt and loose-hanging blouse, hair pulled pack in a ponytail (not an unattractive style on her and yet reflecting an especially casual attitude toward her appearance), she looks like a schoolgirl wearing adult clothes for some obligatory formal affair. "Dr. Han has several appointments this morning, he will be downstairs shortly. Big Uncle Han is already up. Ah-jin and Min-suk stayed the night in Pohang with Min-suk's colleagues; they will return this evening." Mrs. Han says this last part with no particular tone or concern, but Cho Jin-sook is taken aback. The two of them out together overnight? Such impropriety, and at a time such as this! Mrs. Han's casual statement strikes Cho Jin-sook as tacit approval. This new permissiveness troubles her. On the table is a piece of paper, unfolded with creases in thirds. A torn envelope has fallen to the floor by the chair leg.

"Have you been to the post office already?" Cho Jin-sook asks.

"No, no," she says, absently. "That's just something I found in my purse. Something I'd forgotten about. Throw it away. It's not important." Cho Jin-sook bends over to pick up the envelope with one hand and crumple the piece of paper with the other. Before throwing it in the trash can, she looks to see that Han Jung-joo has left the room, then pulls on the ends of the paper to flatten it out. Quickly, before Han Jung-joo returns, she makes out a few typed words: *laboratory, blood count, Han Min-yung*. The rest are numbers.

The morning meal transpires quickly. Dr. Han does not linger much these days before leaving for the office. He mumbles something about a busy day, perhaps late this evening. It is unlike Dr. Han to mumble, to be so unclear about his plans for the day; and even more unlike Mrs. Han to accept the unclarity. Cho Jin-sook knows that she must inquire about the holidays, will they be needing her, and about this evening, who will be present for dinner; about anything she needs to know. Her employers no longer have the scheduling of their household foremost in their minds.

Han Hyun-kyu begins stacking breakfast plates, a habit he is developing which irritates Cho Jin-sook greatly. "*Koman ha sae yo*," she says, pulling the plates away from him. "I will do it." Her words are correct, she uses the formal address, but her manner and tone betray a temper of insolence. Han Jung-joo takes notice.

"Auntie Cho," she says, "*na doh*, I will clear the table. Here is the list for the market. You may go without me. I will stay home today, I have a terrible headache. And please tell Mrs. Kim at the meat counter that I am sorry I will not attend her granddaughter's baptism on Sunday." Cho Jin-sook hands the plates over to Mrs. Han like a scolded child and takes the list. She does not look directly at her during the exchange, but she does catch Han Hyun-kyu's eye to the side and thinks she detects a nervousness, almost a giddiness. Inwardly, she scowls.

"*Kuruh sae yo*. Yes, ma'am," she says, untying her apron and handing it over as well. "I will return shortly."

"It is no rush, Auntie Cho. Dr. Han says he will be late this evening." Again, Cho Jin-sook looks to see Han Hyun-kyu's reaction to Mrs. Han's words, but he has stepped away to gather the rest of the breakfast dishes from the table. Mrs. Han turns to the sink to tend to the dishes in her hands. Cho Jin-sook takes her cue and departs, reluctantly.

Keeping the water running, Han Jung-joo drowns out the silence. Today, she does not think she can bear it. Today, she is on the farther shore, farther than she could ever have imagined. Nothing is as it should be; nothing is as it has been. This much she knows. This is all she knows. She moves through the days, through her house, through her body, as if departed. Floating above and below, everywhere but *in*. She does not feel pain, or sadness, or anger; nor happiness, nor pleasure. She wonders when or if she has ever felt these things. She is feather-light and just barely tethered. A slight shift in one direction or another, and she will slide off the surface of her life. How easily this happens to a person. How little it takes to unhinge what once seemed securely locked. She and her husband were tied together, and now they are not. How foolish to think that a knot cannot simply be untied! Or a lock cut open by something strong and sharp. There is always something stronger and sharper, looming, like a law of nature. The world is like this, she thinks—an arena of aggressive forces, sharpening their blades or licking their chops, cruel and ready to pounce on anything or anyone foolish enough to believe themselves safe or immune. How small-minded, she realizes now, to have never considered it! It is the one plain thought in her head—the terrible headache to which she has just referred—and it spreads further into her mood, her *spirit*, as a weakness and a surrender. There is no return, no salvation, from one's own blindness, a road paved with assumptions. One builds a life, layer upon layer. Things pile up, a few precarious structures protruding, cantilevering out beyond the foundation—haughty in their defiance of gravity. No need to worry, though. All is well. One takes it on faith . . . that the foundation, the rock, is level and whole. And permanent.

It is all a lie. The faith, the confidence. Her daughter is dead. And this man, her husband, he is an imposter, a cardboard cutout of someone she once admired. He folds now, flimsy in reality; bloodless, fleshless. It is not true that she *believed* in it. No, she did not really believe, she has worried all these years, lived with the worry, tamped it down neatly and consistently with propriety and order. Believing not in the house of cards itself, but in her ability to be good and proper, to fend off the blade sharpeners, the chop lickers, with attention and diligence.

She does not hear him approach from behind. He reaches around her and closes the faucet. He takes her hands, still standing behind her, wipes them one at a time, kindly, thoroughly, with flannel shirtsleeves. He steps back and turns her slowly by the shoulders to face him. She does not pull away. He takes her hands again, and they stand there, like teenagers at the front door, awkward before saying good night. She does not look up. If she did, she would see that he beholds her as a child.

He is sorry for her. It is unthinking, an intuitive burst, this surge of pity that fills him. It is a kind of joy, this fullness. He has an urge to crush her delicate hands in his massive ones, or to squeeze them until she cries out. *We must feel things*—this he has come to in the last weeks. *Our blood must flow, one way or another.*

If she looked up, she might also see the boy child in *him*: the promising young man who left home alone, in search of some elusive largeness of life, and has returned now with nothing but a ringing, radiating energy—willing, hungry, indiscriminate— and an enormous empty heart. *He.* He is flesh and blood. He has brought his carnage with him, he wears it shamelessly. He is not afraid of his hunger but pursues it with abandon. He ran from here, and now he runs back. He is not afraid. I am not afraid.

She is flush with heat. She lets go of one of Han Hyun-kyu's hands and squeezes the other, turning now to lead him. Through the living room, up the stairs, they move quietly and briskly, hearts pounding. Han Jung-joo does not know who, or what, leads *her*. She has no script, no plan. As they ascend the stairs, time washes over her, a backward wave. Her stake in this place, her home, as owner and keeper, recedes. She and Han Hyun- kyu are now teenagers on the run who have happened upon this place, stopping over for a brief interlude; except there is no real danger. Nothing immediately threatens. They are borrowing these identities, these other lives, just temporarily. Who would have imagined that the notion of consequence could be so read- ily suspended?

Who will know the difference?

Near the top of the stairs she is aware that she must decide something. She follows the reverse flow of time into her daugh- ter's room—untouched since Min-yung's death, except to put away her bedclothes and a few other signs of an imminent return. Han Jung-joo sits down on the bed and pulls Han Hyun-kyu by the hand to sit next to her. His other hand is large and warm on her cheek; it is rough and smells of damp wood.

She closes her eyes, yielding. His hand moves to the back of her neck, his other hand now wrapped around her small shoulder. He moves his hands over her—arm, back, now her thighs. His hands move with great care, minding her fragility (and his). Now he drops slowly to his knees by the side of the bed, holding her firmly by the hips, his head buried fiercely in her lap, like an animal. Like a child. She holds his head, her fingers spread through his silver hair. There is nothing but deep, heavy breath for a moment. She pulls his head into her belly; he rears up, then nestles into her like a pup searching for a teat.

Her eyes still closed, time continues to wash over her. Now she is young again, a girl of fourteen—her body tired, always tired, from household work, from tending to chore after chore, at the service of her brothers, doing as her mother requires of her. She is lying on the bare floor mat in the bedroom alone after a long day, a hot summer day. Her mother has been away tending to her grandfather, and the bulk of chores has fallen to her alone. Her older brothers have had their supper and are off somewhere, perhaps at the new *guk jang*, the first movie theater in town. Min-suk is working quietly at his desk, drawing. Her body throbs, moist with the humidity of the day and the steamy kitchen. She smells on herself the sourness of mop water. From where she is now, both girl in the flesh and visitor from the future, the feeling and the smell are not unpleasant. But as she lies there, sprawled out like a chalk outline of the dead, a body acquiescing to all of its new smells and bulges and sprouts like food going rotten, something strange begins to happen. The heat she feels, the aching pulse, is suddenly a longing. Her heat seeks heat, more heat, the throb and ache of another. The heat now begins to fill her head, she drifts into dream. She pulls at her clothes, runs her hands over herself, feels them as the hands of another, someone large and heavy and dark. A dark visitor, a powerful stranger. Everything is damp now—her hair, her clothing, the dark warm area between her legs. Her fingertips are wet and slimy.

Nu-nah! Nu-nah! She awakes to Min-suk calling her. He has spilled a bottle of ink.

The stranger came to her once, only that once. So rarely was she ever accessible for such a visit again. Good Jung-joo, industrious and efficient Jung-joo. No time, no place for lazy daydreams. Now the warm and heavy stranger is back. Now, here, in the time that is no time, the place that froze in time when her child passed from this life. Good Jung-joo is now futile Jung-joo, failed Jung-joo, who could not supply her child with health. What now but to yield? What now but to give herself up to the stranger, to the ravaging that awaits her, hateful wife and mother? Yes, she hates. She hates him, her husband, the man who allowed her, thoughtless and complicit, to become this woman. The man who keeps her—has kept her—in this lifeless life. He. Her father. Her father's father. They have all *kept* her.

And yes, she hates *her*, too. She hates the daughter who dared to die on her watch.

Min-yung! She sees her now, stepping out into the street, a car speeding toward her. The child has a doll in her hands, is talking to the doll. Han Jung-joo has a full sack of food from the market in her arms, a heavy jar of kimchi. *Min-yung!* She drops everything, glass breaking and red pepper juice splattering everywhere. She reaches out, a miraculously long arm, grabs the child by the fingers and yanks her back into the red spray.

Min-yung!

Han Jung-joo opens her eyes. The man who has wrapped his arms tightly around her waist, kneeling before her, is squeezing the breath out of her, crushing her bones. His hands underneath her sweater and camisole fumble with the hooks of her brassiere. His head is buried in her breast, he is an enormous oaf of a man. At this moment, she cannot help but laugh. A strange and deep sound comes from her middle, and it jars him from concentration. He ceases, releases her slowly, falls back on the floor, kicking knees up into crossed legs. He groans slightly with the ache of aging bones and muscles. She purses her lips, holding back more laughter. He looks up at her, red with effort, and now embarrassment.

"I am sorry," she says. "I am very, very sorry."

"Is everything all right?" he asks.

"Yes. Yes. It's just . . . this is foolish. Like children." A sadness comes over him. Then a deep sigh. He recovers himself, stands with much effort—a further reminder to her that he is most certainly not a child, but an old man—and sits by her on the bed.

"Yes. Like children." He sighs, rubs his hands over his face, then through his hair. "Though I am not so sure they are any more foolish than adults." She holds one of his hands between both of hers. Suddenly she feels sorry for him. Something in his recklessness, his readiness to plow forward and outward, into an unknown, wholly untethered. There is something saddening to her about his fearlessness—about having nothing to lose. As if speaking to her thoughts, he says, "Do not think I am unaware of how I must seem—to you, to my brother. My wife, my children. *Foolish.* Of course. But self-consciousness is for the young. For an old man, there are worse things than foolishness. There are worse things even than dissatisfaction or loss. There is . . . the kind of homesickness that has no place, no kin, as its objects; mourning of ghosts . . ."

"My daughter was like a ghost to me at times," she says. "She did not fear her death. She did not fight it." Han Jung-joo raises her head to fight back tears, and in doing so sees where she is. Min-yung's room. Min-yung.

"I understand there was nothing really that could be done for her." Han Jung-joo bristles at these words. *Doctors.* Those doctors, and their science and medicines and pronouncements. Experts in illness, in death and pain, ignorant of human *life*. They keep themselves in business with their complacency, their smug expertise. How she hates them all right now.

"I would like to be alone now," she says. "Please excuse me." She does not move, signaling to him that she would like him to go. He stands, again with effort, and leaves her.

When she awakens, it is nearly dusk. Her head is heavy with the tender throbbing of unintentional sleep, her clothes twisted about her like a straitjacket. The room has darkened and stilled. She sits up quickly with a rush of blood to the head and becomes aware of an intense thirst. *They'll all be home soon. I must . . . I must . . .* Her light-headedness converges with lingering shame from this morning's episode, and an uncharacteristic reluctance to manage her household's evening rituals comes over her. This disconnect, this lack of motivation, is a misery. The worst misery imaginable.

She sits, dazed and paralyzed. Her eyes fix on nothing. Then the objects in the room appear to spin and move toward her. One object in particular finds its way into her line of sight, catches focus. A plain black notebook on the floor, near Min-yung's desk. She reaches down to pick it up; a slip of paper falls out.

Downstairs she hears the back door open and close. Her husband has arrived. Whispering voices—Cho Jin-sook and Han Jae-kyu conferring—indicate to her that Han Hyun-kyu told Cho Jin-sook not to disturb her. She sits still, holding the slip of paper in her hand, listens for her husband's footsteps ascending the stairs. He pauses in front of Min-yung's door, then continues on to their bedroom.

Han Jung-joo unfolds the piece of paper and begins reading. The words, at first, appear opaque and primitive, like hiero-glyphs. She closes her eyes, then opens them again, reads over what her daughter has written, in a neat and deliberate hand, on this torn-out sheet of lined notebook paper. She mouths the words silently as she reads:

To My Family:

   I am dying. I will be gone soon. I am trying to live just a
little longer, so that my child can live. If he survives, my baby
boy, I give him over to be raised by my cousin Han Ah-jin.
She will be my baby's mother. She may take him to America,
she may do as she wishes. We have discussed it, and she has
agreed to this. I entrust my baby's life to

The note is not dated and trails off.

Han Jung-joo is no longer dazed, no longer sluggish. She
comprehends the words, a red-hot slap to the face. It is done.
The house of cards. Collapsed.

She does not hear Min-suk and Ah-jin downstairs. They have
returned, from their overnight who-knows-what. Nor does she
hear the downpour outside, the heavens raining down a preamble to the mounting disturbance within. Han Jung-joo is standing now in the hallway at the top of the stairs, a folded piece of
paper in hand, eyes wild. Strands of tangled hair hanging around
her face, her clothes rumpled and twisted. She is not herself. Her
husband emerges from their bedroom and beholds the sight.

"*Aigoo!* What is it? Look at you! What is happening?"

At the bottom of the stairs, Cho Jin-sook looks up to see
her employer in her disheveled state, takes her cue from Han
Jae-kyu, who stands at a distance, stupefied by this wife-turned-
banshee in the hallway. "*A-ya!*" she exclaims, unable to hold back
a response. Terrified, she steps back out of sight. Chae Min-suk
and Ah-jin, hearing the commotion, take her place at the landing. In a moment, Han Hyun-kyu is also there.

"*Nuh,*" she says, pointing at Ah-jin, the storm now gathering
in her eyes. Slowly, she descends the stairs toward them. "*You.*
You get out now. Get out of my house. Go away! *Na ga!* Get out!"
She reaches the landing and sees Han Hyun-kyu now for the first
time, behind the banister. "And *you. You* too! *Na ga!* Both of you.
You bring this upon us. *You* did this. You come from somewhere,

something . . . *terrible*. And you bring this to my house. Get *out*. Get *out*! Go back where you came from!" Han Jung-joo's fists are clenched, her veins blue and bulging in her neck. She reaches out for the wall now. Han Jae-kyu rushes down the stairs to her side, braces her up with both hands and all his weight as she falters. She uses her remaining strength to push him away.

"*Yobo*, calm down. *Calm down*. What has happened? Why are you like this?"

"They must go. They must go *now*. You must force them to go. They are no longer welcome here."

"*Yobo*, be reasonable. What has happened? You must explain yourself."

"It's all right," Han Hyun-kyu says to his brother, holding Ah-jin's arm and looking down. "We will go. It's all right." Han Jae-kyu takes a moment to understand—that his brother is taking responsibility for something. A faint light of comprehension begins to dawn over him, the seeds of misunderstanding ready to germinate.

But before he can grasp on to a false cause, Chae Min-suk, whose absence no one has noticed until just now, returns, telephone receiver in hand. The blank look on his face, a pallid gravity, takes the air out of the moment, injects a chill into the heat of fear and confusion. All eyes look to him.

"There is a phone call. The *ajjummah* thought someone should take it. It is from America." He looks to Han Hyun-kyu first, then to Ah-jin. He says the last words he will say to her for a long time: "There has been an accident."

Book Five

Hearts and Minds

1

The child, Joon, faces the pavement from just a few inches away. Hands spread, weight on wrists. Likely a scrape on the knee, scratched palms, perhaps a bit of blood. But he feels nothing yet, nothing except the sensation of having *hit*, the earth rising to a hard stop. There was the stumble, then the fall, then: a loud silence. He learns that there is no sound to *stop*. It is this silence that is most terrifying, that is the pain of the fall. And so, before the silence destroys him, before it has the chance to wrap him completely in its grip and leave him breathless, he cries out. No one hears the low moan from which the cry originates, the gradual rise in pitch. The other children, the nannies, his mother—they see the fall. Perhaps they see blood on the pavement. Then they hear the wailing. No one knows that he feels no physical pain, not yet. The scrapes won't register for another minute, after they've come running. After his mother sweeps him up in her arms, twists his wrists, pokes and prods at his knees, kisses his hands. The kisses hurt the most; don't they know this?

2

Every so often, Joony does something that reminds me of Henry. Like when he's thinking hard about something, he puckers his lips and rolls his eyes up into his brow, intense and comical at the same time. Or when he runs, he hunches over a little, like he's a running back for the Giants or something, and I think maybe he'll be jock-y, like Henry was.

But other than that, other than those moments, those reminders, I have thought of Henry, these past few years, surprisingly little.

I think Joony sometimes reminds Dr. Lee of Henry as well. Her affection for her grandson knocks me out still. It is no exaggeration, I think, to say that he saved her life. But every so often, I'll watch the two of them together, and I'll see her disappear for a moment, composed as a statue but lost to some distant vision; I see her looking at Joony, I see her looking through him.

In the mail today, another invitation. Tacoma, Washington, a gallery there that has recently picked up my show. They will fly me out, put me up. My father, if I tell him about it, will offer to watch Joon so I can go. But I will decline—as I've declined all the others.

We're getting ready for a different trip, Joon-bo and me. We're going back to Korea, to Seoul this time. Joony is old enough now, he's three, and he's talking about all kinds of things, wondrous complex things that shock the heck out of me. Like recently, something about the scrape on his hand, the way blood *looks* like ouch but *tastes* sweet and warm. That's when I knew; I knew it was time for us to go back, for Joony to meet his father.

The show is called *Accidental Family*. It's a modest assemblage of twenty or so photos taken during that time, during my hiatus, after the blast. It includes photos of Henry, looking indifferent and doughy in his apartment, and shots taken, mostly candids on the sly, of Dr. Han Jae-kyu and family—*the photographer's uncle, aunt, et al.*

I'd put the photos away, for a couple of years, and didn't worry too much about what to do with them. When I started developing and mounting the prints, playing with arrangements and groupings, it was a kind of kitchen-table craft project, something to do while Joon was napping or at playgroup. I'd been ashore since Joon's birth, working a staff position with the City beat of the *Times*, getting my bearings in motherhood. At my father's urging, I sent the proofs to Julien, who sent them to a curator he knew in L.A. I didn't quite know what to make of it when, within weeks, the show was booked in five cities.

And, to my surprise, it has received a fair amount of critical attention. One writer described it as "an intimate look at the personal life of a young war journalist, who brings her sensibilities for danger and devastation into her family story." Another piece, written by a cultural historian, a popular professor type, read "powerful Cold War and anticolonialist subtexts" into the images. I even received an e-mail from Paul, who had brought his wife and stepson to see it, saying he thought it was my best work.

I have received invitations to attend openings and give talks in all the cities but it doesn't interest me, and it's not the point really. The photographs aren't about me, or my hope is that they aren't. They are, you could say, intimate, yes; but my intention, in putting them out there in the first place, is of course something more universal.

The other day, I pulled out the three-ring binder that holds contact sheets and proofs from the series. I lingered over the photos of Chae Min-suk. There were a handful, but only two made it into the show. I wondered: Is it evident? Did I somehow betray the truth? Might a viewer detect an invisible subtitle, *The Father of the Photographer's Child?* Accidental family, indeed. I decided to try a test. I called Joony over, interrupted him in the middle of his dancing dinosaurs video (his favorite, a gift from Dr. Lee). "Joony, look at this." We sat together and I held out the notebook, half on his lap, half on mine, the two photos from the show laid out opposite each other. He looked. I waited, said nothing more. "Dog!" he said, smiling and pointing to Bear, a photo from the day we first met, when I happened upon him

and the shepherd, howling crazily at the sky. The other photo—
he and my uncle standing together in the backyard, facing each
other from a rather awkward distance at a V-angle (bright noon-
day light, mountains rising up in the distance and the shimmer
of the lake), one man gesticulating with his hands the shape of
something, the other listening intently with arms folded across
his chest (title: *After My Cousin's Passing*)—registered nothing. He
was getting restless sitting with me, eager to get back to the
dinosaurs, so I let him go. It was a good reminder that my son—
brilliant and precocious as he is—is just three years old.

There was one photo—just one—from Henry's funeral. A
black-and-white of Dr. Lee in profile, at the small gathering held
after the service, sitting alone in an armchair in a corner of
the living room. Her posture perfectly upright, her graying hair
swept back in a low bun, there is no other trace of movement,
internally or externally. It is, I think, a truly breathtaking rendering of my mother, more like a painting than a photograph.
Her unprecedented stillness (an enduring metamorphosis, as far
as we can tell) tells the story of her heartbreak; of an irregu-
lar sort of empathy, mother and son, maintained, and perhaps
misunderstood, to this day; and of the end, finally, of all that
buzzing, all that pouncing. Ironically, Henry, I think, would have
liked this portrait very much.

In the show, I had the photo hung side-by-side with another
portrait, discovered and contributed by my father, of his elder
brother's wife. She'd died long before our visit, but I'd heard the
stories of her many times: she was Lee Woo-in's youngest aunt,
and the resemblance really was uncanny. The woman in this second photo is pretty and unadorned, with a flush in her cheek.
She is posed as for a formal portrait and yet seemingly restless,
uncomfortable with the attention paid by the photographer, and
eager to be done with it; she has . . . *things to do* (by this time,
her husband has become chief administrator for the schools in
Kyongju, and she's not yet fallen sick with the cancer that took

her life at the young age of forty-eight). The two women are starkly discrete, save for the physical resemblance—the effect being an even stronger sense of disconnection than if they bore no resemblance at all. And yet . . . perhaps this is where the show is not so universal, this is where I, the photographer, put my stamp. My mother and her aunt *belong* together, they are not discrete nor disconnected; I know this, in my gut. They cannot live without each other.

When I do recall them, the events of those days after Henry died are clear and present to me the way a vivid dream is when you first awake: it's right there, in the front of your mind, and yet slipping away rapidly, like sand through your fingers. By the time my father and I had arrived home, Dr. Lee, mother of the deceased, had identified the body, filed a police report, and assured the driver (a Barbadian cabbie who buried his head in his hands, weeping, repeating over and over, *He just came out of nowhere)* that she would not be pressing charges. She had also authorized cremation, made arrangements with a funeral home; and then collapsed in the hospital waiting room. She'd been running on adrenaline those thirty-six hours, and it wasn't until she stopped—waiting for us, waiting for us to see Henry—that she gave out. When we arrived, we found Henry in the morgue, and Dr. Lee in the ER, glassy-eyed and rehydrating intravenously.

The day we went to scatter Henry's ashes—my father, Dr. Lee, and me—my father took her arm and hooked it into his, held it firmly with his other arm, propping her and guiding her along. I was leading them to the creek behind the house, where I thought Henry would be at peace: he'd never have to remember the way again. It was an unusually warm day in early February, the creek flowed with the vigor of first thaw, and the air was humid. Dr. Lee was not well, she wanted to turn back halfway, but my father would not allow it.

Since our return, since her collapse, my father has taken full charge of Dr. Lee. I have watched this transformation, this man-turned-husband, this woman-turned-wife, with puzzlement; and also, I admit, relief. Despite the fact that she is fragile, she is often confused, it has gotten worse and not better in the years since Henry's death. For a time, her colleagues kept after her, pressed her to return to her work; but eventually they relented, and it all fell away from her, quietly, almost elegantly, like a satin robe spilling off her shoulders, a glimmering puddle at her feet.

I have no good reasons, really, for not much thinking of Henry. Except, perhaps, that it seems to me what Henry meant, what he *did*, when he walked into the path of that speeding cab: he unburdened us, by unburdening himself. If it is possible for a single act to be staggeringly selfish and selfless at the same time—clouded and lucid, desperate and free—I believe this is what Henry achieved in his last moments. He didn't want our love anymore, not on the old terms; he set new ones. *Let me go*, he seemed to be saying, *let me be*. And for me, ultimately—perhaps surprisingly—it was easy to do. It was what I'd been trying to do for a long time: to see him as Henry—*Han Han-soo*—a being completely separate from me. To see the *him* beneath his baby brother–ness. Not unlike who and what I saw that day, in the woods, when I left him. All those years ago.

And so now I've given all that thought, all that energy, to Joon. The feeling—the ache in your chest, the impulse to pro-tect—is similar, but there is at least one difference: I look after Joony, I would do anything to keep him from harm; but in the absolute, I know that he is stronger than me. He is a force of life, making his way, busting out at every turn, while I recede, emp-tying out everything I can to help him along. I am the guardian, the protector, and yet he trumps me in every way; I run along behind him.

My son was conceived in a sterile hotel room. I've managed

to be philosophical about this—*he'll be at home on the go, just like Mom.* The day I found out, the day I took the test and the line on the stick turned purple, was the same day that we scattered Henry's ashes. It was not long after our return from my uncle's house. It was not long after my cousin died. It was not long after the blast. It was not long after Gereida.

The first one was a Syrian girl, pockets full of stones.

Some people are not long for this world. The rest of us survive. For whatever reason, we are still standing, the lasting ones. Why us and not them? No one knows, and no one speaks of it. We are us, we are not them, we feel perhaps we should move about gingerly.

The day I found out about Joony, I thought, *I am here, I am still standing.* And soon after, my full hearing returned, inexplicably. I could hear again; more accurately, I was reminded that I hadn't been hearing clearly—fully—for some time.

A tiny life fights, sees daylight . . . life, this world—looming and luminous. Another drains away in a pool of black blood.

We are us, we are not them. We don't know the answers, but we will give our love, our devotion, nonetheless. We will ask, *What's next. . . .*

3

Over the last four years, Chae Min-suk has come and gone frequently to his sister's home in the country, staying for several weeks at a time. The studio they built has become his most productive work space. In Seoul, he takes care of business, keeps up social and collegial relations, and sees his daughter as often as possible—which isn't often since she's become a cosmopolitan "tween," her attentions turned toward a legion of distractions (her mother's star is rising in the arts world, just as his is falling, and Soo-young is often left to herself with a housekeeper or her grandmother. But, as always, he is powerless to interfere). At his sister's home, he has embarked on an intensely productive period—productive in terms of ideas and development, if not finished paintings. He is experimenting with new forms and subject matter with a new freedom, pursuing, in a word, simplicity—the stripped-down basics of whatever native facility he possesses for line and color. In moments of reflection (he's taken to staring out the window of his studio for prolonged periods), he flashes back to childhood, when he drew and painted whatever came to him, thoughtless of idea or pattern or design. He has for so long wanted to recapture this capacity for pure receptivity, for *vessel-ness*; and the unencumbered ability to transform inspiration into form and beauty.

Arriving at his sister's home now, by foot as always, Chae Min-suk walks briskly and savors the pleasure of a heart beating hard in his chest, the pressure of air in his lungs. The day is warm and moist. Low clouds, white and wispy, circle just below granite peaks like ballerinas' tutus. The heavens have choreographed a whimsical show, and his hope just now is that many in the valley are able to attend and share in its delight. A moment is all that is required.

The house is showing its first signs of age. A gutter hangs an inch or two off the edge of the roof on one end, white paint has yellowed a shade, slate slabs on the walkway have cracked from the freeze-and-thaw of seasons. The shepherd was put down recently; they'd found him lying on his side in the pen, unable to stand and breathing with great difficulty. Two stray kittens have since been adopted into the household, regarded with supreme apathy by the queen feline, now fat and smug with seniority. The grounds have grown nicely into their own, a lush native grass and large flowering shrubs surrounding, like a moat in bloom. Dr. Han acquired a new car last year (a gift from his sons), the latest Hyundai SUV, black with leather interior. His sons urged

him toward a European make—a Volvo or perhaps Mercedes—
but Dr. Han begged off such a notion. The finest domestic-made
car was what pleased him most.

Arriving with a particular mission in mind, a mission related
to his sister, Chae Min-suk brings with him a hyperawareness of
the air that surrounds and fills her home—its weight, its color
and tone. With the whimsy of skirted mountaintops lingering in
his mind and tickling his senses, he is struck now by a feeling of
vacancy and pallor. What he has previously accepted as peace-
ableness seems now desolate.

It is mid-afternoon, Saturday. He stands at the gate looking
into the backyard. His brother-in-law, reading glasses at the tip
of his nose, reclines on a lawn chair with the newspaper. He
takes the rustling of the paper's page-turning, a sharp disturbance of the silence, as a call, to which he responds. *"Hyung-nim!
Anyong ha sae yo!"*

Han Jae-kyu lowers his head and looks over the top of his
reading glasses. *"Uy! Owhat sumnida!* You've arrived!" He rises with
some effort and moves to greet Chae Min-suk. Walking now
with exaggerated bowlegs, the addled shuffle of a hardworking
man past sixty, he fiddles with the gate latch and steps back when
at last it opens. "You came by foot?"

"Of course, as always."

"Ahh, you mind your health very well. I should do better to
find some enjoyable exercise. Look, I am so lazy, lying here and
reading the paper."

"My *hyung-nim* is in great demand, with such a busy schedule
during the week. All day long you give yourself to others. It is
good that you rest."

"Well . . . it is true, I suppose. But I am slowing down. Come
inside, my wife is preparing something. Have you eaten?"

"A little something. But I have saved room for my sister's
cooking."

"Ha, ha, good man. Let us go then." The rapport between

the two men is easy. It could be said that during Chae Min-suk's creative transformation, as he fell out of favor in fashionable arts circles in recent years, his brother-in-law became his most loyal benefactor. Han Jae-kyu welcomed him unconditionally to come and work in the studio and afforded him an atmosphere of quiet respect and interest. Chae Min-suk showed Han Jae-kyu almost all of the works he produced during this time: pencil sketches and unresolved studies in color and shape, full canvases devoted to experiments in texture and layering techniques.

Han Jae-kyu regarded each piece with serious consideration. From time to time he might inquire, in a word, about a particular effect, or comment on a preference. By the time Chae Min-suk began producing works he felt were complete, Han Jae-kyu, to his own surprise, found himself quite attached to them. He was no art aficionado by any stretch, and these pieces were markedly different from anything Chae Min-suk had produced in the past. They were abstract, often developed around a central geometric form; faint in tone, even when color was applied; and overall made an underwhelming impression. The paintings called for a discrete attentiveness, an inclination, from the viewer. At first glance they might be perceived as tentative or amateurish, a youth's rendering of newly learned shapes and colors. But Han Jae-kyu, having been privy to phases of the process, felt that possibly he understood them; that he could hear their music and feel the undulating rhythms of the artist's experience in both conceiving and executing the work. He did surely feel something intimate and personal in their presence—sadness and joy together, simply put, and this he did not take for granted. Thus the process and experience of art came anew into Han Jae-kyu's life, without fanfare or event, and he counted it a private blessing—something precious as he looked ahead toward the denouement of life as he'd known it.

ꝏ   ꝏ   ꝏ

Han Jung-joo knew little of what transpired between the two men or the nature of her brother's projects. She regarded them as boys, tinkering in the outbuilding together. They may as well have been discussing lawnmowers or car engines. She never did approve of the studio itself, she thought it an eyesore. Beneath this aesthetic opinion lay also the association of its inception with her husband's apparent callousness toward the death of their daughter, whom she had come to think of, in those days, in the wake of the tragedy, as *her* daughter. But these were unspoken claims, and a firm détente developed between Han Jung-joo and her husband as a matter of course. She tolerated the presence of one of her brother's new paintings in the living room (and was not aware of a second which hung in her husband's office at the clinic), a medium-sized canvas of white on white on white, circles in overlapping layers. She considered the painting innocuous and granted that it was not *dis*pleasing to look at. At times she even drew a kind of assurance from the thickness of the paint, how certain sections where the white was especially thick and gloppy seemed to defy gravity, the laws of viscosity. At any rate, the arrangement proved harmonious for the two men and thus incited no argument from her.

The state of détente between Han Jung-joo and Han Jae-kyu was so solid, however, it became like a stone around their necks. Han Jung-joo was aware of her husband's impression that she harbored an immovable anger toward him—if not holding him responsible for, somehow associating him with the death of their daughter. And while this was not the case, not really, Han Jung-joo was neither determined nor able to clarify the misunderstanding; upon misunderstanding, she had come to feel, relied much of the ability to go on.

Four years ago, after expelling the American relatives—the incident of her rage never again mentioned by her, by her husband, by her brother or housekeeper—Han Jung-joo did not return to her daughter's room. The following day, she asked her husband to pack up Min-yung's things in boxes. The clothing could all be given away. The rest was to be sealed and stored in the shed. Her husband obliged and understood that with his wife's request, something was finished. He had no way of knowing the nature of this finality, as his wife never did reveal to him the source of her rage in the first place; and so he accepted it as a distance, a wound, between them. Han Jung-joo was no longer angry with her husband, she was somewhere beyond anger; but conceded this wordless nonunderstanding. And with supreme discipline, she did not once admit the American Hans into her thoughts again.

Until her brother's visit, on this occasion four years later.

In fact, the seed of thought was planted a few weeks before, when the letter from America arrived for Chae Min-suk. The writer had taken a risk in not penning a return name or address, given the unreliability of international mail in their region. Han Jung-joo had, with all other memories of that time, locked away any notions about her brother's relationship with her husband's niece. And yet, when the letter arrived, Han Jung-joo knew—she knew both logically and below the rational level—that the letter came from Ah-jin.

For days after the letter arrived (it sat for nearly two weeks on a small table in the front entryway of the house, awaiting Chae Min-suk's retrieval), Han Jung-joo busied herself with superfluous, physically demanding tasks, refusing the help of Cho Jin-sook or her daughter (who now also worked in the Han household to earn extra money for her family); and with social appointments, lunching and shopping with people she normally avoided. She fended off, for as long as she could, whatever torrent might come over her. She felt no particular curiosity in regard to the contents of the letter—unlike her husband, whom she caught one day holding it up to the light—only a submerged, emerging anxiety about recalling, reexperiencing, the measure of rage and sorrow of those days. At least once a day, a fatigue came over her, a gaping feebleness. She swooned, like those soap opera characters on TV, and would have to sit down, wherever she was. How she hated this absurd vision of herself, and yet she could not overcome it.

Finally, her brother came. Han Jae-kyu handed him the letter with little exchange. Chae Min-suk stayed with them that time for a shorter duration than normal. Something in the letter, it seemed, made him decide to return to Seoul.

Chae Min-suk's departure, and with him the departure of the letter, relieved Han Jung-joo for the moment. But then, when her brother telegrammed shortly after to let them know he'd be coming again in a few days' time, something collapsed—or converged—within her: the strength of resistance waned, and a new strength, of facing forward, rose up, allowing bits of air and light into sealed caverns of memory. She felt herself falling, falling, picking up speed toward a dreaded confrontation, and yet exhilarated, welcoming crosswinds into the stale spaces. Time and circumstance had marched on, the planet had continued to spin. Inertia now tipped into acceleration, and she felt a force stirring up and releasing what she was too weak to hold hostage any longer. The force was a benevolent one, she felt—potent and wise and gentle. Or at least this was what she chose, and what she needed, to believe.

"Your brother has arrived." The announcement from Han Jae-kyu is of course unnecessary, Han Jung-joo heard their greetings from the kitchen. She has anticipated her brother's arrival with hesitancy, but now, seeing him in the flesh, sensing something in his own manner—a purposefulness, a searching—she is emboldened.

"*Yobo*, we are in need of some things for dinner. I sent the girl yesterday but she is absentminded, always daydreaming, she forgets things. Here is my list, please hurry before the markets close so the meal won't be ruined." She scribbles on a scrap of paper as she says this, inventing more items than she really needs.

"All right, then. We will talk more of your latest work when I return," he says to Chae Min-suk, visibly disappointed to be sent away just now.

"There will be plenty of time for that," Han Jung-joo says, shooing her husband away. Han Jae-kyu rolls his eyes comically as he departs.

Chae Min-suk stands a moment looking around the room. "Have you changed something, *nu-nah*? Something feels different."

"Wallpaper," she says, looking up and around, her posture noticeably open, more so than Chae Min-suk has seen in a long time. "You can barely tell, but see, there is texture to it. The color is similar."

"Ah, yes. These tiny pinstripes."

"We needed a change in this room. Something."

"Yes," he says. The affirmation is an aggressive one, given his sister's vagueness. With it, he sets a tone of understanding between them. "Have you been well?" Han Jung-joo pulls a chair out from the table to sit down and motions for her brother to sit as well. It is unusual for Han Jung-joo to sit in her own kitchen. The kitchen is her place of *doing*. Others sit while she moves. Chae Min-suk recognizes the significance of her invitation.

"I am well, yes. As well as could be. Perhaps I might be better." She speaks in a light tone, a hint of singsong. "I was thinking the other day . . . it's silly . . . I was thinking how much I miss that noisy dog. I notice his empty pen every time I go out now. Maybe it's time to get a new one. A puppy. A *jindo-geh*? Maybe another shepherd. Or else break down the pen and plant a garden. I don't know. What do you think?" She asks him in an offhand way that tells him she is not seeking an answer necessarily. "How is Soo-young?"

"She is fine, I think. Her life seems very busy, like an adult's.

And she is showered with gifts by her mother's relatives. They spoil her with things no child of twelve needs—telephones, music players, blue jeans that cost more than . . ."

"You should not begrudge them, or her, those things. She is always loved, always remembered. Our parents did not have the time or luxury to shower us in that way. Father never remembered our birthdays."

"That's right. But you always did."

"That was Mother. She would tell me to go buy extra rice cakes or a small trinket. She was always too tired, but she did remember." Han Jung-joo looks away, finding her way to the thoughts, the questions, that stir and move to the fore. "I am thinking of taking a trip. Maybe with Won-soo. With the new baby, you know, he is feeling a little ignored. Three children"— she sighs—"it's not how it used to be. Hae-sik and Ji-eun are out of their minds, I think."

"That may be a good idea. Won-soo loves his dear grandmother. And you have not traveled much, this is a good time for that. Kyoto would be nice this time of year."

"I was thinking of going to America. Won-soo should see the place, don't you think? Maybe San Francisco. I hear Seattle is a nice place."

"Mm." He registers this idea with surprise, and curiosity.

"Will you stay long? When will you come again? I will feel better leaving my husband if you are here with him. Lately, he forgets things." Chae Min-suk is happy to hear his sister speak this way about Han Jae-kyu. He sensed it before, in the comic shooing, but now detects most certainly an almost-forgotten affection in her voice, returning from a long absence. His sister strikes him as flush with warmth and color, but he recognizes that she has simply regained a loss, attained to baseline. That she has lived and moved about with the vacant composure of a ghost for some time.

"I will stay only through next week. But then I must return

to Seoul and prepare . . . for some exhibitions. My plans are . . . a bit uncertain right now."

"Oh, don't worry then. Auntie Cho takes good care. And the girl is sweet, though not much of a housekeeper. My husband thinks we should pay her more so she can work less and go back to school."

"That is a generous idea."

"Yes, I agree." She says this somehow both firmly and distractedly. "The girl should go back to school. Her father wants that more than anything. He is a good man. We should do what we can to help."

"And is my *hyung-nim* in favor of the trip to America?"

"Oh, yes. It may have been his idea, in fact. For me to take a trip with Won-soo. It seems a good time, as you say. I will speak with Hae-sik and Ji-eun. I imagine they will be glad to send him. And the school has a spring vacation coming up. I only hope I can get around all right. It's been so long. . . ." The two are silent for a moment, giving the reference its due. A gravity descends.

"Is everything all right, *nu-nah*?"

Han Jung-joo does not seem to hear the question but proceeds on her own train of thought. "I have thought . . . I have wondered, lately . . . about our American relatives. Do you think of them as well?"

"I have thought of them often, yes."

"We've not spoken of them."

"No."

"My husband has attempted to speak of them, but I have preferred not to. He hears from his brother, just once in a long while, I think."

"What news?"

"Last time something about a photography exhibit. Pictures of *us*. I did not catch the details. . . . It has been . . . too unpleasant for me to think of them."

"I bear them no ill feelings."

"Mm." He cannot tell whether she disapproves of his state-ment. But her thoughts, her considerations, seem to be in motion. He senses permission to proceed.

"And you, *nu-nah?*" She pauses markedly and furrows her brow, more bemused than disturbed. It is the first time she has considered the question straight-on and finds herself relieved by the directness of it.

"I cannot say what feelings I bear them. I think perhaps I pity them. And pity is a rather hateful feeling, is it not?"

"I suppose it might be. . . ."

"But I do not think I hate them. Hate runs its course, it would seem. Whatever the feeling, I do think that we share something . . . we share . . . *tragedy*. And loss. At a minimum, we share this. And the burden . . . of survival. Of continuing on." She finishes these thoughts with great effort. It is more than she knew she wanted to say. "I assume," she says softly, "that they continue on. . . ."

Chae Min-suk says nothing to this, betrays nothing. He takes his sister's words as reckonings with the past, exorcism of ghosts. Her pain, her anger, *running its course*. He gives his sister, his good sister, the gift of bearing witness, a silent *amen* to her confes-sions and to her hard-fought acceptance of the burden she car-ries. Will always carry.

Chae Min-suk keeps to himself his news, his secrets. He did not come to speak of himself. He does not say anything about Ah-jin, about the fact that he has thought of her often these past years, and now every day since receiving her letter. He does not say that something new has grown in him these last weeks. He does not say that the only word he can conjure for what he feels is *choong shil*—fidelity, faithfulness—and that it is as myste-rious and inexplicable to him as anything; and for that reason, he trusts it. He says none of these things, not now. For now, he wants simply to speak with his sister, to understand her heart. This is why he has come. The future will have its day, after all. It will arrive as the present, soon enough.

"I have returned!" Han Jae-kyu is buoyant. It is that time of day, a leisurely day, when preparations for mealtime tease the senses and promise satiation. Brother and sister arise, turn their attention happily to the new arrival.

"Have you got everything? Did you remember both kinds of peppers?"

"My wife thinks I am suffering from premature senility, Min-suk *shi*." Chae Min-suk relaxes into an old familiarity and is reminded of those days, years ago, when he was an art student and a regular guest, enjoying the comfort of his sister's home, the rest and warmth he always found here. For some time, a chill has seized the climate in this house. . . . How they have all hoped and waited, unconsciously perhaps, for the thaw. Here is grace, he thinks: that unconscious hope is as good as any.

"*Hyung-nim*, I have been wanting to ask you . . . about the old man, the bus driver. I have not seen him the last few times. What has become of him?"

"The bus driver . . . Mr. Yoo? Oh yes, he was a patient of mine. About a year ago, I saw something and sent him to a cancer clinic in Taegu. They diagnosed him and put him on aggressive treatment. He met a nurse there, a widow, and after the treatment was done, he had no more reason to go see her. So he asked for a transfer to a route in Taegu. Now I hear from the new driver, who came in the other day for a checkup: they are married, and Mr. Yoo is in remission."

"What a good story," Han Jung-joo says. "A happy story."

4

The boy sits quietly in the car, shoulder slumped against door, face inches from the window. He looks out, sees dark smooth road, wide lanes with bright yellow lines, small cars mostly. Such ampleness, and speed, plenty of room for everyone. Alien line shapes on green road signs, happy stick figures. Everything different from home, but this is as far as the thought goes, as far as he can take it, in his three-year-old mind. Beyond the highway, he sees flatlands dotted with construction equipment and the broad, low steel beginnings of who-knows-what. The boy's mind is active and burgeoning. He registers image and tone and sound, but his cognition is yet still flat (like this road, from Incheon to Seoul), all information equal and bite-sized as it passes from world to thought. He does not yet know the web of connectedness, the implications of what he sees—equipment, land, steel, ownership, production, labor, wages, trade, power, treaties, alliances, enemies . . . violence. He does not know what kinds of pictures his mother takes with her *cam-ra stuff*, the mound of black bags and shiny boxes she carries with her always.

Nor does he understand the extent of peculiarity surrounding this visit. Most of the children he knows have a mother and a father, but not all of them. Some of the mothers and fathers live together, some of them live apart. His friend Jorie has two mothers. He understands that he has a father, a father exists, this father is the figure at the end of this long journey. He senses, but does not *know*, that his life is a jumble and a hodgepodge, that the constancy of motion and change is only just beginning. He does understand, full well, anticipation. *We'll have a cookie later, Joony; hang on just a few more minutes, we'll find a bathroom soon; after you put your toys away we can watch the video.*

Villages like tiny Monopoly houses in the distance. Cranes and backhoes side-by-side with swampy rice paddies, and old women with broad-brimmed hats and pants folded to the knees crouched over yellow stalks. All information of equal import and flying by his eyes. *Not far now, Joony.* He anticipates the figure at the end of this journey.

❧   ❧   ❧

It was late fall when she came last, four years ago; now it is spring. She looks over her son's head into the thin haze, yellow dust from China. The driver's window is slightly cracked, her eyes sting from the pollen and dust. Joon sneezes, wipes his nose with the too-long sleeve that hangs over his hand, the one he's been favoring since his scrape-up at the playground. Too entranced to notice now, he resumes focus. Through the window, through the haze, she sees the same motley juxtapositions he sees, speeding by . . . but with different eyes, adult eyes, fighting the essential disenchantment that looms. A quote from Carlyle comes to mind, it was the epigraph for Eloise's book: "The beginning of all wisdom is to look fixedly on clothes . . . with armed eyesight, till they become transparent. . . . All visible things are emblems. . . ." Her son is concentrating, pushing the limits of his child's vision and thought. Will he see, will he learn that the true emperor never has any clothes? Yes, he is trying to freeze what he sees, to stop the motion so he can apprehend the *what*. She does the opposite, loosening her vision, allowing the blur to blur, giving over to the power of impression. She rests her hand on the boy's head, the only real thing at this moment. Her son. Will *he*, the anticipated figure at the end of this journey, be worthy of a son's love? Will she fear for the boy's heart, will the father be more enemy than ally? She holds lightly the crown of Joon's head, then squeezes with a quick pulse, her long fingers wrapped over top and ending just above his forehead at the hairline. He has his father's hairline, the early signs of an eventual widow's peak.

They enter the city from the west. Joon sits up taller and closer to the window. "Bridge . . . bridge . . . bridge," he says, as they drive along the south bank of the Han River. Silver high-rises gleam in the early-morning sun, the reflections hit Jane's eyes in flashes like a secret code.

Rush hour is just beginning. The car slows to join commuters—a largely homogeneous legion of black Hyundais and Kias—in their daily choreography of merge and pass, all quite orderly and deferent in comparison to the American analogue. Traffic loosens and speeds up again as they follow the highway east. She notices the entrance to Seoul University, her eyes follow the winding road up to a motley collection of massive buildings dotting the broad hillside. They must be close.

Click click. The camera is out quickly, by reflex—as if provoked.

"What, Mama?"

"Your daddy works there sometimes."

"Works?"

"Yes, Joony. At the school." He turns back to the window, thinking on this. *He's being so quiet,* she thinks. *Too quiet.*

At Kangnam, they turn off the highway and drive through a series of mini-mall areas, all brand-new, interspersed with luxury condo complexes. The streets are pristine and impossibly wide. Along the sidewalks, women in impeccable business suits walk with arms hooked through the elbows of tiny hunch-backed grandmothers in *hanbok.* The younger women are impatient with the pace, some of them double-minding even more impatient children who skip ahead, their bright pink and yellow backpacks gleaming and reflecting off the sun like the buildings rising up behind them. Farther on, the driver turns onto a narrow road, which takes them up a steep hill into an older neighborhood, tree-lined and denser with homes. In a moment, they have entered a different world, a world that seems to exist and remain as an impotent yet stubborn relic, a survivor of progress. They turn into a driveway, where the driver puts down his window and punches a code into a silver box at the side of a black iron gate. The gate opens and they continue on, down a long drive which descends slightly into a wooded area, lush with ginkgo and chestnut trees, flowering pear, and groves of bamboo. The house—low and rambling—is a traditional-style home, modest in size at first glance and striking in its refinement. Jane exhales, despite herself. She had committed to caution and skepticism, but this home presents itself to her as nothing short of a mirage . . . an oasis.

The driver opens the doors for Jane and Joon and unloads their luggage from the trunk. They gather up their ensemble of duffels and totes, Joon's miniature versions of each, stray toys and food wrappers spilling out of his pockets. At the sound of the car doors slamming shut, there is movement in the house. Chae Min-suk emerges from a side door toward the far end. As he approaches, Jane's exhalation reverses almost completely, like a cartoon rewind. She steps back and pulls Joon in front of her, a human shield, gripping his shoulders. Joon twists and cranes his neck to look up at his mother, who stands erect and still as the bamboo, and takes his cue from her expression: something remarkable is about to happen.

Acknowledgments

For their support and assistance of many kinds throughout the creation of this book, I'd like to thank: Lisa Nicholas-Ritscher, Alice Quinn, Blas Manuel De Luna, Amy Williams, Alexis Gargagliano, Gillian Bagley, Jess Manners, David Shields, Karen Cooper, Jin Auh, Shashi Khorana, Linnea Hasegawa, Robin Holland, and John C. Woo.

Thank you also to the staff and writers' communities of the Bronx Council on the Arts and the Gotham Writers' Workshop.

Finally, thank you to my family and friends, near and far, currently in touch and long out of touch, for persisting through pain and chasing beauty; each and every day you inspire me.

About the Author

SONYA CHUNG's short fiction and essays have appeared in *The Threepenny Review, BOMB Magazine, Cream City Review,* and *Sonora Review,* among other publications. She is a recipient of the Charles Johnson Fiction Award, a Pushcart Prize nomination, and the Bronx Council on the Arts Literary Fellowship and Residency. This is her first novel.